THUNDERDOG

Also by Doug Solter

Tomorrow Always Lies

Spies Like Me

Season of Speed

My Girlfriend Bites

THUNDERDOG

BOOK 3 OF THE GEMS SPY SERIES

Doug Solter

Thunderdog. Copyright © 2019 Doug Solter.

First Trade Paperback Edition

ISBN-10: 0-9981466-6-8

ISBN-13: 978-0-9981466-6-9

Cover Art Design by Travis Miles

Website: www.probookcovers.com

To Ellen, the best grandmother ever.

THUNDERDOG

CHAPTER 1

Miyuki looked too cute to die. Her long black hair was dyed cotton-candy pink, and her face was powdered white with pink lipstick and pink hearts added to her cheeks. She wore pink pants with white polka dots and pink high-top sneakers. Her white T-shirt had the cutest puppy dog with the words LOVE ME printed above.

She stood in a narrow street filled with pedestrians as far as the eye could see. Covered with reds and pinks, each store along this street advertised cakes, candies, and sweets of all types. It projected cuteness to the tenth power.

Miyuki adjusted her pink-rimmed glasses and observed. Some of the pedestrians were "normal" while others wore similar clothing to hers. The Harajuku Province was the absolute center of Japan's youth and fashion culture, inspiring fashion designers from around the world with its eclectic style. A cute and childish style called Kawaii in Japanese. And here on Takeshita Street was the center of it all.

Miyuki finally spotted her target, a young woman with a Sailor Moon canvas handbag. The woman dressed normal and plain, fitting in with all the other normal and plain people. When the young woman walked by, Miyuki waited until she was farther down the street before tailing her.

Takeshita Street was crowded, but manageable. As Miyuki weaved back and forth among the people, she always presented a pleasant Kawaii smile on her face. When people held up their phones to snap a pic of her outfit, Miyuki waved and blew them each a kiss. But she didn't stop walking.

When the young woman with the Sailor Moon bag ducked inside a nearby business, Miyuki followed her inside.

It was a small local boutique which had a section of bright Kawaii-style clothes on a row of metal racks, but there was another section full of Western-inspired fashion as well. Glancing at the tags on the clothes, Miyuki could tell they were all done by local Japanese designers. She liked this boutique and would love to hang out and shop, but she was here on business.

Sailor Moon acted nervous. She pretended to shop, but wasn't doing a good job of selling it. Fidgeting, looking around the store, barely glancing at the clothes her hands were separating. Miyuki could tell she wasn't a professional.

Sailor Moon then slipped something in the back pocket of a pair of white jeans before hanging up the garment on a different rack to make it stand out. Sailor Moon didn't linger. She raced out of the business like a scared rabbit.

Miyuki resisted the urge to shake her head in dismay. She stayed in the Kawaii section of the store for a couple of minutes, just to make sure Sailor Moon wasn't coming back. Then she moved over to the other section. Miyuki picked through some of the jeans, making a face as if they were too boring for a fun Kawaii girl like herself. Then she clapped her hands together as if she "discovered" the white jeans. Miyuki took them off the rack and put them over her own waist, pretending to see how they looked. When she did this, Miyuki slipped her fingers inside the pocket and felt the thumb drive inside. She palmed the drive before making another face, as if she didn't like the jeans after all. She placed the white jeans back on the rack.

It was all a big production in case anyone was watching.

As Miyuki searched through another rack of clothes, her eyes scanned the business. Since she saw no one paying attention to her, Miyuki took her time moving towards the exit. She was almost through it when a Chinese woman blocked the doorway. On instinct, Miyuki backed away and bowed, letting the older woman come inside.

The Chinese woman sighed like a disgusted horse before moving around Miyuki to enter the boutique.

And that was when it hit her. Miyuki knew that woman.

Her heart pounded. Miyuki knew she should head down the street immediately and not look back. But she couldn't help herself.

Miyuki turned.

The Chinese woman had reached the white jeans and checked

the back pocket. Confused, she checked all the pockets.

Now she was certain. The woman was one of the three Chinese intelligence agents who kidnapped Robert and Nadia on that train in Utah. The woman was always angry and serial-killer crazy.

After she finished searching the white jeans, her eyes went straight to Miyuki, as if the woman could smell another operative in the room. The always angry woman tilted her head, and her stoic facade switched to pure hatred.

Her cover now blown, Miyuki sprinted out of the boutique and weaved through the thick crowd on Takeshita Street. Not hiding the fact that she was running for her life.

Miyuki glanced over her shoulder.

The always angry woman was on her like a police dog, weaving just as fast through the crowd and keeping an excellent pace. The woman concealed something in her right hand.

Miyuki convinced herself it was a weapon.

She had to circle around a group of kids holding hands before Miyuki could look over her shoulder again. Now she could see the knife the woman was holding.

Miyuki gripped her woven handbag tight. It contained the only weapons she had on her. But the always angry woman was only keeping pace with her, not gaining. If Miyuki was lucky, she could lure the woman inside the Harajuku train station bathroom and knock her out. Then Miyuki could jump on the next train to escape.

But that plan fell through the moment a large Polynesian man in a blue suit impeded her path. His name was Kawiki.

He has also been on the train in Utah.

Miyuki swallowed. This made things complicated. Now two Chinese intelligence operatives were closing in on her from opposite ends of the street. Each operative quite capable of killing her. Ducking into one of the local shops could be an option. But Miyuki didn't like the idea of getting trapped in a corner. She always preferred the freedom to maneuver.

Then what should she do?

Miyuki spotted the white rubber tire of a pink bicycle, its rear end poking out from behind one of the businesses. Most likely it was a little girl's bike. Hope filled Miyuki's chest. She headed straight to the business. It was an outdoor candy shop. There was a man behind the counter.

A little girl asked the man something in Japanese. It convinced Miyuki that the man was her father.

Miyuki went up to the counter and gave the man all the money she had.

"What's this for?" the man asked in Japanese.

"For borrowing your daughter's bicycle, *Aragoto*."

Before the man comprehended what she meant by that, Miyuki grabbed the pink bicycle and hopped on.

When Miyuki looked back up...the always angry woman was ten feet away.

She raised her arm. The knife's blade gleamed as it left her hand.

Miyuki ducked.

The knife sailed over her head and bit into the wood wall behind her.

The always angry woman lunged for her.

Miyuki stood on the right pedal, rolling the bicycle to her right as she brought up her left leg to kick the woman hard in the stomach. This pushed her out of the way, allowing Miyuki to pedal her way through the open end of the street.

After weaving through some pedestrians and making progress down the street, Miyuki glanced behind her. No one was in pursuit.

Miyuki's heart slowed down and she allowed herself a grin. It was only a quick chase, but Miyuki quite enjoyed the rush of adrenaline it created. Being a Gem opened up many situations that required heavy amounts of adrenaline. She couldn't wait to tell Emma and the other girls about her mission.

Miyuki reached the end of Takeshita Street and stopped. Here, there was a busy intersection of passing vehicle traffic. If she biked down this cross street, Miyuki was confident she could find the next train station that would take her back to downtown Tokyo. There, she could deliver the thumb drive.

Miyuki made the turn and merged into the public bike lane. These special lanes were a part of every Japanese road system since bicycles were a popular way to get around the city. Miyuki traveled a little more than two blocks before she heard an engine rev behind her.

She noted a driver was getting too close to the bike lane. At first, Miyuki thought the driver was only careless. But when she peered through the clear windshield, Miyuki noted Volleen Woo behind the right-side steering wheel. His dangerous eyes focused on her like a snake. Miyuki's heart raced again and she pedaled as hard as she could. Her bicycle flew down the bike lane as she passed other bikes like they were cardboard cutouts.

Miyuki took a hard left, leaning her body into the turn and allowing her sneaker to scrape across the pavement to create enough friction to turn her bike a little quicker.

As she completed the turn, the squeal of tires echoed behind her as the Mitsubishi SUV whipped around the corner and accelerated towards her.

Other bicyclists complained about the road hog by slapping his side windows as the vehicle moved up the bike lane, causing most of them to veer out of the way.

Miyuki pumped her legs as hard as she could, her butt rising from the seat as she used her leg muscles to squeeze every kilometer of speed out of the bicycle.

It wasn't enough.

The engine raced behind her. So close that she didn't dare peek.

Miyuki felt a hard bump that almost made her wipe out.

Another shove from the SUV and her bike wobbled.

The car horn blared. The shrill it made stabbed her eardrums.

Miyuki's heart was pumping out so much adrenaline she knew she would be high for at least a week.

The excitement.

The fear.

She raced along the narrow ledge between them.

Loving it.

Wanting more and more of it.

But Miyuki knew she would die if she stayed in this bike lane. She veered right, sending her bike straight into oncoming traffic.

There were three lanes of cars going in this direction. Miyuki aimed for the space between the lanes and pumped the pedals as hard as she could. She weaved between the three lanes of traffic as best she could. Luckily, traffic in this part of the city was heavy, so it wasn't moving fast. Still…one wrong move and Miyuki would crack her head through a windshield.

Left, right, left again. The traffic whipped by.

She was doing well. Defying the odds. Staying alive.

The Mitsubishi raced along the left side of the street. Trying to keep pace with her. Hoping Miyuki would either crash or come to her senses by veering back to the legal flow of traffic. But the Chinese didn't know her very well.

Miyuki kept weaving through oncoming traffic. Determined to make this work. Getting addicted to the rush of danger. Getting used to the idea of not dying.

As she approached a side street, the Mitsubishi was to her left. A clear lane to her right.

Miyuki gambled. She made a hard right at the side street, leaning her body into the forty-five-degree turn and leaving the Mitsubishi behind as it sailed through the intersection going in the wrong direction. Volleen Woo would have to do a quick U-turn, move through traffic, then take a left at the intersection against traffic to resume the chase.

Miyuki had bought herself some—

The other car came out of nowhere. Miyuki barely had time to register its existence before the Toyota pulled out in front of her and she felt herself flying over the hood like a bird. Miyuki didn't think about it, but her gymnastics training kicked in automatically as she tumbled forward into a roll, letting herself tumble over and over to dissipate the forward momentum before her body came to a complete stop.

Miyuki stared at the sky. Yes, she was still alive.

Her hands stung, most likely due to her palms rubbing against the pavement. But otherwise, she was good. Miyuki slowly got to her feet. The pink bike lay on the ground with its front end crushed. It had taken most of the impact while Miyuki sailed over the hood. The driver was out of his vehicle. He looked surprised, as if amazed that this teenage girl wasn't dead.

Miyuki heard more squealing tires. It was the Mitsubishi clearing the intersection and racing towards the accident.

Miyuki needed to run. She took a step forward and almost fell on her face. Her knees ached. They weren't broken, but hitting the pavement still made them stiff and sore.

The Mitsubishi slid to a stop. Volleen Woo, the always angry woman, and Kawiki got out of the car.

Miyuki hobbled away, getting about three steps before Kawiki restrained her. She was so exhausted after her bicycle-chase workout that there was no way Miyuki could fight back right now.

The always angry woman glared at her. "Bitch," she said in

Mandarin Chinese before slapping Miyuki across the face. All Miyuki could do was hold her chin up in defiance. The woman raised her hand again.

But Volleen Woo stopped her. "Focus on the task, shall we?" he said in Mandarin.

The always angry woman restrained herself.

"Hello there," Volleen Woo said in English. "Ruby, isn't it? You're a long way from Utah, aren't you?"

Miyuki didn't answer.

"Do you remember us? Well, we certainly remember you."

"You threw us off a train," the giant Polynesian man said in English, as if the girl had hurt his feelings.

"Where are your friends? Should we be expecting them to come save you?"

Miyuki said nothing.

"Give us the thumb drive and we'll be on our way."

"What thumb drive?"

The always angry woman slapped Miyuki again.

Volleen Woo sighed. "I bore of such repetitive games. It's a ridiculous waste of time. We know you have it, but fine. We'll go through the motions if you wish." He addressed Kawiki. "Give the young lady a full body search and don't be a gentleman about it."

CHAPTER 2

The warm California sun greeted Emma as she emerged with the other students just released from the clutches of West Berkley High school. Some students went off to the line of idling school buses while others headed for the designated pickup areas for parents. Emma was one of the lucky ones. She had a car.

"Nadia forgot again," a girl with an English accent called out to Emma. "If she misses the bus this time, your grandmother will have to come pick her up." Olivia had brown skin accented by cool, bronze undertones. Her layers of curly golden-brown hair were pulled back with a cute hair ribbon that Emma forgot to compliment her on this morning.

Emma wanted to correct that. "Okay, tell the bus driver to wait for her. Did I mention that I absolutely love your hair ribbon. It goes with that outfit so well."

Olivia stopped walking. "Are you messing with me, love?"

"Oh my God…can't I give you one honest compliment when I feel like it?"

"Sure, but you'd better warn me first so I can prepare myself." Olivia showed her a sly grin before leaving.

Emma quickened her pace towards the student parking lot. Her white Mercedes AMG Coupe glistened in the sun. Emma had had it washed and detailed over the weekend and it looked beautiful.

Another girl with warm, orange-brown skin waited near the trunk as she glanced down at her phone. A light breeze teased Nadia's dark hair and the purple headscarf she was wearing.

"Hey, I'm not going home," Emma said. "It's Wednesday. Remember?"

Nadia's eyebrows shot up. "Shoot, I completely forgot. See you at dinner?"

"Probably not." Emma sighed.

"Have fun training." Nadia waved goodbye as she rushed towards the waiting buses.

The route was so familiar to Emma's Mercedes that she could release the wheel and the car would find the place on its own. Northbound on I-80 out of Berkeley. North through Vallejo until she hit California State Highway 29 and took it into Napa Valley. Once there, a large welcome sign greeted the tourists: *The Burlington Winery, one of the world's finest producers of Cabernet Sauvignon.*

Emma skipped the public parking lot and stopped her Mercedes near the hidden entrance the public didn't know about. A long-haired hippie with round glasses came up and checked inside Emma's car before asking for her driver's license. Once satisfied, he nodded. "Enjoy your afternoon, my sister." The hippie walked away. His gun holster was slightly visible just under his grape-stained smock.

Emma drove the Mercedes through the gate and into the small garage. The doors closed and a hidden elevator in the floor lowered her car to the underground parking lot.

After clearing all the Authority's security checkpoints, Emma walked through a sprawling, open area with two levels. A large circular staircase climbed up to the second floor, which had glass walls separating most of the offices and meeting rooms. It was bright, using yellow, white, and light brown as primary colors. The bottom level had a cafeteria, a relaxation area, and a section designed like a jungle with green pod-looking structures surrounded by fake trees. The pods were meeting rooms.

Emma stayed downstairs and walked through an unmarked entrance that led to another part of the bottom floor.

Emma soon found herself inside a maze of dark blue walls, floors, and ceilings, where the only light source was a series of white strips running along the top and bottom of each wall. Glowing white letters pressed into the walls identified different destinations. The Labyrinth was the most sensitive area of the facility.

Emma didn't need the directions. Her sneakers had been to the TR division so many times over the last few months that they automatically knew the way. The TR division was a massive area carved out like a giant cave. There was a full gym, indoor gun range, hand-to-hand combat area, simulators, and other pieces of training equipment.

A large Russian woman with blond hair was waiting. Her code name was Lioness.

"I take it that gushing over our favorite episodes of *Riverdale Creek* while having milkshakes is out for today?" Emma asked.

Lioness refused to smile. "Your jokes provide me hours of amusement, Black Opal."

Black Opal was Emma's code name in the Gems. She didn't much care for the name at first, but it was slowly growing on her.

Lioness continued. "Today's training agenda is as follows…first you'll take your qualification test for personal firearms level one. Then we'll work on your sketching skills."

"Sketching? Isn't that like drawing?"

"It's precisely like drawing."

"Why does a spy need to know that?"

Lioness stopped writing on her clipboard and leveled a stare.

Emma instantly regretted talking.

"Sketching helps you see details," the woman said. "The details of a human face. The details of a room you've been inside. Knowing such details could be crucial to the failure or the success of any mission."

Emma pulled out her phone. "But if I need to gather intelligence inside a room, all I need to do is snap some pics on my phone. Isn't that faster?"

Lioness grabbed her phone and tossed it on the floor. As the woman lifted her boot—

"I got it!" Emma yelled. "I understand. Sometimes I won't have a phone available to use."

Lioness smiled and gave Emma back her phone. "If you can memorize the details around you, then you can recall them. Sketching gives you that skill."

"Got it. After sketching, can I go home?"

"Yes," Lioness said before handing her a pistol.

Lioness and Emma moved through a set of double doors that slammed shut behind them as they entered the underground gun range. The ceilings, floors, and walls of the range were heavily soundproofed.

"What weapon did I give you?" Lioness asked.

"A gun. I think."

"Black Opal…"

"Okay, fine. You gave me a Glock 43 single stack, 9 mm Luger caliber pistol."

"Next, demonstrate the correct firing stance for the shooting range."

After Emma showed her the proper stance, Lioness checked that off. "Now, disassemble your weapon."

"Didn't I already pass that on my last phase of gun training?"

Lioness waited for her to continue.

Emma sighed and got on with it. Luckily for her, Aardvark worked with her extensively on disassembling pistols, so the task wasn't a huge issue. Soon Emma completed it.

Lioness examined the disassembled pistol on the table. "Excellent. Put it back together."

Emma did and presented the pistol back to Lioness, with the muzzle pointed at the floor and her finger far away from the trigger.

Lioness took the Glock, pulled back the chamber, and checked it. She handed it back to Emma. "Excellent. Load the weapon and prepare for the qualification test."

Emma loaded a ten-round magazine into the Glock, leveled the pistol at the target area, and waited.

Lioness didn't speak.

What was she waiting for?

Did Emma forget something?

Emma noted the protective eye shades and the earmuffs hanging on the wall. She activated the trigger safety on her pistol before setting it down and putting on her eye and ear protection. She picked up her pistol, got back into her stance, and removed the trigger safety.

"Now you can begin," Lioness announced.

A target moved to her left. Emma aimed and squeezed the trigger. The Glock kicked back and the target was hit dead center. More targets presented themselves. But Emma didn't panic; she focused on each target and fired. Soon it became a rhythm. Spot the target. Aim at the target. Squeeze. Spot. Aim. Squeeze.

After ten rounds Emma replaced the empty magazine with a full one.

Spot. Aim. Squeeze. Repeat.

After firing on forty targets, Lioness ordered her to stop.

Emma pointed the gun towards the ground and moved her finger away from the trigger.

"Forty targets. Thirty-five hits," Lioness said. "That's excellent, Black Opal. If this was a qualification test for military weapons level one, you would be classified as a sharpshooter."

"Cool. What's a sharpshooter?"

Lioness sighed. "Congratulations, you have passed personal firearms level one."

It was close to eleven when Emma arrived home. But as soon as she closed the front door, Emma could smell sage burning in the kitchen. Grandma must still be up. A Jack Russell terrier came over to greet her, his tail wagging like a weed trimmer. Snoopy barked and Emma leaned down to give him some love. Her fingers could feel the plastic brace that still supported the dog's weak back. A pang of guilt still went through her.

Emma put away her backpack, slipped off her sneakers, and made her way across the polished wood floor to the kitchen, where she knew her grandmother would be.

"They have you keeping hoodlum hours, young one. And on a school night no less," Grandma said as she chopped vegetables near a Crock-Pot. Her white hair was braided into two white ponytails that hung over a Grateful Dead T-shirt. "Is Laura training you to be a spy or a Navy SEAL?"

Emma picked up a piece of celery. "She says it won't be too much longer before I catch up with the other girls." Emma crunched the end of it and chewed. "What are you making?"

"A vegetable soup for dinner tomorrow. I'll be on campus all day. The philosophy department is having a meeting right after my three o'clock lecture, so I have to do my office work late."

"You don't have to make soup. We can order some carryout for dinner."

Her grandmother raised an eyebrow. "I know what you girls will do. You'll go through the drive-thru at some fast-food garbage factory and eat junk. Nope, even if I'm not here, you girls are eating a good meal made with fresh ingredients." Grandmother returned to her food prep. "Just remember to turn the slow cooker off and rinse it out when you girls are done. Now…why haven't you kissed your grandmother yet? She missed you tonight."

Emma kissed her on the cheek.

"Thank you. Now get out of here and get some sleep, young one."

Emma finished the rest of her celery and picked up Snoopy as she headed upstairs to her room. She rubbed Snoopy's throat and kept him calm so he wouldn't wake up Olivia or Nadia as she passed by their room.

Emma changed clothes and got ready for bed. She made Snoopy comfortable on his favorite chair that sat next to her bed before leaving to go brush her teeth.

As she moved down the hall towards the bathroom, Emma paused beside her friend's room. Miyuki's name was on the door covered with bright fake flowers and a few slogans written in Japanese. It was a door overflowing with happiness. Just like the girl who normally occupied it.

Emma missed her happiness.

Wherever she was in the world, Emma only hoped Miyuki was being careful.

CHAPTER 3

Miyuki swallowed her fear as the large Polynesian man named Kawiki circled behind her. His large wrinkled hands pressed against her waist. His fingers were about to go to places that Miyuki wanted to stay private and personal. She looked around her. The side street was empty. Even the driver of the Toyota had disappeared. In a country of over two hundred million people crammed together on an island, Miyuki thought there'd be someone around to yell help to.

But it wasn't her day.

A back kick or even a stomp on the man's foot was out of the question because Miyuki's thighs were still screaming from the bicycle chase. She could elbow him in the stomach, but Kawiki was so fat, her sharp elbow would only tickle him. All she could do was collapse to the ground and passively resist his search. It was the only defense she had.

Unless…Miyuki realized that in her native Japan, it was always custom for people to bow when they first met. *Hei*, it would be rude not to show her guests from China the proper respect.

With Kawiki hunched over her and his hand reaching inside her knee, Miyuki bowed. She bowed at such a sharp angle that Kawiki rolled over the top of her like a large beach ball. His massive body gaining momentum as it rolled into Volleen Woo and the always angry woman.

Miyuki stood up and pushed herself down the side street.

"Get her!" Volleen yelled.

Miyuki took the thumb drive out of her pocket and palmed it. She was unable to break into a run because of her legs, so it wouldn't be long until they caught up to her again. But Miyuki did reach the end of the side street where it met with the main street.

Out of the corner of her eye, Miyuki saw a right-side-driven Sako Cakes delivery van. The van's passenger-side window was halfway down.

An idea popped into her mind and Miyuki went with it. As the van passed her, she tossed the thumb drive through the open window. As Emma would say, touchdown!

But then Kawiki grabbed her and threw her to the ground.

Volleen Woo stepped out into the main street and watched the van make a turn. "She tossed it into the van. Come." The man ran down the side street towards the Mitsubishi. Kawiki and the always angry woman flashed her dirty looks before they retreated towards their car. The Mitsubishi flew out of the side street and did a perfect power slide as it raced to catch up with the delivery van.

Miyuki was pissed at herself. All she did was postpone the inevitable. Volleen Woo would stop the van, take the drive, and her mission would be a huge failure.

But a car horn pulled Miyuki out of her pity party. It was from a small Honda. Inside were four young women, each wearing pink hair and wearing Kawaii-style clothing. They all looked adorable.

"Would you like a ride?" the driver asked politely in Japanese.

"Love your outfit!" another girl in the back said out the window. "So cute!"

"Are you walking over to Takeshita Street?" a third girl asked.

Miyuki smiled. Her luck had just changed. "*Hei!*"

"We can squeeze you in!" the driver said, stopping the car.

Miyuki walked up and bowed to them slightly. "*Aragoto.*" And then she had another idea. "I was heading to my cupcake bakery when a man showed me a knife and stole my van. He just left me here."

"Oh no," the driver said, actually meaning it. "Do you want us to call the police?"

"Actually, may I ask a favor?"

A minute later, Miyuki was behind the Honda's right-side steering wheel as the car zigzagged through some traffic. She could see Volleen Woo's Mitsubishi in the distance. He was closing in on the Sako Cakes van. Miyuki popped the little Honda into a higher gear and gunned it. One of the girls inside the car cheered as Miyuki veered around another car.

"You're a better driver than Suki!" a girl in the back said.

Suki nodded from the passenger seat and watched Miyuki with awe as her little Honda acted like a tiny Formula one car as it made another sharp left turn with precision.

Miyuki could see the Mitsubishi on the right side of the van. Kawiki's hands were outside the SUV, trying to get the driver's attention to pull over the cake van. But for some reason, the driver kept going. The Sako Cakes van veered left and took the entrance to the expressway.

The cake van was in the middle lane. The Mitsubishi was on the right, so Miyuki pointed the little Honda down the left lane. She reached the opposite side of the cake van and honked the high-pitched horn. But the driver didn't react.

"Cupcake crook!" a girl in the back yelled.

"Give this girl her van back, you criminal!" Suki yelled out the window. "Oh, the driver is wearing headphones."

Ah, so that was why the driver couldn't hear them. That made sense to Miyuki. She considered pulling in front of the van and slowing him down to a stop. But then Volleen Woo would simply pull out a gun and take the thumb drive. Miyuki needed to get creative.

She took off her seat belt. "Switch places with me."

"Sorry, could you repeat?" Suki asked.

"Take your belt off and come sit on my lap," Miyuki said. "I want to switch places with you." Suki was a small girl and Miyuki had had to push her seat back to drive, so fitting the girl in should be possible.

"While we're moving?" Suki asked, unsure if Miyuki was serious.

"*Hei*, just like in the movies."

The girls in the back were intrigued. They were up for anything. But Suki wasn't so sure.

"Please, I must get my van back."

Suki reluctantly took off her seat belt and awkwardly slipped on top of Miyuki's lap.

"Take the wheel," Miyuki said.

The girl grabbed it.

Miyuki contorted her body, like she did in gymnastics class, rotating her pelvis to the side and using her hands to pull herself out from under Suki. The Honda zigzagged as the driver exchange bumped the steering wheel left and right. The engine noise dropped off as the little Honda lost speed and fell behind the van.

"Put your foot on the gas!" Miyuki said.

"Oh, *Hei!* Sorry." Suki found the gas pedal and the Honda surged forward once again.

Miyuki was now in the passenger seat. "Faster!"

"Go, Suki!" her friends in the back yelled.

Suki looked terrified but she held it together and drove faster as the little Honda caught up to the cake van and the Mitsubishi.

Now came Miyuki's favorite part. It was a tight fit, but she climbed through the small moon roof and crouched on top of the little Honda as it swerved back and forth.

"Oh, she's like Wonder Woman!" a girl in the back said.

"And she loves her cupcakes," another girl added.

Miyuki motioned Suki to get closer. The girl sped up. The dashes on the pavement flew by so fast that they blurred. If Miyuki miscalculated her jump by even a meter, she would slide off the van and most likely get flattened by a truck.

But she wasn't afraid. Far from it. Excited was more like it. The adrenaline flowed inside her and she felt invincible.

Miyuki coiled herself like a python and jumped.

She landed on the cake van's roof, but farther back than she wanted. Her hands tried to grab something. But the roof was smooth, allowing her body to slide towards the roof's edge.

She was about to fall off.

But Miyuki grabbed on to a large mirror for dear life. The mirror itself pointed down at the van's back doors. She was lucky that the cake van was old and not equipped with a backup camera.

Miyuki took a deep breath. The high-pitched horn tooted as the girls poked their heads out of the Honda's moon-roof and cheered. They loved the show she was putting on for them.

The Mitsubishi pulled in front of the van and slowed down. Miyuki held on tight as the van's driver swerved to the next lane to avoid it. But the Mitsubishi switched lanes and blocked him again. Kawiki's massive body hung out the window as he pointed a gun at the windshield.

The van quickly slowed down and pulled over to the shoulder.

Miyuki was too late. Or was she?

As the van stopped in the emergency lane, Miyuki dropped to the pavement, ran over to the driver, and knocked on his door.

The driver opened it. "I don't understand what's going on. Are you the police?" he asked in Japanese.

"*Hei*, go talk to those undercover officers over there." Miyuki pointed to the Mitsubishi now parked a few car links ahead.

The driver walked toward the SUV as Volleen Woo, Kawiki, and the always angry lady hopped out. They started running towards the van.

Miyuki climbed behind the wheel and put the cake van in gear. The three Chinese agents stopped running. But Volleen Woo pulled out a gun.

The van's windshield cracked as a bullet punched through it, causing Miyuki to duck. She stomped on the gas and lined up the left side of the cake van to the right rear corner of the Mitsubishi. Miyuki closed her eyes and braced herself as the van smashed into the SUV.

As Miyuki veered back on to the expressway, she checked her rearview mirror. The Mitsubishi's left-side tires were hooked on top of the guardrail, preventing it from going anywhere.

Miyuki drove to the nearest train station and retrieved the thumb drive from the passenger-side floorboard.

The ride to downtown Tokyo was quiet and peaceful.

* * *

The sky was a dark purple. The last afterthought of daylight was a fading pink line on the horizon. Far below, the Tokyo streetlights were on, outlining the city's road system in orange as it traced around the endless amount of multistory buildings.

Miyuki gripped the metal railing as she stood on the observation deck of the Tokyo Metropolitan Government Building. The deck was open to the public and was the perfect meeting place for her contact.

A middle-aged Japanese man with a crisp dark suit joined her along the railing. She handed him the thumb drive.

"Any difficulties?" the man asked.

Mr. E was the head of the Authority's Tokyo Station. Miyuki noticed that he often sucked on candy that left a hint of cinnamon on his breath.

She liked that scent.

"A small pursuit by Mr. Woo and his friends," she said. "And the local police might be looking for a girl with pink hair who stole a cake van. Otherwise, no complications to speak of."

Mr. E placed the thumb drive securely into a canister and pulled a tab. There was a sizzling sound as a special acid devoured the plastic drive. After a few minutes, Mr. E opened the canister and dumped a pile of granules that blew off the observation deck railing and sailed over Tokyo.

"Congratulations," Mr. E said. "That was the last backup file to the Red Storm VX formula."

A woman's voice with a crisp British accent echoed from Mr. E's pocket. "Excellent work. Last week we wiped out the Russian lab and the scientists creating that dreadful biological weapon. Now, Red Storm VX will never exist again."

Mr. E smiled. "I forgot she was in my pocket." He pulled out his phone. It was on speaker. "Ruby has done an excellent job for us, Mrs. B. Thank you for loaning her out to us."

"You're welcome, Mr. E," the voice said. "I think you deserve a reward, Ruby. Since you're already in Japan, why don't you take a brief holiday to go visit your family?"

Miyuki scanned the horizon. Osaka would be off to the left, over by Mount Fuji. It would be nice to see her little sister again. But dealing with everything else…

"It would be most inconvenient for me to visit my family at this time."

There was a pause.

"Why would it be inconvenient?" Mrs. B's voice asked. "On the contrary I would think."

"My division will gladly arrange whatever transportation you need," Mr. E added.

"Thank you for your kind offer," Miyuki said. "But I have schoolwork to get back to. Perhaps another time."

"Are you sure, Ruby?" Mrs. B asked. "I can talk to Black Opal's grandmother. I'm sure it won't be a problem for you to take a couple of days off due to the circumstances."

"With all due respect, ma'am, I don't think it's convenient at this time."

"As you wish," Mrs. B said. "See you at the end of the week, then."

Mr. E ended the call and put up his phone.

"Can you arrange to fly me back to San Francisco as soon as possible?" Miyuki asked.

CHAPTER 4

Miyuki woke up to the sound of her alarm. She pulled herself out of bed and checked the time. She'd received only about five hours of sleep and it felt like it. Miyuki told herself it would have to do as she began her normal morning routine.

After an hour, Miyuki went downstairs. A small Jack Russell terrier scurried across the polished wood floor with excitement, his spine supported by a plastic brace. Even with the limitation, the dog made the effort to greet her with boundless enthusiasm.

Miyuki went to her knees. "Good morning, Snoopy." The terrier licked her like a tasty Popsicle, making her laugh. After a minute of petting and kisses, Miyuki headed into the kitchen.

"There she is," Emma's grandmother said, her white hair braided into two ponytails as she cooked over a griddle. "I made pancakes for you."

Miyuki loved pancakes. Breakfast, lunch, or dinner. Miyuki thought they were the best food America ever invented. Emma's grandmother was so nice to her.

She clapped her hands. "Thank you."

Done with her breakfast, Nadia was at the table folding her headscarf. "When did you come in last night?"

"Yeah, we didn't hear you at all, love." Olivia was still working on her pancakes. Her curly golden-brown hair was pulled back with a cute hair ribbon Miyuki had never seen before.

"It was late." Miyuki joined her friends at the table. "About one in the morning."

"Laura works you girls too hard." Emma's grandmother built a pile of three pancakes and brought the plate over to Miyuki. "How she expects you to do all these missions and then go to school is beyond me." Emma's grandmother was the only one Miyuki knew who used Mrs. B's first name. None of them would ever dare call her Laura.

Emma's grandmother sat down. "Where did you go this time?"

"She's not allowed to tell you that," Olivia said.

"Even we don't know where she went," Nadia added.

Emma's grandmother sighed, then showed Miyuki a smile. "Well, you're here. Safe and sound. And that makes me happy."

"Your pancakes make me happy," Miyuki said, spreading fresh butter in between the layers before smothering the stack with maple syrup. The first bite was always her favorite and this one didn't disappoint.

Yes, pancakes made the world a much happier place.

After Miyuki made good progress with her pancakes, Emma came inside the kitchen with Snoopy, his little tail wagging. She waved at Miyuki before yawning.

"It's about time, young one," Emma's grandmother said. "Miyuki had only five hours of sleep and she's already halfway done with her breakfast."

"Pancakes? Isn't that a little heavy for a school day?" Emma asked, subconsciously touching her waist.

Emma's grandmother sipped her herbal tea. "Make something else if you want, but you're cleaning it up."

Emma made a face, but took a plate and put one single pancake and one turkey sausage link on it.

"This objection is coming from the girl who eats little chocolate donuts every day," Olivia said.

Emma sat down and grabbed the plastic maple syrup bottle. "I only eat them in the afternoon, when I've burned off most of my calories for the day."

"Told you to stop eating that junk," Emma's grandmother said. "You know what kind of food additives they put in those donuts?"

Emma squinted at Olivia, saying thanks for bringing up the subject.

Nadia checked her phone. "I do like the new lemon-flavored ones."

"Lemon-flavored donuts?" Emma's grandmother shook her head. "The junk they sell in those vending machines these days."

Later that day, the students of West Berkeley high school gathered inside the commons area for lunch period number one. The Gems claimed one of the many circular wood-topped tables crowding the area.

Miyuki heard her phone laugh as she received a text from one of her new gamer friends. The laugh was from her favorite anime character, Yuki Luki Abuki, a precocious ten-year-old girl who always got into trouble, but could always count on her magical cat Aiko for help.

Miyuki read the text. After school, her gamer friends were planning a joint mission on the new online *Star Trek* game and wanted her to join. Miyuki wasn't much of a Trekkie. However, being a communications officer for a starship sounded like fun, so she texted them back with a yes. Miyuki nibbled on a carrot as she watched her friends at the table.

Olivia looked pissed as she read a novel by Ernest Hemingway. The book was an assignment for her English lit class and the girl was not happy about it. Mostly because Olivia hated reading, period.

"Everyone's so quiet today," Emma said, checking for a reaction from the table. She had already polished off half of her mini chocolate donuts for lunch.

Olivia took a moment to drink some milk, then returned to her book.

Emma glanced at Miyuki, who flashed a supportive grin.

"World-renowned astrophysicist Jules Vernon came up with a new theory about comets," Nadia said. "I'm reading about it now on this astrophysics website. It's fascinating."

"Oh, yeah?—he's a—he's good," Emma said. The girl didn't have a clue about science. "What about you, Miyuki, anything going on?"

"I'm playing *Star Trek Online* after school."

"*Star Trek*, huh? Have you seen the new movie?" Emma asked. "I love that girl Jedi, she rocks."

Nadia lifted her eyes from her phone. "You're referring to *Star Wars*, a fantasy set in outer space. *Star Trek* is a science fiction series that stays within basic scientific principles. There's a large difference between the two."

Emma shrugged. "I'm only saying that I love the girl Jedi."

Olivia shot a knowing look to Nadia, causing both of them to grin. Miyuki wished the girls weren't so hard on Emma. Maybe she was ignorant about *Star Trek*, but it still didn't mean she was a stupid blonde.

Emma's phone chirped with a message. She read it and rolled her eyes.

"Bad news?" Miyuki asked.

"Not really, it's just—okay, there's this sweet girl in my business economics class who transferred here from Seattle. She doesn't know anyone, so she's kind of glued herself to me. I feel like she sees me as, like, a mentor."

"Poor girl," Olivia said.

Emma fired a look.

"Just kidding, love."

"Did this girl text you?" Miyuki asked, trying to keep the harmony of the table intact.

"Yeah, she wants to know where I'm sitting," Emma said. "We must have the same lunch."

"You should invite her over."

"Do you think I should?"

"When we came to this school, you introduced us to your friends," Miyuki said. "We should do the same for her."

"You're right. We should," Emma said. "Okay, I'll text her."

Emma typed a message and hit send.

As soon as she looked up, a short girl with red hair rushed up to their table. Her skin had freckles and her eyes had this sparkle about them, hinting at a boundless energy that couldn't be kept inside one human being.

Miyuki instantly liked her.

"Wow, were you over at the next table?" Emma asked.

"Thank you so much for the invite, Emma. You're the best person ever," the girl with freckles said. Her delivery was so fast her voice sounded like she was on permanent fast-forward. The girl waved. "Hi, Emma's friends. My name is Kayla and I'm from Seattle. I love music and art. I love kittens and sewing. I love pizza and Thai food. I love boys and girls." She paused. "I mean, I love girls in the sister sorta way. Although, my cousin is gay, which I'm fine with because she's always liked girls her entire life and it was way too obvious to my aunt and uncle, who didn't make her pick boys over girls. But anyway, as far as me, I like guys."

Nadia froze. She appeared overwhelmed by this girl.

Olivia had stopped reading. Her mouth was slightly open. Her eyes amazed.

Emma smiled, as if delighted by everyone's reaction.

Now even Miyuki wasn't too sure about this girl. In Japan, talking like that in public would get Kayla admitted to a mental hospital for evaluation.

"Is it cool if I sit?" Kayla asked.

"Be our guest," Emma said. She introduced everyone at the table to Kayla. The Gems replied with polite hellos.

"I love that book," Kayla said, referring to the Ernest Hemingway novel. "I didn't think I would like it, but I really did."

"I hate reading it," Olivia said.

"Oh," Kayla said.

"Why don't you read the CliffsNotes version?" Nadia asked.

"Better yet, go online and copy someone else's book report on it," Emma said.

Olivia closed the book. "But I want to write this paper myself. When I go to college, I'll be expected to write papers all the time and read a large number of books. So I'd better get on with it and learn to tolerate things like—reading." Olivia glanced at Emma. "And I won't take shortcuts because I do want to learn, not skate through life because my father died and left me millions of dollars."

Nadia covered her mouth out of shock.

Miyuki almost did the same.

Kayla ate corn chips. She was savoring those and the drama unfolding at lunch.

Emma glared at Olivia. The girl had crossed a line.

"Excuse me?"

Miyuki could feel the harmony of the table cracking like a bridge made of plywood. It was her job to save it. "None of us has a right to judge anyone at this table. It's not our past that will dictate our future. We have control over our lives. Emma will choose her own path. The same as I. The same as Olivia. The same as Nadia. We must help—not hinder—each other in that journey."

Olivia absorbed Miyuki's words. She glanced at Nadia, who approved with a nod. That gesture made Olivia shift in her chair and take another drink of milk before she addressed Emma. "Sorry, love. I'm just a bit irritable today. No offense to your father intended."

Emma paused to consider it. "No offense taken."

"Oh my God. That was so beautiful," Kayla said as she crunched down on another corn chip.

Once lunch period was over, the Gems cleared their table and threw away their trash. Olivia pointed to one of the vending machines near the entrance to the commons. "Has that always been there?"

Miyuki noted a Thunderdog energy drink machine sitting next to the school's normal line of vending machines.

"That one's new," Nadia said. "Think I saw that drink in Australia when we were there."

"Wow, when did you go to Australia?" Kayla asked.

Olivia shot the Gems an uncomfortable look. Kayla was already asking questions they didn't want to answer.

However, Nadia didn't bat an eyelash. "Oh, when I came to this country from Saudi Arabia, I flew east through Australia and noticed the beverages at the airport. Do you like energy drinks, Kayla?"

Nadia was smooth. Her question threw Kayla into a large spiel about her feelings about energy drinks and soda pop in general, making the girl forget all about her original question as the bell rang for fifth hour.

The lunch group began separating.

"Remember, you'll have to ride the bus today since I have to go —you know where—after school," Emma said to the rest of the Gems.

"Where do you have to go?" Kayla asked.

"It's nothing. Just this thing I can't get out of."

CHAPTER 5

The driver training facility was a few miles away from the Napa Valley underground headquarters. In the daytime, it was a public stunt-driving school. At night, it trained Authority operatives how to handle evasive driving maneuvers to combat kidnappers, assassination attempts, and, of course, road rage. Tonight would be the facilities' ultimate test…teaching Emma Rothchild how not to destroy a car.

The twelve-year-old Crown Vic police cruiser she drove was in great distress. Emma had already sheared off its right fender, busted out the glass in the back window, and punctured two of its tires, which were replaced before her latest attempt through the obstacle course.

"Accelerate into the turn," her instructor said.

Emma did, but she wanted to shut her eyes.

"Turn the wheel more."

"More."

"More…stay with it."

The wheels squealed as she turned the wheel sharply.

"Keep your foot on the gas."

Emma's foot was scared. Her whole body was scared as she felt the Crown Vic wanting to break away from her control.

Another fake car popped into view.

"Evade!" her instructor said.

Emma panicked.

"Stay off the brakes!"

Too late. She stood on the pedal, and the Crown Vic rammed the fake car, ripping the Styrofoam body to pieces.

"Civilians!" The instructor pointed at the Styrofoam family ahead.

Emma turned the wheel, but her foot wouldn't release the brakes. The car obliterated the family before it slowed to a stop.

Emma closed her eyes. What was the point? She was a horrible driver. Simply avoiding non-moving objects was enough of a daily driving challenge for her. But Lioness was determined to improve Emma's driving skills. Even if they had to destroy another car.

"I'm sorry," Emma said. "I'm so sorry. I keep doing that. Can we try it again?"

Her instructor stared out the window as if his mind were somewhere else. He didn't say a word.

"Mr. Albatross?" Emma asked. "Can we try that again?"

The man closed his eyes. He was breathing so fast Emma wondered if he was having a heart attack. But the man took in a final breath and his body relaxed. "Again?" he asked. "You want to try that again?"

"Yes, sir."

"This is pointless," Albatross said. "You can't drive a car."

"Well, I'm okay under normal driving conditions. It's only when we go fast that I—"

"No," he interrupted. "It's abundantly clear that you fail to grasp even the most basic concepts of controlling a motor vehicle."

"That's not true. I drive home every day from school without hurting anyone."

"Black Opal, you're a ticking time bomb just waiting to go off on the public roads of the world, and I refuse to encourage you any longer." The instructor got out of the car.

"Mr. Albatross?"

Lioness walked up to the Crown Vic. "What's the matter now?"

"I'm done."

"Done?"

"She'll never pass escape and evasion driving or any other course involving four wheels and an engine."

Lioness groaned to herself. "I know your patience is wearing thin in regard—"

"*You* don't understand," Albatross said. "I refuse to train her anymore."

"Is that really necessary?"

"Lioness, I've been training operatives escape and evasion driving for ten years. Before that, I was a wheelman for criminal and legit organizations. But I have never come across anyone who is so unable to learn…even the basics of what I do."

"Is she really that bad?"

"She's hopeless. I'd have more luck teaching a puppy."

"Lower your voice."

It was too late. Emma could hear everything Albatross said through the open window. The tears were already falling. She knew how bad a driver she was. But hearing it from her instructor was like a slap across the face. A realization that no matter what, Emma would always be a hopeless driver. Why did she even have a car? Her grandmother should take it away from her so she wouldn't kill some poor family on the road or hurt another cute little dog or cat. Maybe Albatross was right. Maybe she shouldn't be taught how to drive.

"Change of plans, Black Opal," Lioness said near Emma's window. "Tonight, I'll teach you how to drive a vehicle with a manual transmission. Every operative should know how to do that."

Later that night, Emma took it easy driving back home to Berkley. Her nerves were still frazzled after the driving fiasco with Albatross. The only highlight was when Lioness calmed Emma down and showed her how to drive a stick using her own Jeep. It was a huge sign of trust in light of how many cars Emma had destroyed so far in her training. But Lioness was patient and Emma didn't do too bad. At least the Jeep stopped making those awful grinding noises when Emma finally changed the gears correctly.

On the outskirts of Berkley, Emma received a text. It was from Kayla.

Are you up?

If she said yes, Emma could feel a conversation coming on, and she felt tired and wanted to crash. But Kayla had never contacted her this late before. Maybe it was important. Emma could spare a few text messages.

When a red light stopped her progress, Emma texted her back. And then her phone rang. Kayla had broken protocol and gone straight to the phone call, bypassing a text conversation altogether.

Emma waited for the Bluetooth in her car to pick it up before selecting the answer button. "Hey, what's up?"

"Nothing much. I'm kinda bored," Kayla's voice said.

"Why don't you go to sleep then?"

"Oh my God, did I wake you? I didn't mean to wake you up. If I did wake you up, please tell me and I'll leave you alone. I don't wanna be a nuisance by constantly—"

"Kayla?"

"Yeah?"

"You're not being a nuisance," Emma said. "And I'm not in bed. I'm in my car."

Why did you say that? Why don't you just tell her about your weapons training? And about all the missions you've been on because you're a spy for a secret organization that even the head of the CIA wants destroyed.

Emma dumped those thoughts from her mind. She was tired and a little cranky. But she agreed that having a decent excuse would be a good idea.

"I had to go pick up some medicine for my grandmother."

"Oh, wow. Is she okay?"

"Nothing big. She has this problem with her stomach. This medicine should take care of it."

The light turned green and Emma moved through the intersection. "Now, what's really bothering you? I know something is."

There was a long hesitation before Kayla began sobbing through the car's speakers. "I miss Seattle. I miss my friends and my school." The sadness poured out of the girl. "Sorry, I'm dumping on you."

Emma caught herself sharing in that sadness. She empathized with Kayla more than she knew.

"You're not dumping on me," Emma said. "Tell me more about Seattle."

Kayla told Emma about her school's hiking trips to Mount Rainer and Olympic National Parks. The rainy weather. How much the people of Washington hated the Twilight books. Kayla also told her about one of her Canadian friends who spoke fluent French. About how she worked at the original Starbucks in Seattle, but then got fired for telling a customer that they smelled.

"But he did smell," Kayla said. "It was disgusting and the customers all noticed it too. Okay, maybe I should have said it in a more pleasant way. At Starbucks, they always want you to be pleasant."

After listing to Kayla for a half hour, Emma pulled into her grandmother's driveway and put the Mercedes in park. She could tell her new friend was still hanging on to her past life, just like Emma did after her father died and she had to move to California to live with her grandmother.

Emma sat back inside the car and relaxed. "Do you know what I miss about New York? The sounds. The constant sounds. Here...it sounds different. Does that make any sense? Maybe it's because I have to drive everywhere instead of taking the subway." Emma thought about it. "But I've walked around Fisherman's Wharf and down along Haight-Ashbury and across the USC campus where my grandmother works and—it all sounds different. And that makes me sad sometimes."

"Because you grew up in New York?" Kayla asked.

"Yeah. I mean, you grow up in a place and you think—this is the world. This is my reality or how I understand that reality to be, right? Then you go to a different place and it doesn't feel real. It's not comfortable or familiar to you. Like, the ground you took for granted is no longer under your feet."

"Yes! That's how I feel, Emma. That's it exactly."

"Manhattan has this distinct sound that made me happy. Even in the five boroughs of New York I could close my eyes and tell you where I was using only my nose and ears. Seriously, each borough has this distinct vibe that's so unique. And other places too, like Coney Island or the beaches way out in Long Island. They're not at all like the beaches in California. But all of that felt real to me. I felt comfortable there."

"What about your friends?"

"I had my one clique at Van Dorn Hall. Well, Hayley and I did. We shared power as equals. We were tight. Did everything together. Kind of like that hiking club you were in."

"And you miss them too?"

"A few months after I moved here, my friend Hayley posted a selfie of her and all my friends together at Horowitz's Deli, which was our after school hangout. Like, every day we were there since elementary school," Emma said. "And when I looked at that picture, I realized that I wasn't in it. I was used to seeing my image in all those pictures with my friends. And suddenly, I wasn't."

"That hit you hard, didn't it?" Kayla asked.

"Yeah, because I realized that...my friends had moved on

without me. I was no longer a part of their lives, and they seemed to be okay with that."

"Oh, I'm sure they were very sad when you left."

"No, that's not my point. I know they were sad, but my friends moved on with their lives. And that picture helped me realize that I needed to move on with my life too. Like, if I let go of the past and welcomed the future, it would help heal that wound. Do you see what I'm saying?"

"Oh, wow. I so get what you're saying," Kayla said. "You're, like, a genius. You should be a school counselor or something."

"Hey, I was the new girl once. So I know. And it'll get better, Kayla. Trust me on that, okay? Things will work themselves out."

"Thank you, Emma. This has really helped. You don't realize how much this helps."

Emma could feel Kayla's honesty through the phone, and that made her feel really good. "Come find me at school tomorrow and we can talk more if you want."

"Yes! That would be awesome. See you then!"

* * *

The next day at school, Emma was still feeling the positive vibes from last night's call with Kayla. She hadn't realized how similar their situations were. That they both were transplants. Girls who had to leave one life and embrace a new one. Emma finally found someone who could empathize with her. The Gems tried to understand. They too had to adjust to a new school when they first came to California. But Nadia, Olivia, and Miyuki had already lived together in two different homes and had each other for support. This was long before Emma had joined them. Also, those girls had been separated from their families for a while now. They were all used to it. Meanwhile, Emma was still having dreams about her father being alive.

Emma popped open her locker. She checked her face and hair with a mirror and decided her hair needed some combing. After a few rounds with her favorite prickly brush, her blond hair looked amazing. Her lips felt dry, so she applied more gloss. Perfect. Emma took what she needed for her next class and slipped it in her backpack before zipping it up.

After shutting her locker, Emma saw Kayla in the hallway. She navigated through all the student traffic to intercept her.

"How's it going?"

Kayla's face was tight, like the girl was holding something in. Her eyes snapped to Emma. "What do you want?"

The girl's tone made Emma pause. "I—I wanted to check up on you after last night."

Kayla only glared, like Emma was a stranger or a girl who just stole her boyfriend. It was bizarre.

"I'm fine," Kayla said, marching off towards class.

Emma stood there for a moment. What was with Kayla this morning? She was blowing Emma off like they had never spoken last night.

Whatever. Emma followed Kayla into their business economics classroom. Mrs. Carmichael wasn't there yet, but some of their classmates were, hanging around some of their desks and talking.

Emma placed her backpack on top of her desk and sat down before noticing Kayla's simmering eyes. What was she so mad about?

Josh, one of the gamer geeks who knew Miyuki, was parking his butt on top of Kayla's desk.

Kayla waited for him to move, but didn't say anything.

But once Josh noticed her, he jumped off the desk. "Sorry, my bad."

Instead of saying thank you or just sitting down at her desk without a word…

Kayla shoved Josh so hard he lost his balance and fell down. Then Kayla stomped on his face with her sneaker.

A collective howl of disbelief went up from the students as Kayla whaled on Josh with both fists, her hair flying around like a wild animal.

Emma jumped up from her desk. At first, her mind was unable to process what was going on. Why was Kayla beating the hell out of Josh?

"Stop it, Kayla!" Emma rushed over and tried to pull her off the boy.

Kayla rolled over and pushed Emma away. The girl's cheeks were red, her eyes looked crazy, and her teeth clenched together like a police dog.

"What's wrong with you?" Emma asked.

Kayla didn't reply. Her victim moaned on the floor with a cut on his face that was bleeding. The crazy girl heard him and went back on the attack, this time taking her backpack and shoving it against the boy's face. Josh now struggled to breathe. Was Kayla trying to smother him to death?

Emma looked around the classroom. The boys were all cheering, thinking this was hilarious. The girls looked horrified. But no one was doing anything to stop it. Emma thought about rushing into the hallway to find a teacher or a security guard. But the way Kayla was smothering Josh, he wasn't going to last.

Emma had to do something.

She grabbed her backpack, took out her purse, and opened the secret pocket inside. Emma took out the mascara pen and rotated the body, revealing a dart at the end. She checked the room. Everyone was watching Kayla, not her.

Emma slipped the mascara pen in the palm of her hand and knelt beside Kayla. As the crazy girl switched her attention back to her, Emma stabbed her neck with the pen, releasing a tranquilizer into Kayla's bloodstream.

But Kayla gripped Emma's throat and pressed down hard, closing off her windpipe.

Emma tried to push Kayla off, but the girl was crazy strong, more than Emma would have ever thought.

She couldn't get her to stop.

"Kayla," Emma said, but the word came out in a whisper.

She didn't have enough air to form words.

Josh crawled along the floor, trying to escape while Kayla was distracted with Emma.

Kayla wouldn't let go.

Emma tried to plead with her, but she couldn't speak.

Or draw in air to breathe.

Was she about to die? Was this how her life would end? At the hands of a girl she thought she was friends with?

Why was this happening? What the hell was going on? If she was about to die, Emma wanted to know why.

Kayla's grip around her neck loosened. The girl's eyelids drooped.

Was the dart finally working?

Kayla could barely keep her eyes open now as Emma gave her

one last shove. Kayla rolled off her, and a rush of cool air filled Emma's lungs.

With Mrs. Carmichael's permission, Emma gathered Kayla's things and took them down to the nurse's office. There, she found Kayla recovering on one of the three exam beds. A school security officer stood watch over Kayla while the nurse on duty asked Emma a few questions.

"Is Kayla on any type of medication that you know of?"

"I don't know."

"I've tried calling her mom, but she didn't answer," the nurse said.

The vice principal came into the office and asked Emma to tell him exactly what had happened. Emma did, but she left out the part about using a dart from her secret spy kit. The school district wouldn't like a student carrying around tranquilizer darts, a mini flamethrower, two smoke bombs, or a nail polish grenade hidden inside their purse. Even though Emma was trained on how to use each device properly.

"Thank you for telling us, Emma. You can go back to class now," the vice principal said, before addressing the nurse. "When her mother calls, please forward her to me, thanks."

The vice principal left the room, but Emma wanted to stay and find out why Kayla freaked out.

The girl in question moaned as she woke up. Her eyes blinked as they looked around. "Where am I?"

"You're in the nurse's office," Emma said.

The security officer stepped forward, ready to react if Kayla freaked out and attacked anyone.

The nurse came up and felt Kayla's forehead. "She's not warm anymore." The nurse flashed a light into each eye, checking them. "How do you feel, Kayla?"

She smiled. "Good, I think. Did I fall asleep in class?"

Emma and the nurse exchanged a look.

"Is she serious?" the security officer asked.

"What's the last thing you remember?" Emma asked.

Kayla tried hard. It took her a minute to focus. "I was headed to class." She paused. "Our class. The one we have together."

"Business economics."

"Yeah, that one." Kayla took another moment. "Didn't I see you in the hallway?"

"Yes, and I asked you how things were going, remember?"

Kayla shook her head. "I don't remember that part."

"Do you remember seeing Josh sitting on your desk?" Emma asked.

"No, but he does it all the time before class. I've been meaning to ask him not to."

"Well, today you did more than ask him."

Kayla didn't understand.

"Kayla," the nurse said, "you attacked Josh in class today. Do you remember that?"

Kayla sat up, her face distressed. "You mean that wasn't a dream?"

"Did you dream about attacking someone?" Emma asked.

"Yeah, I was angry about something. Really pissed. Like furious. So furious I wanted to choke him."

"It wasn't a dream, Kayla. Josh Overton was sitting on your desk and you freaked out and tried to kill him."

Tears streamed down the girl's cheeks. "Are you saying, I did try to kill someone?"

"Are you on any medication, dear?" the nurse asked. "A drug that you might have forgotten to take?"

Kayla shook her head as she wiped off a tear. "Will Josh be okay?"

"He's fine. Just a little shaken up," the nurse said. "I have to ask this, Kayla, but, are you taking any drugs like meth, cocaine, or marijuana?"

"Not at all. I'm not a druggie," Kayla said.

She began sobbing.

"She needs rest," the nurse said. "You should go back to class, Emma. There's nothing more you can do here."

"Okay." Emma stepped over to Kayla and gave her a hug. "Let me know if you need anything."

Kayla sniffled. "Thank you."

CHAPTER 6

In the kitchen of her grandma's house, Emma finished scraping food off the last dinner plate before inserting it into an empty spot in the plastic dishwasher rack. She closed the washer and locked it before rotating the knob to turn it on. Emma opened the fridge and checked for something to drink. There was one can of Sprite left and she claimed it.

Emma felt the cool wood floor under her bare feet as she parted the wall of blue beads that acted like a door between the dining and living room. She found a seat on the couch with her grandma, who was reading term papers with her feet curled under her. Emma drank her soda and checked out all the action.

Nadia balanced her laptop on her knees as she worked on computer programming code, her long dark hair freed of its headscarf. The glow from her laptop highlighted her Girl Scientists Rock T-shirt.

Olivia lounged on the other couch with a frown on her face as she concentrated on her Ernest Hemingway novel.

The only one missing was Miyuki, who was upstairs in her room, most likely playing something online with her gamer friends from school.

"How's the book?" Emma asked.

"It's bloody awful. I hate it," Olivia said. "I want to throw it across the room."

"Mr. Hemingway would be sad to hear you say that," Emma's grandma said.

"Piss on him and his book."

Emma's grandmother took off her reading glasses. "I know not everyone's a fan of his work. However, I don't feel he's that bad a writer."

"All writers are a bunch of flipping passive-aggressive twits who write only for people who are themselves passive-aggressive twits," Olivia said. "They should burn the whole lot of them."

"The people or the books?" Emma's grandmother asked.

Olivia slammed her book shut. "Yes, of course I meant the books."

"Your observations interest me. Why should we burn books?"

"And what do you mean, passive-aggressive twits?" Emma asked. "I love reading. Am I a passive-aggressive twit?"

"In the information age, books are ridiculous," Olivia said. "All the information we need is all on the internet. We don't need these books anymore, so why force students to read the stupid things."

"The internet doesn't teach empathy, Olivia," Emma's grandmother said. "But books can."

"Why do I want to empathize with a man? They control everything in this world anyway." Olivia's voice was getting louder and angrier. "They control all the governments. Our bodies. Our future. Why should I empathize with them?"

"Since when did you start hating men?" Emma asked.

"They keep women down. We should be more pissed off at them."

"I find it interesting how much of an effect reading Ernest Hemingway's work has had on you, Olivia," Emma's grandmother said. "I'd like to examine this anger you have towards literature and men—"

Emma could tell when the college professor inside her grandmother came out. She couldn't help herself when it came to helping any young person make sense of the world.

"You should add that anger into your book report." Nadia lifted her eyes from her laptop and flashed a grin. "Mrs. Fields should find it a gripping read."

"Don't make fun of me." Olivia threw the book at Nadia, who ducked before it flew over her head.

Emma couldn't believe that she did that.

"What on earth has gotten into you?" Emma's grandmother said. "Take a moment to relax and breathe."

Olivia's eyes burned. "Piss off, you old bitch!"

"What did you call my grandmother?" Emma asked.

There was a madness boiling inside Olivia's eyes. Something weird and bizarre. The observation cooled Emma off. Something didn't feel right about how her friend was acting.

Emma's grandmother pointed. "Go upstairs and put some ice in your sweatpants, young lady."

Olivia hesitated.

"Sit down, Emma."

Emma didn't want to, but the stare her grandmother leveled made her do exactly what she said.

Olivia and Emma's grandmother had a face-off.

Each trying to wear the other down.

"Well?" the older woman asked.

Olivia balled up her fists and ran up the stairs. Emma heard a door slam shut.

The tension drained from the living room.

Nadia put away her laptop. "I'll go talk to her and find out what's wrong." The girl acted unfazed by her best friend throwing a hardback at her. Nadia soon disappeared upstairs.

"Maybe I should go up there too."

"Stay right here, young one," Emma's grandmother said. "Nadia will talk some sense into that girl. Those two understand each other."

Maybe her grandmother was right.

Emma sipped her can of Sprite. That was when a large crash echoed from upstairs.

Then Nadia screamed.

Emma looked to her grandmother, and they both moved off the couch. Emma took the lead as she ran up the stairs as quickly as she could before reaching the upstairs hallway.

Nadia's butt was on the carpeted floor and her back was against the far wall, like she had been thrown there. Olivia stormed out of her room in a rage. Her jaw tight. Her eyes wild. She jumped on top of Nadia and yanked her long hair, pulling the poor girl's head at an awkward angle.

Emma froze. Was Olivia fighting Nadia? This was insane.

Nadia used her foot to push Olivia off her. "She's gone crazy!"

Olivia tumbled to the floor. Nadia scrambled back to her feet while combing her long hair back into place.

"What's going on?" Emma asked.

"I just asked her what was wrong and she went crazy," Nadia said. "She literally threw me out of the room."

Olivia lunged toward Nadia, and the two best friends wrestled on the floor.

"Please help me!"

Emma went to Nadia's rescue by wrapping her arms around the crazy girl's stomach to pull her off. But Olivia ducked forward and Emma found herself rolling over Olivia's body and smacking into Nadia, causing both girls to wipe out across the floor.

Olivia's jaw tightened as her crazy eyes burned into her friends.

"Go downstairs, Grandma!" Emma said. "We got this."

"No, you don't have this," her grandmother said, standing near the edge of the stairs. "Let me talk to her."

Olivia swung around and lunged towards Emma's grandmother.

But Nadia and Emma reached her before she could get there. They pulled their friend away and dragged her across the floor.

Olivia fought back, shoving Nadia and then Emma against opposite walls. Despite this punishment, the two girls clung to Olivia like cowgirls breaking a horse.

"Miyuki!" Nadia called out.

"We need your help!" Emma added.

Miyuki's door remained closed. Emma was certain she was using her headphones again.

Olivia slammed Emma hard into the wall, making her finally let go. This allowed Olivia to attack Nadia again.

But Nadia used her leg again to shove Olivia out of the way.

Olivia's next target was Emma. After sweeping her legs out from under her, Emma dropped to the floor. Olivia wasted no time. She jumped on top of Emma and they wrestled. Olivia grabbed a handful of Emma's blond hair and pulled. Emma heard herself yelp in pain. It hurt like a mother-trucker.

Nadia pounded on Miyuki's door. "We need your help!" She tried the door, but it was locked. "Miyuki!"

Emma felt Olivia's teeth biting into her skin. Emma couldn't believe it. Olivia was trying to eat her like some cannibal. Emma didn't want to hurt her friend, but this fight was getting way too serious.

"Should I call Miyuki's phone?" Grandma asked.

"Yes!" Emma yelled as she shoved Olivia off.

Nadia went in a fighting stance as her best friend closed in. Olivia didn't bother with a stance, she ran straight into Nadia, and they struggled again.

This was already tiring Emma out, but they didn't have a choice. Emma got back up to help Nadia.

"Why are you wrestling Olivia?" Miyuki stood inside her open door with a pair of headphones hung around her neck. She then smiled. "Oh…is WrestleMania on television? I love those wrestlers! Can I wrestle Olivia next?"

Olivia then flipped Nadia over her head. The girl had a boundless amount of energy.

Miyuki clapped her hands. "Nice throw, Olivia!"

"We're not wrestling each other. Olivia's gone nuts and started attacking—" Emma found herself being dragged to the ground again.

Nadia rolled to her feet and grabbed Olivia around the waist. "Please help us!"

Miyuki's enthusiasm changed to seriousness as she ran over to help.

Olivia greeted her with a strike in the face with her palm.

"Stop it!" Nadia said.

Emma didn't know what else to do. Olivia had gone insane. Acting crazy like—like Kayla.

Emma ran down the hall to her room. She grabbed her purse and realized she was out of mascara darts. She ran into Miyuki's room and found her tiny purse. But it was all real makeup. She ran back out into the hallway.

"Where are your mascara pens?"

Miyuki grunted as Olivia struck her in the gut.

"Sorry, I can't hear you," Emma said.

"Go to the side of my bed," Nadia said. "I have mine there."

Emma rushed into Nadia and Olivia's room and hopped over a broken vase. Emma found Nadia's bed and her makeup bag. She took a mascara dart and headed back out.

Nadia was on top of Olivia, who was still hitting Miyuki. "Hurry!"

Emma yanked off the cap that exposed the sharp dart. She then stabbed the dart into Olivia's neck.

The effect on Olivia was quicker than Kayla. The girl rolled off Miyuki as her eyes drifted closed. The physical exhaustion of fighting and the drug itself worked quickly on her.

Finally, Olivia passed out.

The three remaining Gems sat on the floor, each breathing hard and trying to digest what had just happened.

"Do we need to call the cops?" Emma's grandmother asked

from the top of the stairs.

"That tranquilizer dart should keep her out for an hour," Nadia said.

"Why was she acting like a crazy woman?" Miyuki asked.

"I only asked her if anything was wrong," Nadia said. "And she attacked me. This isn't Olivia. Something's affecting her."

"I think it affected Kayla too," Emma said. "Today, I watched her attack a boy in class. And Kayla was also acting weird before she snapped."

"You think they're related?" Miyuki asked.

"Too much of a coincidence not to be," Nadia said. "We should find out."

As Emma's grandmother and Miyuki kept watch over an unconscious Olivia downstairs, Emma and Nadia searched the upstairs for clues. They started in the bedroom shared by both Nadia and Olivia. There were two beds, and each girl had added their own decorative touches to the room, but it was still a joint project. Nadia checked Olivia's backpack while Emma searched her dresser. They found nothing strange. Nadia had Emma search the closet she shared with Olivia. Again, they found nothing out of the ordinary.

Emma peeked into the trash can. She pulled out a fresh tissue and used it to grab an empty drink can. The label said Thunderdog. She glanced over at Nadia. "We don't have any of these in the fridge. And my grandmother isn't a fan of energy drinks."

"She must have bought that at school," Nadia said. "Remember that new vending machine?"

Things began to click inside Emma's mind. She used her phone to dial Kayla's number. Emma put the call on speaker so Nadia could hear.

"Hi, Emma! How are you? I'm so happy you're calling me. I haven't thanked you for helping me today. It was so scary, and you were so awesome for making sure I was okay. You rock so hard it's not even—"

"Kayla, I'm so happy you're feeling well," Emma interrupted. If she didn't get a word in now, they'd be on the phone until midnight. "Can you answer a quick question? Did you drink anything at school today?"

Kayla paused on the phone. "Um—water and my normal apple juice. I so love apples. Have I told you about my mom's apple—"

"Would love to hear more about it at school tomorrow, but this is important. Did you buy anything from the vending machines?"

"No, my apple juice is from home—oh, wait—my mom gave me two dollars to spend, so I tried one of those new Thunderdog drinks. It was good. I liked the grape flavor with the—"

"Wait, so you drank one of those before fifth hour?"

"Yeah, why?"

Emma and Nadia shared a look.

"Do me a huge solid and stick to apple juice, okay? I gotta go." Emma ended the call. She thought about it for a moment before addressing Nadia. "Can energy drinks make you go crazy?"

"Chemically they boost your energy levels, but they shouldn't make kids crazy." Nadia sniffed the inside of the can and peeked into it. "There's still some liquid inside that I can test."

"Did someone spike the drinks?"

"We can't jump to conclusions yet," Nadia said. "First, we need to go to Authority headquarters and test this drink."

"What do we do with Olivia?"

CHAPTER 7

It was late by the time Emma drove the Gems out to Napa Valley. A large bald man with black eyes and a deep scar running down his throat met them in the underground parking lot. His code name was Aardvark.

Olivia was groggy and in restraints as she was carted off to the Authority headquarters medical unit for observation. Meanwhile, Aardvark led the remaining Gems into the Labyrinth. Not many people knew where Mrs. B's office was inside the Labyrinth, but Aardvark did and led Emma, Nadia, and Miyuki straight to it. He pressed a button that released a low chime.

The door's lock clicked and Aardvark held the door open for the Gems as they stepped inside. Mrs. B sat behind a vintage steel pink desk straight from the set of the television series *Mad Men*. The room itself had a vintage '60s office feel to it with all the furnishings. On the walls were a mixture of modern artwork, along with concert posters from The Beatles, The Animals, Jefferson Airplane, and The Byrds.

Emma and Nadia selected the two vintage white metal office chairs, while Miyuki picked the vintage couch.

"This is way cool," Miyuki said before pointing at the desk. "I love your phone!"

Mrs. B had a powder-blue rotary phone on her desk. This office blew Emma away. She'd had her grandmother Laura pegged as more of a *Downton Abbey* duchess with an all-walnut study complete with a fireplace. Here, she was more the female version of Don Draper.

"Have I not brought you girls into my private office before?" Mrs. B asked. "I apologize for how informal it is. Over the years, I've tended to decorate it to suit my personal taste since I do spend an enormous amount of time in here working."

"It's wonderful," Miyuki said.

"Very unique," Nadia said politely.

"This doesn't seem like you," Emma said.

Mrs. B revealed a slight grin. "Did you already put me in a box, Black Opal? Shame on you. You should know better. Is that what we taught you in psychological assessment? That human beings are simple to figure out?"

"No, ma'am," Emma said.

Mrs. B held her stare for a couple of beats to let her point sink in. "Alright, let's dig into why you girls are here. Tell me everything that happened to Emerald and this girl Kayla."

Emma told Mrs. B about Kayla and her happy-go-lucky personality. About how Kayla had freaked out and tried to kill a student. About how she'd had no knowledge about the attack afterward. Nadia explained how Olivia had been behaving at Emma's grandmother's house and the vicious fight upstairs.

"It was like she was a zombie wanting to munch on our brains," Miyuki added.

Mrs. B sat back in her chair. The woman's brilliant mind analyzed the information. "Your suspicion involving the drink is sound. A correlation between the two incidents seems plausible, but we need more evidence."

"With your permission, I'd like to analyze this sample I brought using our labs," Nadia said. "If I can break the drink down chemically, it could give us some answers."

"You know how to do that?" Emma asked.

Nadia's back stiffened. "Of course I know how to do that. I'm a scientist."

"We appreciate your offer, Sapphire. However, I'm confident our Authority scientists can handle the analysis," Mrs. B said. "Besides, you girls have school in the morning."

"I understand, ma'am," Nadia said, her enthusiasm wilting.

Emma could relate. Adults always loved using the school excuse when a girl wanted to do something she thought would be fun.

Mrs. B used her powder-blue rotary phone to contact the lab; then she summoned Aardvark. The large man appeared within seconds.

"Please take Nadia's drink sample to the lab. They're expecting it."

Nadia hesitated, but still gave Aardvark the Thunderdog can.

The man nodded in silence before leaving the room.

"Please be careful driving home. When I receive any information about Emerald or the drink, I will contact you."

"May we see Emerald before we leave?" Nadia asked.

"It's late. You girls should head back home," Mrs. B said. "Don't worry, Sapphire, we'll take good care of her."

* * *

The next morning, Emma woke up tired. The Gems didn't get home from Napa Valley until way past midnight, and Emma's body was screaming in protest. Nadia and Miyuki were in the same situation. Both girls dragged themselves into the shower, each trying to use the cold water to wake up. Emma decided to rely on her old favorite. On the way to school she stopped at the Kaffee Cadre for a triple-shot vanilla latte.

"Please order me one too," Miyuki said.

That surprised Emma. Miyuki usually went with a tea. But Nadia held firm and ordered her normal black tea, but with two bags this time instead of one.

As Emma pulled into the student parking lot of West Berkeley High School, there was a crowd of kids gathered nearby. Curious, the three Gems sipped their beverages and walked over for a look.

It was a fight. Students were shouting encouragement as two boys wrestled on the ground. One guy from the varsity football team had pinned down a small freshman kid. It was an unfair mismatch. But the little freshman kid was trying to fight back with all the strength he had.

Finally, the small freshman broke free of the football player's grasp and launched himself like a tiny missile at the player. The small kid let off a series of punches into the player's gut. They were hard and vicious enough for the varsity player to back up. The football player did manage to push off the freshman, only to have the kid attack him again.

Emma had to look away. She found the fight too disturbing to watch. As she surveyed the crowd watching the fight, Emma noted a few of the students drinking cans of Thunderdog. And it was those students who were cheering the loudest, wanting more blood and more violence.

"Shouldn't we find a teacher?" Nadia asked. "That small freshman will get killed."

No sooner than she said that, the freshman landed a punch that spun the varsity player to the ground.

"Or not," Emma added.

"Show's over, everyone." The vice principal parted the sea of students as he made his way to the student boxers. "That's it. Get up, Binkman." The varsity football player managed to stand. His face had taken a beating. "I've had it with you."

"But he started it." The football player pointed at the freshman. "I swear to God."

The little freshman didn't talk. He only yelled and punched the player again.

"I said the fight is over!" The vice principal grabbed the freshman. But the student now turned on the vice principal and hit him.

A collective wow floated over the students. Did he just do that?

The freshman had this crazy look in his eyes. A look Emma had seen before. She checked with Nadia and Miyuki. Their looks confirmed what Emma was thinking.

Finally, two security guards came in and took the freshman down to the ground, managing to put on handcuffs. The vice principal frowned and shook his head at the situation. He faced the students still watching. "Go to class now. It's over."

The students began disappearing into the building as the security officers escorted the freshman to their office.

Emma, Nadia, and Miyuki traded knowing looks. Their vice principal was wrong. This was far from being over.

CHAPTER 8

After school, Miyuki and the Gems drove back to the Authority headquarters in Napa Valley, where they were greeted by a familiar face. Olivia waited for them on the bottom floor, near the stairs that led up to the threat assessment division. Nadia ran over and hugged her. Miyuki and Emma each took turns too.

"How are you feeling?" Nadia asked.

"We were so worried," Miyuki said.

Regret overwhelmed Olivia's face. "Mrs. B told me what happened." The girl paused, unable to find the words. "I—I can't believe I did all that. But what I do remember—it was like a nightmare. I wasn't too sure if it was really happening or not."

"Oh, it happened," Emma said. "I have the bite marks to prove it."

Nadia fired off a look.

"But you weren't in control of yourself," Emma added.

Olivia gently folded Miyuki's hands into her own. "I'm so sorry, love. I could have killed you." Her eyes watered, but Olivia didn't cry. "Can you forgive me? Can any of you forgive me?"

"Of course we forgive you. You're our friend," Miyuki said. "Usually, you only think about killing us."

"I've never lost control of myself like that before," Olivia said. "I didn't know I was capable of doing—what I did."

"Oh, you're capable," Emma said. "But next time, please do it to the bad guys."

"Did I hurt your grandmother, Emma?"

"Not physically, but you did tell her she was a—"

"I remember that part," Olivia said. "I'll bring her a peace offering later."

"Sorry to cut the reunion short, but we have a problem that

48

needs to be fixed immediately," Mrs. B said as she walked up to the Gems. "If you please, ladies."

The Gems followed Mrs. B into the jungle where all the green pod meeting rooms were. Waiting inside one pod was Aardvark, two men, and one woman. Miyuki only recognized Mr. O. He was an older Indian man in charge of the threat assessment section of the IT division. The other man wore a lab coat while the woman wore slacks. Once Mrs. B and the Gems stepped inside the pod, it closed and the cone of silence mode activated to prevent any type of surveillance equipment from penetrating the interior.

The Gems sat opposite the four adults as Mrs. B began the meeting. "What do you have for us, Mr. O?"

The older Indian man read from his tablet. "The threat analysis section looked into the number of incidents at not only the school in question, but at any American school that has a Thunderdog vending machine on campus. We used that data and compared it with the same number of American schools that do not have a Thunderdog machine. We found some interesting results."

The pod went dim as an animated chart floated in the air above them.

Mr. O continued. "Schools with a Thunderdog vending machine on campus had a fifty percent rise in aggravated assaults on campus compared to all non-Thunderdog schools."

"Fifty percent?" Mrs. B asked.

"Yes, and there's more. Thunderdog is being tested in six countries. We compared our American data with all foreign schools and universities that also have Thunderdog vending machines."

The chart disappeared and the lights inside the pod went back to normal.

"The threat analysis section concluded that a violent spike has occurred over the past month on all university and school campuses that have a Thunderdog vending machine. The country or the culture does not matter. The data all points to a strong connection with the new drink and violence."

"I see," Mrs. B said. "Thank you for the report, Mr. O."

The man with the lab coat jumped in. "The science section examined the sample of Thunderdog that Sapphire brought us and compared it with a new can of Thunderdog that we bought on the University of California campus. The chemical makeup of both samples are identical, so there was no poisoning or tampering with the beverage that Emerald purchased at school. There was no chemical or biological attack in play here."

"Next time, when you address a senior station officer, you wait until she calls on you," Mr. O said to his colleague in the lab coat.

The man with the lab coat frowned and bowed in Mrs. B's direction. "My apologies."

Mrs. B gave the man a good stare, enough to make him uncomfortable. She turned to the woman. "What do you have for us, Doctor?"

"I think I can shed some light on the violence," the doctor said. "This Thunderdog drink has a chemical that supercharges the amygdala in the brain. You see, in normal teens, their prefrontal cortex isn't fully developed, so they are more vulnerable to this drink because it supercharges the part of their brain that deals with their emotions and feelings. Basically, it causes intense emotions, such as aggression or fear, to be magnified."

"What about getting pissed off?" Emma asked. "My friend Kayla freaked out because she was pissed off a kid was on her desk."

"Conceivably, it could magnify any emotion, depending on how much of the chemical is in a young person's bloodstream."

"I remember being worried about my book report," Olivia said. "And then everyone kept hassling me about my opinions about the book, so I felt pissed off and wanted people to leave me alone. But when Sapphire came upstairs to talk to me—I went off on her."

"Doctor," Mrs. B said, "what you're telling us is the young victim isn't in control of their emotions because the drink manipulates their mind?"

"Precisely. Emerald and Black Opal's friend unwittingly lost control of their emotions due to a chemical alteration of their minds."

"This drink sounds extremely dangerous. Who makes Thunderdog?"

"A Japanese beverage company called Shiawase Nomi—Nomi —" Mr. O hesitated as he struggled with the name.

"Shiawase Nomimono International," Miyuki said with little difficulty. "Their headquarters are in Osaka."

"Wow. How did you know that?" Emma asked.

"Because my father works for Shiawase Nomimono."

Mrs. B tilted her head. "That's right. What an interesting

coincidence." She addressed the room. "Thank you for the briefing. To prevent further violence, we'll leak this information to the health officials of the affected countries and see if we can get these vending machines pulled out of schools and universities as quickly as possible. That is all."

The green pod opened up, allowing everyone to leave.

"Do you mind staying for a moment, Ruby?"

Miyuki shook her head and stayed seated.

Emma and the other Gems hesitated.

"Only Ruby, please."

The remaining three Gems stepped out of the pod, and it closed back up again, leaving only Miyuki and Mrs. B. The older woman used her cane to move over to where Miyuki was.

She took a moment before speaking. "I wouldn't ask this unless it was important. I know your history with your father—well, it wasn't pleasant."

Miyuki's thumb found the rough surface of an old cigarette burn under her wrist. Rubbing it was a habit and it was hard to break.

"I want to help," Miyuki said. "If it prevents more kids from hurting themselves or others, I want to help stop it."

"Then I need you to go speak with your father this weekend and see if his company knows about what's happening to their product. And we need to convince them to stop making this Thunderdog rubbish."

"Of course, ma'am. I will do as you ask. May I make a request?"

"You may."

"Can the other Gems come with me?"

CHAPTER 9

On Friday, a Boeing 777 departed San Francisco on time as it gained altitude over the Pacific and leveled off at thirty-five thousand feet. Inside the cabin, Miyuki focused on the beveled partition that separated business class from coach. On that partition were the words *Japan Airlines*. Above the lettering was a red sun on a field of white, the national flag of Japan.

Miyuki's stomach was uneasy. Feeling nervous wasn't quite right. It was more a disturbance in her life force. Miyuki reasoned that if Luke Skywalker could feel a disturbance in the force, she could feel a disturbance in her own life force. Normally, her life force was always in balance. Even during times of extreme danger, Miyuki could always count on her life force to keep her mind and body in balance. But over the ocean, she now felt a shift in that force.

The last time it had happened was when she was all dressed up and stealing the thumb drive on Takeshita Street. The closer Miyuki was to Japan, the more that uneasiness would plague her mind and spirit.

"Can't believe we couldn't at least get business-class seats," Emma said, sitting beside Miyuki. "I need the extra room so I can trick myself into believing I'm not on a plane."

Miyuki turned her attention back to her friend. "If it will help, I can give you my seat and I'll find an empty one in the back."

"No, I can't ask you to do that. Besides, I don't want to be left alone either." Emma leaned in. "Tell me about your dad. Tell me about your family. Tell me anything that'll distract me for the next ten hours."

Miyuki told Emma about her father's tenure as a vice president of Shiawase Nomimono International and how proud the family was of his accomplishments. Emma then asked about her mother.

Miyuki brightened. "She was an Olympic gymnast."

"Really? Did she win any medals?"

"My mother was the captain of the national Olympic team when they won the silver. First time ever for Japan. The team's success brought great honor to our family."

"And your mom was the captain? Wow. Did you ever want to go into gymnastics?"

Miyuki hesitated. She wanted to tell Emma everything, let the truth spill out of her and enjoy the relief it would bring. However, Miyuki didn't want to dump her life story on top of her friend because she might not understand. Growing up in Japan was far different than America. "My little sister Kameko is into gymnastics. She climbs trees like a baby monkey. She's very sweet and kind. My brother Haru is studying business administration in college. He's more like my father."

Emma observed Miyuki for a moment. "You're nervous, aren't you?"

"I'd say apprehensive, not nervous. I haven't seen my family in over two years."

"I'm sure they'll be happy to see you. You're their oldest daughter."

More like the-daughter-who-shall-not-be-named. Miyuki was convinced that her family would welcome home Lord Voldemort with more affection than they would her. Miyuki was correct. Emma wouldn't understand.

"Your mum won a silver medal in the Olympics?" Olivia's head was over the seat in front of Emma. No doubt she was listening to their conversation. "You never told us that before, love."

"I didn't want to brag," Miyuki said.

"I'm looking forward to visiting your country." Nadia was peeking over the seat in front of Miyuki. "I hope we get to look around while we're there."

"I'll show you as much as I can. Hopefully talking to my father will not last long."

"Don't worry about us. We'll be fine," Emma said. "Take as long as you need with your dad. Family is important."

Miyuki's thumb found the damaged skin under her wrist and rubbed it.

Emma didn't understand.

* * *

Ten hours later, Japan Airlines flight 42 landed in Osaka, Japan. Miyuki and the Gems emerged from the Jetway into the crowded international terminal. Through the glass windows above, the Gems could see the sun hanging low over the horizon as it was about to set for the day. Local Japanese time was 18:30, or about 6:30p.m. Because they flew across the international dateline, it was actually Sunday night in Japan. A concept that was always hard to get used to when one traveled to this side of the world.

The Gems made their way through the terminal and found their correct baggage claim. After claiming their luggage, Miyuki called her mother to tell her they had arrived.

"My mother has prepared a meal for us," Miyuki said. "If you'd like, we can go straight there."

"Sounds great. You know, for such a long flight, I feel good," Emma said.

"We're still on California time, love," Olivia said. "Trust me, we won't get any sleep tonight."

Emma blew her off. "I can't wait to meet your mom."

Nadia yawned. "Are your parents picking us up?"

The underground station platforms that served the Osaka airport filled up with people as a long white train approached. The squealing sound of its brakes were amplified by the station's concrete walls. Miyuki led the Gems to an automated ticket kiosk. Searching through the Japanese menus on the screen, Miyuki bought four rail cards with the special credit card that Mrs. B had given them for the trip.

"Is that our train?" Nadia asked.

"No, but it will be here soon," Miyuki said.

Emma gawked at the sea of people waiting. "There's no way we'll make this one."

"The airport trains are always crowded," Miyuki said. "We must slip in as best we can. Follow me, please."

A horn sounded as another train braked into the station. It was already stuffed with passengers. When the train finally stopped, doors on the opposite side of the train opened, letting out people heading upstairs to the airport terminal. A pleasant chime sounded as a lady's voice came over the speakers, announcing for people to step back from the doors in a pleasant Japanese voice. She then repeated the announcement in English.

The doors opened. People pushed through the doors as they filed into the passenger cars. No one wasted space. No one yelled. No one cursed. Everyone filed into the cars as best they could.

Miyuki wedged herself into the doorway and moved forward with the people. Emma was only a few steps away, weaving her way through the cracks. Miyuki came to an empty seat and sat down. The other seats around her filled up quickly. Since people were standing right next to Miyuki, she couldn't see if the other Gems had got on.

But Emma came into view as she forced her way around one old Japanese man, who glared at her.

Emma stood over Miyuki and pointed. "She's my friend."

The man turned his back on her.

"Are the other girls on board?" Miyuki asked. "I can't see."

Emma craned her neck and searched. "I see Olivia."

"What about Nadia?"

Emma frowned. "Hey, you in the hat," she yelled across the car. "Don't be a jerk. Give my friend some room so she can get on the train."

Every Japanese person inside the car stared at Emma like she had no clothes on.

Miyuki could feel her face turn red. She had neglected to tell her friends about Japanese social customs.

"Thank you, sir." Emma radiated confidence again as she turned her attention back to Miyuki. "It's like I'm back home in Manhattan on the W Broadway Local headed uptown."

Miyuki forgot that Emma was originally from New York. No wonder her friend was adapting so well.

The doors closed. The pleasant Japanese voice returned to announce the train's departure and destination. The brakes released with a hiss as the train glided forward a bit before accelerating out of the underground station. Once outside, everyone could see the lights of the city twinkle in the background.

"Osaka looks so huge," Emma said.

"Second largest city in Japan," Miyuki said. The uneasiness returned to her stomach. The disturbance in her life force. Soon they would transfer to the Osaka Loop line. Then transfer again to the Nankai-Koya line that would take them to the Tezukayama station, which was a fifteen-minute walk from her family's home. Miyuki wasn't looking forward to it.

After two hours and one transfer, the Gems arrived at the Tezukayama station. The doors of the train slid open and the Gems walked out into the night. The streets here were clean and the traffic was light in this neighborhood block of Osaka. It was quieter too, with a more residential vibe.

Miyuki led her friends through an iron gate and down the short path to the front door of a residence. The uneasiness inside her stomach was boiling hot, yet Miyuki tried not to let it show. She could feel a part of her reverting back to the little freak who used to live here. The girl lost in her own mind.

Miyuki swallowed and pressed the doorbell.

CHAPTER 10

The front door opened, revealing a young Japanese girl with short dark hair. The moment she saw Miyuki, her body quivered with excitement. "You're here!" the girl said in Japanese as she threw herself into Miyuki's arms.

Her sister Kameko, was taller than Miyuki remembered, and the girl always smelled like flowers. Miyuki's eyes watered, but she held back the emotion. Kameko kissed her sister on the cheek, and the two eyed each other for a long moment. Kameko then noticed the strangers behind Miyuki. The girl bowed and apologized if she had embarrassed them. However, since it was all in Japanese, the apology went on deaf ears.

"This is my sister, Kameko," Miyuki said to the Gems.

Kameko retreated into the house as the Gems entered.

Miyuki kicked off her shoes and placed them in the front entry. "We must take off our shoes here. My family has provided extra slippers for us to use around the house."

Olivia and Nadia slipped off their shoes.

"Your parents are clean freaks, huh?" Emma removed her flats.

"Everyone removes their shoes before entering someone's house. It's custom. A sign of respect."

"We have a similar custom in my country," Nadia added as she put on her fluffy slippers.

After the Gems swapped footwear, they stepped up to the main level of the house. Waiting patiently in the living room was Miyuki's father, mother, and a young man she recognized. Miyuki was surprised how much her brother, Haru, had grown in two years. Wearing a dress shirt and business slacks, he was a duplicate image of her father.

The uneasiness inside Miyuki's stomach increased, but she tried not to show it as she approached them.

Haru greeted Miyuki with a low-key hug and a smile. "It's good to see you again," he said in Japanese. Miyuki could tell he was holding back a little. But she understood why and didn't fault him for it. She was only happy he was here.

Her mother gave Miyuki a warm smile and a deep hug. "It is so wonderful to finally have you home again. You've been away… much too long."

Miyuki hesitated before stepping in front of her father. Right away she noted the uneasiness in his eyes. Miyuki wondered if her father was dreading her visit as much as she was. Unlike the rest of the family, Miyuki gave him a low bow. "*Aragoto*, for inviting my friends to dinner."

Her father bowed slightly. "The organization they represent honors us with the opportunity to host them." Her father's eyes moved to the Gems standing nearby. The family's attention was now focused on them.

Miyuki turned. "This is my father. He is a vice president of Shiawase Nomimono International. His name is Ichirou Kaiko."

Upon hearing his name, her father bowed slightly. "I apologize for my limited English," he said. "Welcome to our home."

"Thank you for having us, sir," Olivia said, bowing.

"We look forward to dinner," Nadia said, adding a late bow.

Emma smiled. "Don't worry, you should try to listen to your daughter's English sometime."

Miyuki knew her English wasn't the best and honestly didn't mind Emma's joke. However, her family might view the comment as an insult.

"What did she say? I do not understand," Miyuki's father asked.

"She said…there is no need for an apology," Miyuki lied in Japanese. Sometimes literal translations were not the best way for different cultures to understand each other.

Miyuki's mother touched her shoulder. "Dinner is ready when your guests have settled in."

"*Aragoto*," Miyuki replied.

A half hour later, the Gems and Miyuki's family sat on their knees and faced each other around a low wooden table. Steaming bowls of white rice, fish, cooked veggies, and miso soup sat between them. Miyuki could feel the stiffness in the air. Normally her family wouldn't be this tense, but *gaijin*, or foreigners, gave most Japanese a hint of anxiety. Especially when the worst sin you can commit here is causing another person to feel embarrassed.

Miyuki knew it was up to her to bridge the gap.

"*Itadakimasu*," she said out loud.

"*Itadakimasu*," her family repeated.

The Gems glanced at Miyuki.

"It means, 'I receive this food.' It's an expression we say before each meal to show thanks to those who have prepared it."

Kameko stood up and began to serve portions of the meal to each person at the table. Next, the little girl poured tea and made sure everyone's cup was full. Then everyone began their meal.

Olivia held up her unbroken chopsticks. She looked uneasy.

Miyuki was about to say something when—

"All you have to do is break them in half." Emma showed her by pulling apart her chopsticks with a crack. She then used them to pick up some fish like a pro.

Olivia frowned and whispered to Miyuki, "Could I trouble your mum for some silverware, love?"

"Seriously, you don't know how to use chopsticks?" Emma asked with her outdoor voice.

Miyuki's family stopped eating.

Olivia let out a slight grumble of annoyance before answering in a lower voice, "I prefer using silverware."

"I'll teach you." Emma opened her chopstick hand. "It's all on how you use your fingers."

Olivia flashed Miyuki's parents a polite grin before gritting her teeth at Emma. "Can't you see that you're embarrassing us?"

"Oh, her family doesn't care." Emma leaned towards their side of the table. "Do you mind if I teach my friend how to use chopsticks?" Her voice was so loud the family's cat rushed into the bedroom.

Miyuki had never seen their fat cat Bobo move that fast.

"They don't understand English, you twit. And speaking louder English doesn't help."

Nadia grinned.

"Well, I'm so sorry for trying to help you," Emma said.

"I'll bring you some silverware." Miyuki jumped to her feet and went into the kitchen. She retrieved some Western-style utensils for Olivia to use.

Finally the table settled down as the meal continued.

"Mom mentioned that you're in the Shiawase Nomimono management training program," Miyuki said to Haru. "How's that going?"

"It's challenging," Haru said. "The hours are long. However, I enjoy the training and meeting new people. I'm with a talented group of young executives. Many of us are close to the same age and have much in common."

"I'm proud of your brother's progress," Miyuki's father added. "He will become a valuable asset to his team. And to the company."

"Father is more optimistic about my value than I. If the company feels I'm contributing well enough to help my team, then I'll be happy."

"Is that what you want to do for the rest of your life?" Miyuki asked. "Work at the company?"

"Why are you questioning him?" Miyuki's father asked. His tone sharp.

Now the Gems stopped eating.

Miyuki bowed low. "Sorry." She focused on her meal.

"Is something wrong?" Emma asked.

"Nothing's wrong. My father was only making a point."

The dinner continued. Haru lifted his miso soup cup to his mouth and began slurping it down in a noisy fashion.

Emma giggled, then tried to hold it in. Nadia cracked a smile. Olivia stopped eating to watch Haru.

Slurp.

Slurp.

Slurp.

Nadia finally broke. She giggled uncontrollably, then tried to hide her face with her hand.

This made Emma giggle more.

Olivia began cracking up too.

Slurp.

Slurp.

Miyuki shot them all a look that said, s*top it!*

But they couldn't.

Until Mr. Kaiko's disapproving gaze hit all three offenders. The girls sat up in unison and wiped the smiles off their faces. Next, her father gave Miyuki a look, as if to say, *control your guests.*

Miyuki flashed him a quick nod. "Are you still taking

gymnastics, Kameko?"

"*Hei!*" Kameko brightened.

"She helped her school win many tournaments this semester," Miyuki's mom said.

"I put up excellent numbers on the double bars," Kameko said with pride. "Without me, our team would have lost."

"Kameko," her mother snapped.

"But it's true."

"Pride is a disease that grows from the inside out," her mother said. "Without your team and their support, you are nothing."

"Just because your sister is visiting," Miyuki's father began, "do not interpret that as an opportunity to act out. If you do so, the consequences will be severe. Do you understand?"

"*Hei,*" Kameko said, her enthusiasm extinguished.

The Gems ate quietly, glancing occasionally at Miyuki to see if she would reveal what her family was arguing about. But Miyuki was stone-faced. It was a tactic she'd developed as a child. A way to mask her feelings. When she left Japan, Miyuki allowed her childhood mask to slip off because she enjoyed the freedom of being herself. In the West, such attitudes were encouraged. But here. Back home. The mask had returned, along with the little Japanese girl who wore it.

"Miyuki," her father announced.

"*Hei,*" she answered.

"Tell me about your friends. You say, they work inside the organization. How so?"

Miyuki placed her chopsticks to the side. "The four of us work as a team. Each girl has special skills she offers to the group. For instance, Olivia is a trained pilot. Nadia is a scientist and knows computer software. Emma is a skilled actor."

"I see," her father said. "And you contribute to the team as well?"

"*Hei,* my gymnastics and martial arts training have been valuable. We all work well together and have completed many missions."

"The Authority is a most honorable organization. It strives to bring harmony and balance to the world of nations. It's a shame that your contributions are kept so secret. But we are proud that you're contributing to their honorable cause."

Miyuki turned to her friends and explained her father's

questions and what she answered.

"How much has Mrs. B told them about us?" Olivia asked, always fearing giving out too much information to people who don't need to know.

"Only how they would use me inside a group of like-minded young women for intelligence work."

"Did you tell your father I can skydive?" Emma asked. "Acting is only one of my many gifts."

"That and modesty," Olivia said.

Emma dipped her hand below the table and pinched Olivia.

"Ouch—you little…" She noted Miyuki's pleading eyes and dropped it. Olivia used her napkin before speaking again. "Can you translate a question to your dad?"

"Sure."

Olivia smiled at Mr. Kaiko. "It sounds like you're proud of your daughter for joining the Authority."

Miyuki paused. It was a question she would never have asked. But her friend did so…she translated it.

Her father took a moment to drink some tea. Miyuki's mother watched him closely, a slight tension in her movements. Her father's eyes lifted slowly as they found his daughter. "Miyuki is… special. Different. Unique in many ways. Her path in life…needed clarification. But now it has become much clearer. I'm pleased that my daughter was chosen to contribute to your worthy organization."

Miyuki could feel her spirits rising. It wasn't a declaration of pride. But from her father, it was praise nonetheless. Miyuki translated her father's words to her friends.

"I love working with your daughter, Mr. Kaiko," Emma said. "She's so funny. I mean, Miyuki makes me laugh so hard I snort coffee through my nose. Seriously, she's hilarious."

Her parents grinned politely and nodded, they waited for their daughter's translation.

Miyuki knew that Emma meant well. To her, being funny was a positive trait. However, to her parents, it would only remind them of the awkward little girl who didn't understand restraint.

"My friend Emma says she enjoys how I keep the harmony inside our group," Miyuki said in Japanese.

Her father nodded with satisfaction.

After dinner, the Gems thanked Miyuki's parents for a wonderful meal. Miyuki escorted her friends back to the front entryway as she watched them put their shoes back on.

"Do you understand how to get to the Kita area?" Miyuki asked.

"The hotel's location and the train numbers are on my phone," Olivia said. "I rode the London Underground when I was twelve. Think I can handle it, love."

"If you become lost, you can come back here. My parents will take you in if necessary."

"No way," Emma said. "You should have some alone time with your brother and sister. We'll be fine."

"Remember, talk to your dad about Thunderdog," Olivia said. "Let us know what he says."

"I will," Miyuki said. "Do you remember how to get back to the Tezukayama station?"

"Yes, and don't worry," Nadia said. "The train system here is quite logical. Getting lost won't be a problem."

CHAPTER 11

After her friends left for the train station, Miyuki's family took a collective breath. Miyuki volunteered to help her mom clean up the table and the kitchen. Then Kameko pulled Miyuki into her bedroom and shut the door for some girl time.

"I love your friends. They seem so nice," Kameko said. "I never met anyone from Saudi Arabia before. Have you been there?"

"Not yet. But I want to," Miyuki said.

"What's America like?"

"It's big and open. Many kinds of people live there."

"Lots of fat people."

"Some people are big. Some people are small. Many kinds of people."

"Father says Americans are crazy."

"They don't hold back what they think. However, we can be crazy too, only we don't choose to show it to each other."

Kameko thought about that. "Emma's not fat at all. She looks like one of those Hollywood actresses."

Miyuki smiled to herself. Emma would've loved that compliment.

Kameko flopped on top of her soft bedspread. "What other places have you been to?"

Miyuki sat on the other side of the bed and thought about it. "I've been to New Zealand, England, Alaska, Tahiti, Korea, China."

"Did you see Harry Potter?"

"Harry Potter?"

"Yes, doesn't Harry Potter live in England?" Kameko asked.

"Harry Potter is a character in a book."

"*Hei*, I know that. But England is full of real wizards. Did you meet any?"

"I didn't see any wizards."

Kameko made a face. Apparently meeting real wizards was a huge priority in her young life.

"In Alaska, I rode on a snowmobile while Emma and Nadia were on a dogsled." Miyuki left off the part about people shooting at them.

"I want to ride on a snowmobile. Father won't let me have a motorcycle. I told him that you had one, but he ignored me."

Their father didn't consider motorcycles would be something a girl could be interested in, but there were many things Miyuki was interested in that her father didn't approve of.

"What did you do in Korea?" Kameko asked.

"I can't say exactly. It's a secret."

"I won't tell anyone."

Miyuki wished she could. Borrowing a North Korean tank and driving it across the Russian border while a group of US Navy SEALs were chasing you made for an exciting story.

Miyuki looked around her sister's room. It was bathed in yellows and pinks. "I like your room."

Kameko rushed over to her closet and showed Kameko all her clothes. Then she dug out all her shoes and her collection of hats. Her sister was so proud of her wardrobe, but a knock at the door ended the fashion talk as Miyuki's father entered.

Kameko stood up straight.

Miyuki did too. Old habits died hard.

"You wanted to speak with me," her father said to Miyuki.

"*Hei*, if this is a good time."

"It is. Join me."

Miyuki followed her father into the living room. He sat down and, for the first time since she had been home, relaxed. Her father took out a cigarette and lit the tip. Blue smoke puffed from his mouth.

Miyuki hesitated, then decided to sit on the opposite couch with her mom.

Her father flicked his thumb against the cigarette, and a piece of ash fell into the glass ashtray. He raised his eyebrows towards his daughter. It was her cue.

"Mrs. B has asked me to come here on behalf of the Authority. They wish to ask for your help in a delicate matter involving Shiawase Nomimono."

Her father took a drag off his cigarette and blew another cloud of smoke in the air. "Your mother and I were under the mistaken impression that your visit home was personal."

"It's good to see you all." Miyuki smiled at her mom. "However, my visit isn't personal. I apologize if I've misrepresented it."

"You didn't. We only assumed," her mother said. "The mistake was ours."

"Since you have been away for two years, the assumption was easy for us to make," her father said, letting the sentence sit there for a moment.

"My work for the Authority, my new school, my new home—it has been a busy time."

"What you do is important. We understand," her mother said. "We do enjoy your phone calls."

"Your mother worries. You don't call her enough."

Her mother kept her smile. "I look forward to your calls, when you can make them. But you're here now and I'm pleased. How long will you be staying in Japan?"

"I don't know. A few days perhaps."

Her mother stood up. She was hopeful. "I'll leave you two to talk. Your old bed is ready, and there are fresh towels in the bath."

"Thank you, Mom."

She gave her another warm smile before leaving the room.

Her father took in another drag of his cigarette and let out another cloud of smoke. "If you have a concern about the company, then you and your friends must schedule an appointment with my office on Monday to discuss the matter. My home is not the proper venue."

Miyuki wondered why her father didn't say *our* home.

"I understand," she said.

The room settled. The clock on the wall ticked off the seconds.

Miyuki's father blew more smoke in the air.

Miyuki touched her thumb to the burn scar under her wrist.

The silence between them grew. There wasn't much else to say.

Her father looked off, acting as if being this close to his daughter was pure torture.

Miyuki took the hint. "It's been a long journey. I should take a bath before bed."

After her father nodded, Miyuki left the living room, but paused at the door frame. Another cloud of smoke rose from her father as the man stared into space. He was obviously thinking. Maybe thinking about his oldest daughter. Thinking about how screwed up she was. Thinking about what a disappointment Miyuki was.

Miyuki doubted her father asked himself why his daughter was so screwed up. Or what role he'd played in creating the disappointment.

What was the point of thinking about it? The past had moved on. She had moved on. And her father had moved on to a different pack of cigarettes.

Miyuki drew water for a bath. She made the water hot. Not enough to burn, but hot enough to make her feel something. She took off all her clothes and submerged herself into the bath. Miyuki gritted her teeth and bore the discomfort as her body adjusted to the temperature. Miyuki then let the tears roll down her cheeks.

CHAPTER 12

Emma took in the view of lush green-leaved trees and the rows of bushes sculpted to perfection. It amazed her how much time and patience it would take for a master gardener to create and keep up such a perfect display of greenery. As far as the streetlights revealed, this perfect display was all over this beautiful city park. Normally, Emma would love to take a book, find a nice big tree to sit under, kick off her shoes, and read.

But it was getting late in the night; the Gems were in a hurry. And more importantly, they were lost in the middle of Osaka.

"This is dumb. Let me call her," Emma said to Olivia.

"No, the hotel should be on the other side of this park."

Nadia appeared concerned. "The correct train station didn't have any parks near it."

"How do you know that?" Olivia asked, her frustration boiling up.

"The Moogle map street view." Nadia held up her phone. "I see streets and hotels. There are no parks."

Olivia glanced at Nadia's phone. "Flipping hell."

"I'm calling Miyuki," Emma said.

Olivia flopped down on a nearby bench. "Those flipping train numbers were correct. We must have gotten off at the wrong station."

Emma dialed Miyuki's number. "*You* made us get off at the wrong station."

"Keep it up, Emma," Olivia said. "Just keep it up."

"It's been a long day. Let's just get to our hotel, please?" Nadia asked.

Emma heard Miyuki's pleasant voice answer.

"Hey, what's up?" Emma asked. "What are you doing?"

"I'm taking a warm bath. How's your hotel?" Miyuki asked.

"I'm so jealous of your bath right now. Us? We're lost in a park. Somewhere in Osaka."

"Tell her we took the correct trains," Olivia said.

Emma rolled her eyes. "Olivia claims we took the right trains, but somehow she got off at a station that's near a huge park."

"Do you remember the name of the station?" Miyuki asked.

Emma covered her phone. "What's the name of the station we got off at?"

"Kawarashima, the correct one," Olivia said with attitude.

Emma repeated it to Miyuki.

"Okay. Let me look." There was a pause. "Oh...you were supposed to take the Kawaramachi station. If you got off at Kawarashima...oh."

"What?" Emma asked.

"Good thing you got off that train. It was headed to Tokyo," Miyuki said. "You took train 381 eastbound. Not 381 westbound."

Emma repeated the information to the other Gems. Olivia crossed her arms and closed her eyes, as if she were pissed at herself.

"It's an honest mistake," Nadia said. "I didn't notice either."

"You need to go back to Kawarashima station and take 381 westbound," Miyuki said to Emma over the phone. "I'll text you the Japanese characters for westbound. Oh..."

"What's wrong now?"

"You'd better hurry. Last train leaves the station in ten minutes."

"Crap, call you later," Emma said, quick as a bunny, before stuffing her phone in her pocket and whirling around to the bench. "We got ten minutes to catch the last train. Go!"

"What train?" Olivia said.

"No time to explain." Emma started running.

"Emma?"

"Come with me or stay here and sleep in the park," Emma shouted as she got up to running speed.

Nadia looked at Olivia before leaping off the bench and running.

"Flipping hell," Olivia said to herself before jumping to her feet and running hard to catch up with the others.

After making the 381 westbound train, the three Gems got off at Kawaramachi station and found themselves among a block of hotels. It was almost midnight and the streets had light traffic on them. The Gems followed Mrs. B's directions from the station and finally found their hotel.

They paused.

The hotel itself was narrow and sandwiched between two other buildings like a book in a bookcase. On the ground floor of the giant book was a large sliding glass door. The words *Eight Hours Hotel* were etched on the glass. The interior beyond was all white and futuristic as it glowed from the inside.

"I think this is it," Olivia said.

Emma was skeptical. "This can't be a real hotel."

"One way to find out." Olivia stepped through the glass doors. Nadia and Emma followed.

"*Konbanwa*," the desk clerk said and bowed enthusiastically.

Olivia bowed slightly and gave the man a piece of paper that Miyuki had written for them with all their booking information.

The male desk clerk read the note and searched for the reservation on one of his tablets on the desk. Satisfied, the man handed them three locker keys along with three capsule numbers. He also gave them a sheet of paper in English.

Olivia studied it. "What's this rubbish? Why do we need to store our belongings in lockers?"

"What's going on?" Emma asked. This was feeling weird to her.

Nadia peeked over Olivia's shoulder. The girl's face lit up like a Roman candle. "This is one of those capsule hotels."

"A what?" Emma asked.

"I watched a documentary about them on Utube. They're famous in Japan. We leave our baggage and clothes in the lockers, then change into robes."

"Is it like some sort of spa?" Olivia asked.

"Oh my God, I hope so," Emma said. Her legs and feet could use a nice rubdown. Maybe even her back too.

"I've always wanted to stay in one. This will be so fun." Nadia took one of the locker keys from Olivia. "First, we put our shoes in one of these public lockers and use slippers."

Nadia looked down. Emma now noticed the black pictorial instructions printed on the white floor. It was like they were at a hotel created by IKEA. Nadia continued. "We then go down these steps to the women's locker room."

"Why can't we just take our bags to our rooms?" Emma asked.

"Because they won't fit."

"Why wouldn't they fit?"

Fifteen minutes later, Emma felt their elevator slow as it reached the fifth floor. The doors opened and the three Gems walked off into a dark and narrow corridor. On one side of the corridor, there were two levels of oblong holes that were glowing from their inside light sources. The bottom row was near the floor and each capsule on the top row was accessible by a few steps jutting out from between the bottom capsules. A series of numbers were on the floor, pointing to the corresponding capsule.

"You must be joking," Olivia said.

"Isn't it wonderful? They gave us three capsules on the bottom so we could be together." Nadia was already leaving Olivia and Emma behind as she walked down the corridor like a kid about to get a big present.

Emma observed a few capsules with a curtain over the glass door openings. They must be occupied. "We have to sleep inside one of those?"

"Apparently," Olivia said.

"This isn't coed, is it?"

"The elevator symbols indicated a female-only floor. Thank God."

"This is stupid," Emma said. "I have my gold Visa card. Let's just go find a real hotel, one with rooms, private bathrooms, and twenty-four-hour room service. What do you say?"

"If Mrs. B hadn't made these arrangements, then I'd say let's do it. But she wants us to stay here for whatever reason, so we'd better not thumb our nose at her intentions."

"Do you really think we'd get into trouble?"

"She could be testing us for whatever reason. I wouldn't put it past her."

Emma thought about that. Grandma Laura always seemed to have something up her sleeve. So secretive. So guarded about giving out her intentions. Olivia was right. Testing the Gems by tempting them not to follow orders would not be beyond her.

"You can go if you want, but I'm staying here."

"Aren't you claustrophobic?"

"Yes. But I'm trying not to think about that," Olivia said.

Nadia ran back to them. "What are you two waiting for?"

Olivia and Emma exchanged looks, then followed Nadia over to their three capsules near the floor.

"Why don't you take four zero five, Emma," Nadia asked. "Olivia and I will take the other two."

"Okay," Emma said with zero enthusiasm. "Hey, if I die inside this thing, please don't let them bury me in it."

"You're so funny, Emma," Nadia said. "Good night."

Emma exchanged glances with Olivia. For once, the two girls agreed. Neither wanted to climb inside.

Olivia held up her fist for a bump. "Don't let them bury me in mine either, love."

Emma bumped it and slid into her capsule. She rotated onto her stomach and shut the glass door. Next, she pulled the curtain across for privacy.

Emma took in her new space. She realized there was enough room inside this capsule to sit up, so she did. Next, she examined the features of her new coffin. There was a video screen recessed into the wall to watch television or movies. To the right of that were some room controls. The occupant could control the capsule's temperature, lighting, air circulation, and sounds. Emma could listen to music, the output of the television, or meditation sounds.

Emma didn't feel like going to sleep. She reasoned her body was still on California time, so it was more like one in the afternoon than one in the morning. Emma popped her purse open and took out the book she always carried along for anti-boredom emergencies such as this. She sat back, relaxed, and began reading.

Emma finished two chapters before her phone rang. Since she now was an Authority operative, Emma had a special phone that could use most cell services around the world. And when needed, access the Authority's covert communication satellite orbiting the Earth. Emma checked the screen. But it wasn't Grandma Laura or her grandma in Berkeley calling. It was Kayla.

Oh crap. What day was it? It was Sunday night in Japan so that made it…Saturday in California. Emma realized why she was calling. On Monday, she had promised to hang out with Kayla on the weekend, and Emma totally forgot.

Emma stared at her phone as the ringtone played and played.

Should she answer? She did promise. How was Kayla supposed to know that Emma had to go to Japan because she had this secret life that no one at school could know about? Emma felt she owed her an explanation, even though it would be a lie.

"What's up?" Emma answered.

"Do you know where I live? I can shoot you some directions if you want to come pick me up," Kayla said. Her voice was so happy and full of hope.

Emma sighed and rested her head on the side of the capsule. Some great friend she was. "There's been a kink in our plan. My grandmother wants me to go to my aunt Laura's house in Oakland with her. I totally forgot."

"Oh." Kayla paused. "How about when you get back?"

"I'm having dinner there and—basically my whole day is ruined."

Kayla was quiet.

"I know. You have my permission to hate me."

"I don't hate you. It's okay. I understand."

"Maybe next weekend?"

"Yeah, maybe." Kayla's voice was quieter. The energy evaporated. "Let me know."

Emma closed her eyes. She felt like garbage.

"See you at school." Kayla's words were so low Emma could barely hear her.

Emma's heart burned. She was such an awful human being and honestly didn't deserve any friends.

"Hey, um, we're not leaving for, like, a half-hour or so. Do you wanna talk for a while?"

* * *

Emma woke up to the sound of her phone ringing inside the capsule. The pillow cuddled her cheek like a soft kitten, unwilling to let her go answer it. Emma felt around for her phone and grabbed it.

"Wha—?" she answered, unable to add the *T* at the end.

"*Ohayou!*" Miyuki said. "I'm on my way to your hotel. Can you wake up Nadia and Olivia so we can have breakfast together when

I get there?"

On her way. The phrase lingered inside Emma's brain for a long minute.

"Okay," Emma answered.

"Great. Be there in one hour. Plenty of time for you to freshen up. See you soon."

The phone went dead.

Sleepiness still clouded Emma's brain. The soft pillow to her cheek. The coziness she felt inside the capsule.

On her way.

That meant Miyuki wasn't here yet. That meant...Emma could keep sleeping, right?

Yes. Her mind reasoned. There was no need to get up. Her mind let go, allowing Emma's body to sink into the bed and fall back asleep.

Someone pounded on her glass door. The shock made Emma sit up like an alert dog. Her heart began racing. Was a rapist trying to get in? Did she need her mace? She grabbed her purse and raced through her cosmetics, looking for a weapon.

"Emma, are you awake?" It was Olivia's strong English accent.

Emma swallowed and tried to relax as she put away her purse. She pulled back the front curtain and pressed the lever that released the latch to the glass door.

"I am now."

"Miyuki's waiting outside. She said she called you over an hour ago."

Emma took a moment. Miyuki's full message suddenly made sense in her mind.

"Damn it. I'm sorry. I fell back to sleep."

Nadia appeared behind Olivia's shoulder. The girl's long dark hair was hanging down. Her face had this joy to it that surprised Emma, especially after someone wakes you up. "I can't blame you," she said. "These sleep capsules are amazing. It was the best night of sleep I've ever had in my life."

"Have to admit," Olivia said, "I was skeptical, but I'm a believer now. It was nice."

"It was so nice Emma fell back to sleep," Nadia said with a grin.

CHAPTER 13

Later that morning, Miyuki and the Gems got off the train and walked a short distance to the corporate offices of Shiawase Nomimono International. Their bright yellow office building had large multicolored Japanese letters printed along the top floor.

Miyuki checked in with the main desk, which told her to go up to office 411. Mr. Kaiko was expecting them. Miyuki bowed to the woman at the desk and the Gems took the elevator up to the fourth floor.

When the Gems stepped off the elevator, they walked into a giant room with neat rows of office desks. The walls were vanilla and the carpet was a drab gray. On one side of the giant room there was a row of glass partitions separating corporate secretaries from the other office workers. Everyone there was busy.

Behind the partition for office 411, a secretary bowed and confirmed this was Mr. Kaiko's office. She invited them to sit while she contacted him.

Miyuki noted the portrait of an older Japanese woman on the office wall. It was quite large. There was a similar one she had seen in the lobby downstairs. Her nameplate said Miss Tenchi, and Miyuki wondered what was so special about her.

"Mr. Kaiko will see you now," the young secretary said in English.

Miyuki and the Gems entered a large executive office. Her father rose from his desk and walked around it to greet his visitors.

Miyuki bowed at a forty-five-degree angle towards her father. Olivia took the hint and did the same. Nadia followed. Emma hesitated. But, she too bowed, but not as deeply as the other girls. Her father then bowed, but only at a slight angle, since he was the most senior person in the room. Everyone then took a seat.

"What concerns did you want to bring to my company's

attention?" Miyuki's father asked with a more official tone.

Miyuki understood. He was no longer her father now. During this meeting, he was a corporate vice president meeting with a bunch of kids.

"It's about your company's new energy drink, Thunderdog," she began. "We have discovered…a serious side effect that the Authority feels the company should address."

"And what serious side effect is that?"

Miyuki explained to him about the unusual effects the drink was having on teens. She told him about the information the Authority had gathered about the schools that had the Thunderdog vending machines on their campuses.

"Do you have this information with you?" her father asked, his facial expression unchanged.

"*Hei,*" Miyuki said. "And Olivia can give you a personal experience of how the drink affected her." While Miyuki translated, Olivia explained how the drink made her incredibly angry and violent. How she knew what she was doing, but still couldn't stop herself from attacking her friends. It was like she was under the influence of a drug. Miyuki also added how hard it was to control Olivia in that state of mind. It was like the drink had turned her into a rabid animal.

When they finished, Miyuki's father was in deep thought. His face betrayed no emotion whatsoever.

Emma was next. She talked about her friend Kayla and how the energy drink caused her to freak out and attack a boy who was sitting on her desk. Emma described Kayla and how nonviolent she was. The drink had done a major rewrite on the girl's brain.

Finally, Nadia explained the more scientific evidence the Authority had gathered. What the chemical compounds in the drink did to a teenager's brain and how it affected their behavior.

After about thirty minutes of giving Miyuki's father every piece of evidence they had about Thunderdog and its effects, the Gems waited for an answer.

Miyuki's father rotated the black thumb drive of information Nadia had given him with his fingers. Miyuki could tell that her father was processing everything they had told him. Then the man stepped away from his desk and glanced out the window that overlooked central Osaka.

Miyuki saw a reflection of her father in the glass. His eyes were closed, his head down to the point where his chin touched his chest. She saw real pain on his face. Why was her father in pain?

"The drink should be pulled before more kids get hurt," Olivia said.

It was an obvious thing to say, but Olivia was trying to drive the point home. Miyuki went ahead and translated it to her father.

He reacted by opening his eyes, lifting his chin, and straightening his stance. The pain was gone from his face.

Miyuki's father turned around to face them. "On behalf of the company, I thank you and your organization for bringing this matter to our attention in such a discreet way. We'll consider your request to remove the drink from our test markets."

Miyuki's heart sank. She translated his answer to her friends.

"You'll consider it?" Olivia asked. "What kind of stupid answer is that? Your drink is dangerous. It should be taken out of the vending machines immediately before more kids drink it and go bonkers. This should be done now." Olivia shot Miyuki a look. "Tell him!"

Miyuki began to translate Olivia's words, but her father told her to stop.

"The decision will be under consideration," he said. "That is the best we can offer right now. Good day."

She checked with her father. His eyes were rigid, unmoving, final. Miyuki knew the meeting was over, so she stood up.

"We should leave now," Miyuki said.

The other Gems looked at each other as they slowly rose to stand.

"How long will it take for them to consider it?" Nadia asked.

"It's time to leave," Miyuki said to her friends as she moved to open the door.

"Miyuki?" Olivia asked.

"I will explain later."

Nadia and Emma hesitated, but then followed Miyuki out of the office, where Mr. Kaiko's secretary was already standing at her desk. The reason was a Japanese man wearing a white business suit and black tie. Pinned to his lapel was an older Japanese flag. It was the rising sun, but with rays bursting from the red center. The man's eyes examined Miyuki's friends.

When the man noted Miyuki, his face brightened. "Hello, young lady, what brings you to our company today?" he asked in

Japanese.

"She is my daughter, Mr. Nagumo." Miyuki's father emerged from his office, his head already bowing to the gentleman. "Her name is Miyuki."

"Ah, I should have noticed the resemblance. The error is mine," the man in the white suit said. "Miyuki…I like that name. You go to school abroad, isn't that correct?"

"*Hei*," Miyuki answered. "I'm visiting my family this week."

"Your father speaks about his family often. It's good to finally meet you." Mr. Nagumo glanced at the Gems, expecting someone to introduce him.

"Allow me to introduce my friends, Mr. Nagumo." Miyuki referenced Olivia first. "This is Lisa Dixon from England."

Olivia only understood the name Lisa Dixon, but the mere mention of her standard alias was enough to clue her in on what Miyuki was doing, and she bowed with a smile.

"This is Shari from Dubai."

Nadia bowed with no protest. She'd figured it out too.

"And this is—" Miyuki realized Emma was so new, she didn't have an official alias yet "—Emily from America."

Emma gave her a strange look. "My name is not Emil—"

"Fine, if you must be so formal about it, love," Olivia interrupted, stepping into the conversation. "Her name is actually Emily Anne. A bit too fancy, if you ask me."

Emma stopped herself. Thought about it. The bulb came on. "I just like how Emily Anne flows off the tongue. Plus that's the name my mom gave me, so why shouldn't I use both names?"

Miyuki began to translate for Mr. Nagumo, but he raised his hand.

"I speak fluent English. I understood what she said. My name is Kori Nagumo, president of Shiawase Nomimono International." The man turned to "Emily." "What part of America are you from?"

"New York City," Emma said.

"I see. Were you there during the terrorist attack on the World Trade Center?"

"That happened before I was born—but I heard it was bad. My father knew some people in the building."

"During World War Two, my great-grandfather was an aircraft carrier pilot. He flew his plane over Pearl Harbor on December seventh and sent a torpedo into the USS *Oklahoma*. It was a direct hit. He helped send hundreds of Americans to their death. He did it for Emperor Hirohito. Those al-Qaeda terrorists on nine-eleven did it for Allah." Mr. Nagumo paused. "The power of an idea. That concept has always fascinated me."

"Even a noble cause can become twisted into an evil one," Nadia said. "Men choose to twist their original intentions to suit their desires."

Mr. Nagumo nodded in agreement. "So, Miyuki, you're here to see where your father works?"

Miyuki hesitated. Calling out her father in front of his boss would be mortifying to him. No, today was not the day to confront these men. "*Hei*, my friends and I were just leaving."

Olivia acted like she wanted to object, but she held herself back.

"Before you leave, Miyuki, I would like to show you something." Mr. Nagumo eyed Miyuki's father. "With your permission, of course."

Her father bowed.

"Wonderful. Your friends may come along if they wish." Mr. Nagumo stretched out his arm. "Follow me."

CHAPTER 14

Miyuki and the Gems followed Mr. Nagumo back across the giant office floor towards a spacious outer office. Two corporate secretaries, one man and one woman, stood up and bowed to Mr. Nagumo as he approached. The man didn't talk to them as he opened a large door and gestured for them to enter.

Miyuki was the first one inside. It was a gigantic office. Miyuki guessed that his office covered the rest of the fourth floor itself. Built in a traditional Japanese style, the office had a meeting table low to the ground with padding around the outside, as if Mr. Nagumo expected his executives to sit on the floor during their meetings. There were also wooden sliding doors that separated different sections of the office. Mr. Nagumo did have an office desk and a chair in the corner, but they were both simple, not at all like a desk you would see in an American executive's office.

A collection of *Space Battleship Yamato* artwork hung on the walls. The 1970s Japanese anime series was ahead of its time. Along with *Speed Racer*, the series was a classic that put Japanese animation on the world's radar. Mr. Nagumo had an impressive collection of items, almost like a shrine to the television series. Full models of the space battleship. Alien ships. Uniforms. Miniatures of all the major characters...

"Are you familiar with it?" Nagumo referenced the artwork in English.

"*Hei*, I know of it well. My brother, Haru, enjoyed the adaptation that was on television recently."

"I prefer the old classic." Nagumo picked up a small framed picture. "This is an actual animation cell from the original 1974 master."

"Very impressive display."

"Why does this battleship have a hole in the bow?" Emma

80

asked. "Doesn't that defeat the purpose?"

"They don't understand," Nagumo said in Japanese. "*Space Battleship Yamato* is not understood by foreigners. They can't see the relevance it had to the children growing up during the new post-war Japan. A world seeping with radiation. A world on the edge of defeat by powerful enemies. A world desperate for hope. A world that rose above the ashes and did the impossible. The series embodies the best things about us. The struggles we've had to endure."

Mr. Nagumo walked along his artwork, continuing to speak in his native language. "If I had it my way, the series would be required watching by every Japanese boy and girl. Only then would they truly understand their country's past. And could see the brightness of its future."

He came close to Miyuki and lowered his voice. "I enjoy talking to young people such as yourself. I seek them out because I feel it's important that our future generations do not give in to those outside influences that move them away from their roots. The roots that have bound Japan to her people for thousands of years."

Nagumo placed his hands on Miyuki's shoulders. His blue eyes glistened with passion. "Our people have taken care of themselves long before the West came to our shores. We even reinvented ourselves after a world war devastated our country. Now we are a major economic power in the world. We are a mighty people who have never tapped into our true potential. Some day, I hope your generation will take us there. To make Japan what she always was destined to become."

Miyuki could tell this was something the man was passionate about. However, she didn't understand why she was chosen to receive Mr. Nagumo's wisdom.

"Your swords are beautiful, Mr. Nagumo," Nadia said.

Mr. Nagumo's passion melted away and a polite smile returned as he switched back to English. "Do you like them?"

He moved to a wooden rack of five samurai swords. Mr Nagumo took one and unsheathed it. The sharp blade glistened in the light. "They are so beautiful. So deadly. A Japanese samurai would wield these weapons like an extension of his arm. Swift. Decisive." Mr. Nagumo swung the edge of the sword down on a nearby table, shearing off the entire corner, which dropped to the floor.

All four Gems froze in place. What the hell?

"That's the fourth table I've injured this year." Mr. Nagumo laughed. He resheathed his sword. "Please forgive me if I scared you. The sword is a seductress. She wants me to wield her. But I must resist her charms or I will not have any office furniture left." Mr. Nagumo put the sword back.

"Aren't we still having lunch with your mom?" Olivia asked Miyuki with a raised eyebrow.

If they were, Miyuki had no knowledge about it.

"Won't we be late for the train?" Nadia asked with both eyebrows raised.

What were they talking about? Miyuki hadn't asked her mom to join them for—then it hit her. Yes, Olivia and Nadia were right. Mr. Nagumo had entertained them with his sword play quite enough for one day.

"Ah, yes—thank you for the reminder. We must leave now if we are to catch our train." Miyuki bowed to Mr. Nagumo. "Our apologies for leaving in such an abrupt way. Thank you for showing us your office. And I thank you personally for allowing my father to contribute to your company."

Mr. Nagumo bowed slightly. "Your father and his team have done well. The company is fortunate to have his services at its disposal. Good day, Miyuki. And think about what I said."

The Gems stepped back on to the elevator. They waited for the doors to close before they let it all out.

"He's a loony," Olivia said. "Did you see how that man looked at that sword? He's in love with it."

"He's eccentric," Miyuki said. "People who are old often become that way."

"Olivia's right," Emma said. "That man has some issues he needs to work out. By the way, what was he talking to you about? He seemed really into whatever it was."

"As I said, he's a bit of an eccentric."

"Did he proposition you?" Nadia asked.

"That cheeky old bastard," Olivia said.

"He did no such thing," Miyuki said. She then told the girls the short version about *Space Battleship Yamato* and Japan. "To be honest, I didn't know what he meant by all that."

"What I want to know is, why did we have to leave your father's office?" Olivia asked.

"Yeah, what does 'we'll consider your request' mean anyway?" Emma asked.

The elevator opened and Miyuki stepped off. She motioned for the girls to follow her outside the crowded lobby. Miyuki found a nice bench and invited them to sit down.

"You see, everything in Japan is designed not to put another person in an embarrassing position. Not losing face is the primary reason we act the way we do."

"What's this have to do with anything?" Olivia asked.

Miyuki held up her hand to pause her. "The one word that's never used in Japan is the word *no*. Telling someone no can embarrass the other person, causing them to lose face among their peers."

"So when your father says they'll consider our request, it actually means no?" Nadia asked.

"Exactly, it's a polite way to avoid using the term *no*. They'll consider our request, but most likely will take no further action."

"And meanwhile more kids will get hurt or even killed while they do nothing," Olivia said. "We should have said something to Mr. Nagumo while we had a chance. He's your father's boss, right?"

"If we had done that, we would have embarrassed my father in front of the company."

"Miyuki," Emma said, "I know you love your father and don't want to see him embarrassed, but—"

"You don't understand how we handle problems here."

"What if your father arranges for us to speak with Mr. Nagumo on official terms?" Nadia asked.

"If my father brings up the problems of Thunderdog to Mr. Nagumo or anyone else inside the company, he will lose face."

"Can't you see that this is more important than your father's reputation?" Olivia asked.

"There are limits to what he can do for us." Miyuki realized her voice rose an octave or two during that sentence. She needed to calm down.

"Perhaps we should check in with Mrs. B," Nadia said. "Maybe she knows what we should do next."

Miyuki and the Gems found a McDonald's in the Osaka business district. Nadia broke out her laptop and inserted her IP scrambler before logging on the public Wi-Fi. Nadia then went to one of the many dummy sites Authority operatives used to access their covert network. After several online challenges to her identity, including a retinal scan using her laptop camera, Nadia gained access and sent a video chat request.

Mrs. B appeared on the screen. "What progress have you made?"

Miyuki explained the meeting with her father and the company's official response.

"That's disappointing," Mrs. B said. "We must double our efforts. The Gems will have to stay in Japan for a little longer. Ruby, you must press your father, convince him to speak with Mr. Nagumo. We must stop them from making this drink."

"With all due respect, convincing my father to confront his boss will be difficult."

Mrs. B hesitated. "Yesterday, a young college student in Oregon rammed his car into a group of people on a crosswalk. Eight people killed. Four injured. The media are trying to frame it as a lone-wolf terrorist attack, but we found out that the student was up all night cramming for a test. Authorities found two empty cans of Thunderdog in his dorm room."

Miyuki's heart dropped. Olivia was right. This was more than saving someone's honor.

"I promise to speak with my father again."

CHAPTER 15

Later that day, Miyuki got off at the Tezukayama train station and walked. The sky above was a deep blue with blotches of clouds drifting in from the west. As Miyuki made the turn into her old neighborhood, she took her time. The road was narrow, with a white stripe running along one side of the smooth pavement to separate the bike lane from the main road. The small two-story houses were all close to the street and crowded together. Most of their front yards were decorated with Japanese maples, plum blossoms, and kobushi magnolia trees that were manicured from reaching out beyond the chest-high fences. Numerous bicycles were parked out in the open. None of them had locks because there was no need. Japan had a low crime rate.

Inside the gardens, many of the yards boasted various ferns and semi-evergreen plants that gave Miyuki's street that distinct smell that she remembered from when she was a kid.

When she reached her family's house, Miyuki opened the iron gate and followed the short path to the front door. Her hand went up to open the door. But it fell back down. A part of her wasn't ready to go in yet.

She turned away from the door and visited her family's small garden. Miyuki spread her body out on the cool grass and took the garden in like a slow-moving sunrise. Admiring the leaves and the plants from every angle. The beauty of it. The simplification. The pleasant scent the plants added to the air. Miyuki allowed herself to become lost in that moment.

Lost in time.

Lost in place.

She didn't even realize how long until Kameko arrived home from school an hour later.

"Miyuki!" Her sister jumped on her with a hug, rolling them both across the grass. This made Miyuki laugh.

"Why are you outside?"

"I'm enjoying the garden. You've done a good job helping Mom since I've been gone."

"Can you play with me?"

"Until Father comes home, *hei!*"

Eight hours later, Miyuki was still waiting for her father. Haru came home around seven and mentioned their father had a late dinner meeting with Mr. Nagumo and some top company executives. After a long workday, it was common for Japanese employees to go out to dinner together. Sometimes these dinners would last a long time, as employees could relax and raise their concerns about work without fear of consequences. Only then, was speaking honestly to your boss allowed. An honesty not tolerated during the workday.

She hoped her father would express his concerns about Thunderdog. It was a more comfortable situation in order to approach the subject.

Miyuki stretched across the couch and watched a new game show on Japanese television. The contestants on this show had to go home for one night and pretend to be an animal in front of their families, who of course were not in on the joke. If the contestant could make it through one night without breaking "character," they would win lots of prizes. So far, Miyuki's favorite was the man who had to act like a monkey. During his family's dinner, the man jumped up and swung on the light fixture while scratching himself and making monkey noises. His small kids loved it, but his poor wife was terrified and called the police.

That was Miyuki received a text from Olivia.

Talk to him yet?

Miyuki sighed. She had told her friends how late most Japanese executives came home after work—midnight was the norm—but Olivia apparently didn't believe her. She typed an answer.

He's not home yet.

Is he seeing a mistress?

Miyuki almost laughed out loud. Her father wouldn't have enough energy after work to keep up with another woman.

Finally the front door opened. Miyuki typed Olivia a quick reply and put up her phone. She glanced up at the clock. It was fifteen minutes before midnight.

Her father took off his shoes and put on some slippers as he came inside the living room. He put up his briefcase before noticing Miyuki on the sofa.

"Waiting up for me?"

"*Hei,*" Miyuki answered.

Her father loosened his tie before coming over to the sofa. Miyuki moved over to one side.

Her father paused, then sat on the opposite side of the sofa, allowing a cushion between them. "Mr. Nagumo talked about you at dinner. You made a strong impression on him the other day."

"Did I?"

"Respectful and confident. Those are the words he used. He asked me where you were attending school."

Miyuki looked at her father.

"Don't worry, I told him what the Authority instructed us to say. This Burlington School for Girls. It's a real place, yes?"

Miyuki told him yes. It was a real place. Somewhere in the American state of Vermont. But neither Miyuki nor any of the Gems had ever been there. It was the cover story that Mrs. B gave all the parents of the Gems. That way they could feel comfortable and not be lying if anyone asked.

"Did you mention anything else to Mr. Nagumo?"

"Such as?"

Miyuki didn't answer.

"No." Her father reached into his pocket for a pack of cigarettes. Then his lighter. He took one out and lit it. A cloud of smoke floated above him.

Miyuki's thumb rubbed the scarred tissue under her wrist.

"Kameko is happy to see you again," her father said. "She has missed you."

"I've missed her too. She's growing up so fast. And Haru, he's a young man now."

"Your brother is doing well inside the company's management

training program. High marks. His trainers are quite pleased."

"And you're pleased?"

"Of course. I look forward to seeing what Haru will add to the future growth of our company." Her father sucked in the smoke from his cigarette. Miyuki could imagine the inside of his lungs struggling for clean air. As Nadia would point out, the scientific evidence was overwhelming. A smoker will most likely develop cancer in their body and die an early death. She knew her mom wanted him to quit, but she always feared that smoking was the only way her father could deal with the stress from work.

"And Kameko—Mom is still involved with her gymnastics training?"

"Your mom works closely with the coaching staff at school. That has helped Kameko focus on improving her skills." Her father paused. "Yet she still fails to motivate herself."

Fails to motivate herself. Miyuki had heard that phrase before. It was one her father would use to describe her.

"Mom should be patient with her. Kameko loves gymnastics. She will come around eventually."

"If Kameko wants to compete in the Olympics, she must come around now."

"I understand. All I'm saying is don't push her too hard—"

"Or she will give up like you did?" her father asked, sharp and to the point.

The air escaped from Miyuki's lungs. The punch was a verbal one, but it still stung.

"I—I didn't give up. Gymnastics no longer interested me."

"Boys and motorcycles interested you." Her father phrased it in a bad way. Yet Miyuki was good at riding motorbikes. The boyfriend part, not so much. Her father continued. "You should have let your mother help you."

Miyuki glanced at the floor.

"You never gave gymnastics a chance," he added.

And you never gave me a chance. Never encouraged me to pursue my interests. Never let me be myself.

Miyuki stopped her angry thoughts and relaxed. "Thank you for allowing me to study judo," she said instead.

Her father took a puff of his cigarette before answering. "You can thank your mother for that. I was against the idea."

Of course he was. Why would a future wife need to know about motorbikes and Judo to help raise a family? Why couldn't he understand? Why couldn't he help his daughter find her own path? Miyuki always knew she was different. Inside her heart, she knew she would never fit into the roles her parents wanted her to play. Her father kept trying to pound her into this round mold, while ignoring the fact that his daughter had lots of corners.

"How happy were you to send me away?"

Her father went silent.

Miyuki wanted to kick herself for letting that slip out. She needed to ask for her father's help, not rip open past wounds. "Forgive me. I didn't come home to—there are more important things we should talk about. You should approach Mr. Nagumo again—"

"We have finished our discussion on that topic." Her father flicked the ash off his cigarette.

Miyuki ignored him. "A college student ran over twelve people yesterday with his car. Eight of those people are dead. Two empty cans of Thunderdog were found in his dorm room."

Her father closed his eyes.

"If you and the company do nothing, more will die."

Before answering, her father took a long drag off his cigarette. "At dinner, I mentioned the negative reports coming out of America to Mr. Nagumo."

"I thought you said you didn't discuss it with him," Miyuki said.

"This is a delicate situation," her father said with frustration. "The company is aware of the controversy. In fact, Mr. Nagumo wants me to monitor the situation and keep him and the other executives informed."

"What does that mean?"

"It means exactly what it means. I keep them informed."

"Did you show them the scientific evidence we presented? Did you stress how serious the situation—?"

Her father jumped to his feet. "There is nothing more I can do," he yelled.

Miyuki clamped her hand over her wrist. The old reaction had returned. And her father saw it too.

He paused before moving away from the sofa. "The company's plans for the energy drink will continue. I'm sorry. I'm not powerful enough to stop them, Miyuki." Her father's eyes softened as he braced himself against one of the walls.

His words shocked her. It was a big crack in her father's neutral exterior. A weakness she had never seen from him. Now Miyuki understood the pressure her father was under. The child inside her wanted to put her arms around her dad and tell him that she loved him. But the fourteen-year-old version could still feel that burning pain on her wrist as if it were yesterday. That teenager wanted to see him crack. To show any sign of remorse for what he did.

Her father stared out the window. "I tried the best I could, Miyuki. However, it still wasn't enough to convince them." He took in another deep breath and let the smoke leak from his nose and mouth. "I have let you down."

"Well, it's not the first time."

Her father closed his eyes again.

Yes, it was a cheap shot. However, the sixteen-year-old inside her just didn't give a shit anymore about earning her father's respect.

Miyuki's eyes wandered around the living room, trying to find an excuse to get out of this uncomfortable conversation. She noted a group of family pictures and walked over to them. One picture had the entire family in it. Miyuki was fourteen at the time. Kameko and Haru were much younger and looked like real kids. Another picture was of her father. He stood by two of his oldest friends. She remembered them from when she was a little girl because their families would do things together.

Miyuki realized something and turned around. "Does your friend Ozawa still work for the government?"

The change of subject pulled her father from the window. He sat on the sofa again. "Last year he was promoted to the foreign minister's office." Her father hesitated. "Do you want him to be your new father? He always did like you."

This was not how Miyuki wanted this discussion to go. Again, her family drama had interrupted the entire reason she was here in the first place.

"I have an idea. What if you told him about Thunderdog?" she asked.

"That's impossible. I will not burden Ozawa with my problems."

"When is the company going to release this drink in Japan? How many young Japanese will die while you remain silent? You must convince the government to act. It's the honorable thing to do."

"Why can't that organization of yours talk to the government? I have heard the Authority has influence over a great many governments."

Her anger returned. "Your company made this product. If they won't act, you must. Father, it's your responsibility to do whatever must be done."

Miyuki's father closed his eyes again. When they opened, he crushed his cigarette out against the bottom of the ashtray before rising to his feet. "It's late and I'm tired." Miyuki's father then disappeared from the living room and shut the door.

Miyuki watched the thin trail of smoke rising from the dying cigarette before heading off to bed herself.

CHAPTER 16

The next morning, Emma felt like she could take on the world. The weird capsule room that she first thought was a coffin was the most comfortable bed she had ever slept in. Nadia was right, once you had everything set to how you liked to sleep, it was perfect.

Emma waited for Nadia and Olivia to wake up before the three of them headed downstairs for a dip in the hot bath located in the female community bathroom. The Japanese women were all very respectful of each other's privacy. That was the one thing Emma liked about Japan. People here showed genuine respect for one another. A sense of community. Everything they did reflected that.

After the three Gems got dressed, they met Miyuki for lunch at a ramen restaurant near their capsule hotel. It puzzled Emma why the Japanese liked whole eggs in their soup of noodles, but she fished hers out and placed it on the side of the bowl. Using chopsticks, Nadia pulled up some noodles and began sucking them up loudly as Emma watched.

"You're fitting in with the culture quite nicely, love," Olivia said.

Nadia finished and wiped her mouth with a napkin. "You know, it's liberating to do that in public and no one even blinks."

"Did you talk to your father?" Emma asked.

Miyuki slurped up some noodles before wiping her mouth and drinking some ginger ale. She wasn't reacting to her question at all.

Emma could tell her mind was elsewhere. "It didn't go well, did it?"

Olivia and Nadia turned to hear her answer.

But Miyuki still didn't respond.

"*Ohayou*, Miyuki!" Emma said loudly.

That woke her up. "Sorry, were you speaking to me?"

"*Hei!*" all three Gems said in unison before laughing.

Miyuki's skin turned a little red as she used her hand to cover her smile. "I'm sorry. What were we talking about?"

Emma dialed down her laughter. "I said it didn't go well, did it? Talking to your dad again?"

Miyuki placed her chopsticks to the side. "My father refuses to bring up Thunderdog again to the company, and I don't know what else to do."

"I bet Nagumo would see you again," Olivia said.

"That would make things awkward for my father."

"I know you want to protect him," Emma said. "But I don't think we have a choice now, do we?"

Miyuki paused. "Actually, we do. My father has an old friend who works for the Japanese foreign affairs ministry. If my father approached him—"

"Maybe he could convince the government to do something," Olivia said. "That might work."

"But my father refuses to approach his friend. I've already asked."

"Have you ever met this friend of his?" Nadia asked.

"Yes, our families are close. We are both originally from Okinawa. In school, I was friends with his daughter and son."

"Then it's a no-brainer," Emma said.

"A no-trainer?"

"She means it's obvious," Olivia said. "We should go warn your father's friend about Thunderdog."

"I can't do that," Miyuki said.

"Why not?"

"You don't understand. My father should be the one who approaches his friend. It's the only way for him to still keep his honor and also do the right thing."

"Miyuki, we've been over this," Olivia said. "Your father's honor isn't worth a human life."

"There's a way to satisfy both."

"When we joined the Authority, we all swore an oath to protect the lives of innocent people. Remember that? If you refuse to do this, I'll have to report you to Mrs. B."

Emma wanted to dump her hot ramen all over Olivia's skirt. The girl needed to chill. "Stop being so dramatic, Olivia. Good God, you have no idea if talking to her father's friend would even change anything. Look, Miyuki is doing the best she can. We're strangers in this country. We don't know how things work here, but Miyuki does. Let's give her a break and stop judging her. Remember, we're here for support. Not to tell her what to do."

Olivia's eyes burned into Emma's.

Emma didn't care. She knew she was right and wasn't going to turn on her friend.

"This is a difficult situation for everyone," Nadia said. "But Mrs. B was clear. She wanted us to support Miyuki. No matter what."

Olivia's eyes wandered over to Nadia. Her friend offered a supportive smile. Olivia loosened up. "Fine, but we still should contact Mrs. B and keep her up to date on what's going on."

"I'll text her," Miyuki said, not happy about it. She pulled out her own sat phone and sent Mrs. B a secure message of her progress through the Authority's spy satellite. Five minutes later, Miyuki's phone rang. It was Mrs. B calling back to talk to her. Miyuki then walked away from the table to speak with her in private.

"Bet you ten dollars she'll make Miyuki rat on her father," Olivia said.

Nadia didn't reply, but frowned.

Emma thought Olivia was probably right. She opened her small purse and found a tissue to wipe off her hands. Emma then noticed her sat phone had a message. It must be from Kayla again. Emma checked the screen and noticed the message was from an unknown number.

Hi Emma. It's Ryan. Been a long time. What are you up to?

Her body turned cold as shock crept into her heart. Ryan? How did he get her new phone number?

Should she answer him?

Emma checked on her friends. Olivia and Nadia were both focused on Miyuki's pacing back and forth along the pavement in deep conversation with Mrs. B.

Emma kept her phone hidden under the table. Before typing back, she had to figure out the time. It should be night in California. Around eleven.

**Going to bed. What do you want? How did you get this
number?**

**Wanted to send you a pic from Egypt, remember? But you
switched phones.**

You took the hint well. Not.

LOL, I won't share your number with them. Promise.

I don't trust you.

You can.

Emma wasn't falling for it. Ryan Raymond was the most
charming and charismatic boy she had ever met. And that made
him dangerous. She had met Ryan on her first mission. Her job
was to cozy up to him and make Ryan fall in love with her so she
could get closer to his father who owned this multibillion dollar
food company. But a funny thing happened. They both ended up
falling for each other. And it was nice for a while. Until she found
out Ryan had a dark side. Working for a criminal organization had
a way of doing that to people. To say their relationship was now
complicated…was an understatement.

A picture appeared in her message stream. Emma tapped on it.
It was a picture of Ryan, his athletic body in tight shorts and a T-
shirt. He wore aviator sunglasses and a big smile on his face. In the
background, the sun was setting over the Egyptian pyramids. She
typed a reply and hit send.

This photoshopped?

**LOL. No I have sunburns to prove it. Egypt was awesome.
So much to see and do. Wish you could have been there.**

Not interested Ryan

? Just talking. Like friends.

Don't want to be your friend.

Yes you do.

**Never take my kindness as a sign of affection. You tried to
hurt my friends and innocent people. You're scum.**

There was a long pause. Emma hoped her meaning was clear
enough.

I can be patient. You're a girl worth waiting for Emma.

Ryan was doing it again. Flattering her. Making Emma blush and get emotional instead of using her brain. She typed.

And you're a boy worth forgetting. Stop contacting me.

Emma put away her phone. She hoped she was clear enough. But a part of her feared this wouldn't be the last time she heard from Ryan.

CHAPTER 17

That afternoon, Miyuki took the crowded train back home. As she stood and held on to the metal bar for balance, her mind was overwhelmed with problems. Mrs. B wasn't happy with their progress. She was frustrated with Miyuki's father and the company in general. When Miyuki told her about the family friend that her father could approach inside the Japanese government, Mrs. B gave Miyuki a direct order. She wanted her to contact Ozawa directly. Mrs. B went on about putting her family's needs aside and to do what was required. No matter what the personal cost. Miyuki thought that was unfair. She was doing her best under the circumstances. However, Mrs. B's last words came back to her…

"The Japanese government won't respond to us about Thunderdog. We need another option. We need your option."

The symbolic box Miyuki found herself in was set up for failure. If she ratted the company out, Mr. Nagumo would retaliate against her father. And it would hurt his close friendship with Ozawa, since her father chose not to come to him with the information himself. And what about her brother Haru's future? Why would Mr. Nagumo want to help the son of a whistle-blower become a company executive? If Miyuki did this, her family's future would be ruined.

Mrs. B and the other Gems didn't understand Japan. Honor was everything. A person's reputation was everything. It was forever glued to the person's soul. Only Miyuki's father could decide to put his own reputation on the line. Doing the honorable thing was not his daughter's choice to make.

"The train is now approaching Tezukayama station," a pleasant female voice announced over the speakers.

Miyuki held on to the bar tighter as the train braked for the station. The doors opened and Miyuki stepped outside. As she followed the other passengers down a flight of concrete stairs, Miyuki bumped into the back of a man ahead of her.

"Excuse me," she said. The man turned and Miyuki recognized him. It was her father.

The two paused on the stairs. Passengers frowned as they went around the irritating human obstacles.

Miyuki's father motioned for her to follow him as they continued to the bottom of the stairs. Her father veered away from the street and sat on a wood bench. Miyuki joined him.

The brakes were released with a hiss as the train rolled forward to the next station. The sound of steel wheels groaning along the rails faded as passengers who lingered at the station finally headed off to wherever it was they were going. Soon, Miyuki and her father were alone.

"Did you leave work early?"

"I'm not feeling well," her father said.

"What's wrong?"

Her father's gaze was far away, as if the man could see beyond the horizon. Miyuki wasn't sure where his attention was, but it certainly wasn't here with her.

Miyuki lifted herself off the bench. "Do you want to go home?"

This broke his attention. Her father nodded and stood up. Together they walked through the neighborhood block. The weather today was pleasant, and small children were out playing in the small yards. Their laughter echoed down the street. One woman was planting in her front garden, her hands crusted with dirt. A retired couple sat in their front yard and relaxed under the afternoon sun. Their hands securely fastened together. Their lives intertwined forever.

Her father's eyes dragged along the pavement, as if he were admiring the craftsmanship the crews had put into the roadwork.

The urge to quiz her father with a million questions pressed hard against Miyuki's lips. But she knew him too well. When she was younger, Miyuki would push him to talk, push him to respond to her, and this behavior would only make her father lash out and lose control of himself.

Miyuki touched the rough skin just under her wrist. The cigarette burn was a reminder that her father had limits.

No, she would not force him into a corner and dare him like before. That fourteen-year-old version of her wanted to rebel.

Wanted nothing to do with tradition. She wanted freedom at any cost. Even a cigarette burn would do. And it did. Miyuki was now free. She was living away from home and doing what she wanted to do. She had won the argument and had accepted the price.

"Does it still hurt?" her father asked.

Miyuki dropped her hands to her sides. Rubbing her fingers under her wrist was such a habit that she was barely aware of it half the time.

"It doesn't hurt."

Her father nodded. "Are you happy?"

Miyuki looked at him.

"With your life now...are you happy?"

"*Hei*," Miyuki said.

As they made the turn into their neighborhood, her father said, "That pleases me."

It did? Miyuki wondered why it pleased him. Was he happy she was gone from his life? Or was he happy that she was happy?

Miyuki followed him down their street. The same familiar Japanese maples, plum blossoms, and kobushi magnolia trees sat in many of the front yards. One neighbor mounted their bicycle and pedaled down the bike lane past them.

They were almost home now. Miyuki had hoped that her father would open up to her and answer some of the questions still weighing on her mind.

But he was so quiet and distant that Miyuki's hope had faded.

As they reached their house, Miyuki opened the front iron gate and stepped into the garden. But her father didn't follow. His right hand rested on the fence post. This seemed to prevent the rest of his body from passing through the gate.

Miyuki retreated to him. This was getting silly to her. "Something is on your mind. Do you want to share it?"

She waited for the standard no or the new excuse that always prevented her father from being open and honest about—

"I told Ozawa about Thunderdog," he said. "This morning I called into work and pretended to be ill, then took the train to Tokyo. I also gave him all the scientific information you provided."

Miyuki's heart soared. She was so proud of him. "I know it was difficult, but under the circumstances you did the honorable thing."

Her words had little effect on his face. The face of a condemned man. His grip tightened on the fence. Something still wasn't right.

"What is it?" she asked.

"This is my fault."

"Thunderdog?"

"*Hei*, it is all my fault."

"How is this your fault? The fault lies with the company. Not with the man who stands up to save lives."

"You don't understand," he said. "Fault lies within the group. Fault lies with the leader of that group."

"What are you talking about?"

"Our company purchased the Raymond Foods Beverage Division six months ago. It was my group that supervised the integration of this new division into Shiawase Nomimono," he said. "The Thunderdog project was already in the advanced stages of development at Raymond Foods. Therefore, we approved the energy drink for market testing."

"But how's that your fault? You didn't know the effect it would have on kids."

Her father was quiet.

"Did you?"

"After our first phase of market tests, there was evidence to suggest that something…unusual was happening with select consumers of our beverage. I brought this to the attention of Thunderdog's creator, Tyler Cho. He's one of the most brilliant young food engineers in the industry. Mr. Cho was one of the main reasons our company bought the beverage division from Raymond Foods."

"And what did this Tyler Cho say?"

"Mr. Cho assured us that Raymond Foods had already done extensive tests on Thunderdog and found no such issues. Therefore, we threw out our company's test results as bad data. To be honest, I trusted Mr. Cho's expertise with the drink and the Raymond Foods data backing it up. I went to Mr. Nagumo and assured him that Thunderdog was ready for the next phase. A limited release in Australia, the Pacific, and North American markets."

That surprised Miyuki. He was much more involved than she had been led to believe.

He looked up at his daughter. "Your information put me in a difficult position. We were already committed to Thunderdog, and any reversal in its development would have had a negative effect upon our company's reputation. Besides, our test data on Thunderdog was still inconclusive. Why did it only affect teens? No one else consuming the beverage was affected. It did not make sense to us."

Her father closed his eyes. The stress pressing against them was intense. "When I first heard the news about the boy in Oregon who ran over all those people...I wept. I knew that we had made a terrible mistake." His eyes opened and they were glassy. He was on the brink of losing it. "Now, I have betrayed my company and my employees. I've also jeopardized Haru's future. I have shamed them all."

Miyuki's heart broke a little. "But you still have your honor. Sacrificing yourself to save thousands."

Her father was now on his knees, facing the house, almost like he was praying to it.

"Telling Ozawa was the honorable thing to do," Miyuki said. "I'm proud of you."

Her father said nothing. His eyes were still under a haze of emptiness.

Young voices echoed from the street. The kids were walking back home from school.

Miyuki knelt and took her father's hands. "Kameko will be home at any moment. Perhaps you should go inside and take a warm bath."

Her father blinked and nodded in agreement before rising to his feet. Shaking off the depression, her father walked into the house and shut the front door.

Miyuki held back her tears. She had never seen her father so broken and it scared her.

"Miyuki!" Kameko yelled from the street and began running towards the house.

Miyuki wiped her eyes and swallowed her worries as she glued on a simple smile. She turned around and waved to her little sister, who quickly arrived at the front gate, excited to hang out with her big sister for one more afternoon.

CHAPTER 18

After brushing her teeth in the capsule hotel's communal bathroom, Emma took the elevator back up to the fifth floor. The long corridor's lighting had switched to night mode, making it dark and very conducive to sleep inside the capsules. The lights to Nadia and Olivia's capsules were still on, so Emma went to her knees and knocked on both glass doors.

Nadia popped open her door, her enthusiasm for this weird hotel still stamped on the girl's face.

"Are you busy?" Emma asked.

"I'm about to start my prayers, but it's okay."

Olivia popped open her door. "What is it, love?"

"What time do we need to be up tomorrow?" Emma asked.

"I'm not sure. Until we hear from Miyuki about how things are going with her father…"

"We could go sightseeing," Nadia said. "There are a few interesting places close to our hotel."

"That sounds fun," Emma said. "Better than sitting inside our coffins all morning."

Nadia's enthusiasm dipped.

"I'm kidding," Emma said. "Actually, its been an…interesting experience."

"These capsules grow on you after a bit," Olivia added.

Nadia's happiness returned. "I'll start researching a few places for the morning, then."

"How about we get ready around nine?" Olivia said. "That way, if we don't hear from Miyuki by then, we'll do the tourist thing. Sound good?"

"Nine it is," Emma said.

"Good night, then." Nadia closed her capsule and pulled the curtain across the glass.

"So you're into this capsule thing after all?"

Olivia lowered her voice to a whisper. "Don't want to hurt Nadia's feelings, but I'm still not a fan. Don't say anything to her."

"I won't. See you in the morning."

Olivia shut her capsule door and turned off her light.

Emma sighed as she crouched down and went feet-first through the oblong capsule door and shut it tight, putting the curtain back in place. She glanced at the video screen, debating if she wanted to watch something or not. She also considered reading her book. However, as Emma sat back and rested on the cushy pillow, she could feel her body wanting to soak right through the mattress. It was acting tired. Maybe it was finally adjusting to Japanese time.

Emma didn't fight the urge. She switched off the light, turned to her side, and her body did the rest.

A few hours later, the call of nature poked Emma awake. She flipped on the light and slid the curtain to the side as she climbed out of her capsule. As she put on the hotel slippers, Emma remembered that she had to go downstairs to use the communal bathroom. Moaning to herself, Emma made her way down the dark hallway of capsules towards the elevator. She pushed the down button and wiped her face before leaning on the cool wall. It was then she noted that her capsule was the only one with a light still on.

That bothered the city girl inside her, who always was security conscious. Emma was good at not leaving things inside her car like phones or purses…anything that would invite a thief to break the glass and steal her stuff. So she jogged back over to the capsule and climbed inside to switch off the light. She even slid the curtain back into place to make it look like she was still inside before climbing out and closing the capsule up. Now she felt better.

Emma summoned the elevator again and took it downstairs. After relieving her call of nature, Emma felt so much better. After washing her hands, she walked out of the women's restroom and passed through the communal lounge. Emma hadn't noticed him on the way in, but coming out she noticed a guy working on his laptop. He was in his early twenties with dark hair, hazel eyes, round and strong cheekbones. He was well-groomed and wore these adorable thick black glasses with a handsome-nerdy vibe.

Emma paused at the elevator. She was sleepy.

But not that sleepy.

Emma wandered into the lounge. She noted a newspaper lying on one table. Emma snatched it and found a seat. The paper was in Japanese. But Emma just looked at the pictures.

She bent the paper down and peeked at the guy.

He noticed and smiled.

Emma's body warmed. His smile was friendly.

She gave him a longer glance and smiled back. Emma's attention went back to the Japanese newspaper. She took her time glancing through it as her brain tossed around the possibilities. What was she hoping for? That this mysterious and handsome man would make a move on her? That he would ask her out on a date? Why would a guy like him ask a teenage girl out on a date? Unless he was a pervert.

However, he might ask out a sophisticated young heiress who's traveling the world with her friends.

Emma stood up straighter. She could tell him that. It wasn't lying. She would be inheriting a large amount of money when she turned twenty-one, thanks to her father's estate. But did she want someone to fall in love with her because she was rich? That implied she was only worth the amount in her bank account. That also implied the person inside her had no worth. She didn't want to be a girl like that.

Okay, Emma wouldn't mention the fact she was an heiress. Maybe a college student visiting Japan with her friends?

Yeah, that was better. He would see her as a normal girl and judge her by what was inside. Not her money.

Emma put down her paper. It was time to act. If she wanted to get to know him, she should go talk to him. Take the initiative. Learn more about him, then see how things go.

But Emma didn't move. Why did she feel so nervous?

Emma needed to summon her acting skills. That would get her over the hill. *Pretend like you're a confident young woman who knows what she wants.* Okay. Emma closed her eyes, breathed deeply, and prepared herself.

When she opened her eyes, a young woman entered the lounge. The man with glasses flashed her a smile. She cuddled up next to him and slid her arm down his back as she asked him a question in French.

Emma's heart sank. The young man wasn't a lonely executive

on a business trip. He was here with his girlfriend on vacation.

Well, that was that. Emma headed upstairs on the elevator.

The doors opened to the fifth floor. She moved into the dark hallway of capsules. When she reached hers, Emma noticed three plastic tubes on the floor. The tubes came down from the ceiling. They ran across the floor and were inserted into three of the bottom sleeping capsules. She wondered why they were there.

There was one tube inserted into her own capsule. The door was shut, but the flexible plastic tube still managed to fit in the gap between the door and the capsule itself. Emma opened the door and heard a hiss coming from the tube, but she didn't smell anything weird inside. Was that oxygen being pumped into the cap—?

Emma braced herself against the door. She felt weak. Like she wanted to faint. Her eyes became heavy.

She slammed the door shut. Surely it was carbon monoxide. The gas didn't have any odor and was invisible to the naked eye.

Emma came to the awful realization. Someone was pumping a deadly gas into their capsules.

Someone was trying to kill them.

CHAPTER 19

Emma began to panic. The bottom two sleeping capsules were filling with carbon monoxide and her friends were breathing it in, slowly dying in their sleep.

Emma forced herself to calm down. She needed to think. She had to pull her friends out, that was obvious, but the gas was strong enough to knock her out if she opened any of the doors. So Emma needed a mask or something to protect her from breathing in too much carbon monoxide.

She looked around. All Emma had was a hotel bathrobe and fluffy slippers. But she did have a cloth belt that tied her robe together. She yanked the belt off and kicked off her slippers. She took one of her slippers and used it to cover her mouth. Then she used the belt to secure the slipper in place, creating a makeshift mask.

Emma rushed over to Nadia's capsule and pulled the latch release. The door swung out.

Nadia's body lay there like a corpse. Emma hoped she wasn't too late. She held her breath and dived inside the capsule. She grabbed Nadia's legs and pulled her out of the capsule. Emma then took her shoulders and gently dragged her away from their group of capsules. Emma wished she had time to check on her, but there was one more Gem she had to save.

Emma rushed over to Olivia's capsule and tried the latch release.

It was jammed.

She noted the tube inserted into Olivia's capsule was interfering with the latch release. Emma tried again, but the damn thing wouldn't release. Next she put on the other slipper and tried to kick the latch release using the heel of her foot, but after several attempts it was obviously useless. She needed something bigger to smack it with.

Emma saw a mounted fire extinguisher near the elevator and grabbed it off the wall. She lifted the extinguisher over her head and slammed the end down on the latch, using all the strength she had.

The impact bent it, but the latch didn't break. Worse yet, it might have jammed it shut.

Furious at the inanimate object, Emma grunted as she lifted the fire extinguisher and slammed it down on the latch again.

This time the latch snapped off and fell to the ground.

Emma flung open the door and grabbed Olivia's feet. She pulled her out of the capsule and gently dragged her over to Nadia, who was still not awake.

Emma noticed the other capsules around her. There were more people here in danger than just her friends.

She ran back over to their capsules. Somehow Emma needed to stop the flow of gas from coming out of the tubes. She picked up the tube from Olivia's capsule and noticed how thin and flexible the plastic was, almost like a shoelace. Emma took the tube and managed to tie the end into a tight knot, stopping the flow of gas. She did the same for the other tubes.

That was when Emma noticed a symbol newly stamped on the wall opposite their capsules. But a cough turned her attention back to her friends. Emma ran over to them and slipped off her makeshift mask.

Nadia coughed again. That was a good sign. But Olivia still hadn't moved.

Emma shook her. "Wake up, Olivia! Can you hear me? Wake up."

She didn't respond.

Emma searched for any sign of breathing and found none. Olivia's chest was still.

Oh God. Her friend was dying.

Emma looked to Nadia for help. But she was half awake herself, still coughing from the gas. Her friend was in no condition to help.

Emma was on her own.

She closed her eyes, telling herself she needed to stay calm. She needed to start CPR on Olivia.

Emma focused and went through the CPR checklist in her mind. She checked Olivia's mouth for anything restricting her airway. Next she took in as much air as she could before placing her mouth over Olivia's and blowing air into her lungs like a balloon. Next Emma placed her hands over Olivia's chest and began chest compressions. She repeated the procedure over and over again.

It seemed to last hours.

Nadia watched. Her eyes were heavy, as if she were still in a daze. But at least she was still alive.

Emma kept going and going. It didn't seem to make a difference.

Emma tasted the salt from her tears as they rolled down her face. But she kept going.

Was she already too late?

Would the Gems be only three girls instead of four? How could they go on without Olivia? She was so strong. So smart. So talented. She was a leader.

Maybe Olivia was bossy and said things that Emma didn't like. But the girl was never fake to her. She was always honest. Someone you could trust.

The tears burned Emma's eyes. She had to take a moment to wipe them off.

Emma would give anything now to hear Olivia give her one last smart-ass comment.

She leaned over and blew more air into Olivia's body. That was when the girl coughed in her face, drawing Emma away from her mouth. Olivia's eyes opened as she coughed. It was like she was a robot and someone had switched her back on.

"Flipping hell—" Olivia's voice was weak, but still trying to burst out of its shell.

Emma heard herself yelp with glee.

Olivia squinted at Emma. "What's going on?"

Nadia sat up, her face returning to normal. "I think Emma just saved our lives."

Olivia moaned and shook her head to wake up. "Saved us from what?"

"Someone was pumping carbon monoxide into our capsules," Emma said.

"You're joking," Nadia said.

Emma pointed at the three plastic tubes tied up on the floor. Nadia's eyes widened. "Who would want to murder us?"

"Whoever left that." Emma pointed.

Opposite their capsules was a large red image stamped on the wall. It was a sword with the rising sun emblazoned over its handle as the rays shot out from its center.

CHAPTER 20

In the morning, Miyuki woke up to Kameko jumping on top of her bed and rolling on top of her like a log. Miyuki countered by smacking her little sister with her pillow. Kameko laughed and rolled on top of her again. Miyuki then put Kameko over her shoulder and carried her around the room like a pet. Of course, her little sister thought this was hilarious.

"Put me down!" Kameko laughed, not being serious.

"You're a menace to my sleep. Go back to your room!" Miyuki said.

"Mom sent me. Breakfast is ready. You slept too late."

Miyuki checked her clock. Her sister was right, but Miyuki couldn't help herself. She didn't sleep well last night. Mostly because she couldn't stop thinking about her father.

"Tell her I'll be down in a moment."

"Your friends are here too. The blond one keeps messing with her hair."

Miyuki wondered why they were already here. Did something happen? Miyuki quickly threw on some jeans, her Nirvana T-shirt, combed out her hair, and wrapped it in a ponytail before leaving her room.

Sitting on their knees around the wooden table were Mr. E and the other three Gems. When he saw Miyuki, Mr. E bowed his head.

Her mom leaned in. "The handsome man in the suit, is he your boss?" she whispered in Japanese.

"In a way, he's one of them," Miyuki said. "I can't really say."

"Too bad he's not ten years younger. You two would look good together."

"Mom…"

"I'll see if he has a younger brother."

"Please do not embarrass me."

"I won't, but I still will keep my eye out for good prospects."

Kameko and her mom placed the breakfast dishes on the table. Miyuki's father and Haru were absent. Most likely they'd already left for work.

"I scrambled eggs. That is the correct term?" Miyuki's mother asked her daughter in Japanese.

Sure enough, there was a plate of yellow scrambled eggs steaming in the center of the table. And Miyuki noticed freshly baked croissant rolls as well.

"*Hei*," Miyuki said to her mom. "The rolls look delicious."

Her mother smiled with pride. "Pillsbury Doughboy. Pop open the can and bake it in the oven. Very easy. I bought eggs and rolls in case your friends came back. Wanted to cook them an American breakfast."

"You did well," Miyuki said.

"Thank you," her mother said.

Kameko served tea to everyone while Miyuki's mom dished out the eggs, rice, and rolls as everyone ate. Miyuki noticed her friends were unusually quiet this morning.

"Does your family speak any English?" Mr. E asked.

"They do not," Miyuki replied.

"We've had a few developments overnight," Mr. E turned to Olivia. "Do you want to tell her?"

Olivia told Miyuki about the tubes inserted into each of their sleeping capsules. About someone pumping carbon monoxide into them in an effort to kill them in their sleep. About how Emma was out of her capsule when the attack occurred and managed to save her and Nadia from carbon monoxide poisoning. And how they followed the tubes up to the roof, where they found a portable petrol generator left running with no one in sight.

"Oh my. That's horrible," Miyuki said.

"And I saved Olivia's life," Emma said with pride. "She was almost dead, like, not breathing. So I did CPR, like they taught me in spy training, and she started breathing again."

"Wow, that's amazing."

"It was amazing." Emma tossed Olivia a smug look. "Don't you owe me something?"

Olivia balked. "What do I owe you?"

"Nadia has already said it."

"Said what?"

"Olivia, you would have died if she hadn't done CPR on you," Nadia said.

"So what do you say when someone saves your life?" Emma asked with a grin, savoring the answer to come.

Olivia sighed. "Thank you."

"You're welcome," Emma said.

"Who could have done such a thing?" Miyuki asked.

Mr. E brought out his phone and showed Miyuki the symbol. "It's from a group called the Emperor's Sword, a radical right-wing group who sees their duty as protecting Japan from all foreign influences. The group has plagued the government for over sixty years."

"Why would they target us?" Olivia asked.

"Good question. I doubt this group even knows our organization exists. I would assume that it was because you three were traveling together. It could have been a random act of terrorism. This group has attacked tourist groups in the past."

"Still, it doesn't make me feel very secure," Olivia said.

"I urge you girls to stay in a safe house for the rest of your visit while Tokyo station follows up on the investigation," Mr. E said. "However, this is not why we're here this morning. The Japanese foreign minister has announced an unscheduled meeting today with Mr. Nagumo and the Shiawase Nomimono management. I was able to secure an invitation from the government for us to attend."

"Did your father say something?" Nadia asked.

"He told me yesterday that he spoke to his friend Ozawa."

"Well done, Miyuki," Mr. E said. "Did your father say anything else?"

Miyuki ditched her Nirvana T-shirt and changed into a more sophisticated set of clothes. As she left the house with her friends, a black Nissan van rolled up and parked. Without hesitation, Olivia opened the side door, allowing Mr. E and the Gems to jump inside.

As the van took them across Osaka, Miyuki filled everyone in on what her father had confessed. "He was more involved in the Thunderdog program than I originally thought." She continued, telling everyone about her father managing the Thunderdog team. Her father's trust in Tyler Cho, the creator of Thunderdog. The poor choices he and the top executives made in an effort to protect the company's reputation. Then Miyuki told Mr. E how her father finally broke down and approached his friend in the foreign minister's office.

"I see," Mr. E said. "The pieces all fit into place now."

"What will they do to your dad?" Emma asked. "Will he be arrested?"

"Why would he be arrested?" Miyuki asked. "He did nothing wrong."

"He knew the drink was dangerous and did nothing about it," Olivia said.

"The company wasn't sure. This Tyler Cho assured them that the drink had already been tested."

"So this Tyler guy lied to the company?"

"I don't know. My father was under a lot of pressure and he was receiving conflicting information about the drink. You don't understand. Japanese companies do not make decisions by the seat of their pants."

"I can't believe he kept the truth from us in our meeting," Olivia said.

"That was his mistake and he admits it."

"On top of all his other mistakes."

"Damn you, Olivia. My father's a human being. He's not perfect like you."

Nadia and Emma froze.

Olivia squinted. "When did I say I was flipping perfect?"

Mr. E glanced towards the ceiling of the van. "Do they always fight like this?"

A familiar voice echoed from inside the van's speakers. "I'm quite appalled at their lack of respect. My sincere apologies, Mr. E. I thought I trained my young women to exercise better manners." It was Mrs. B. She had been listening the entire time.

All four Gems sat up.

Miyuki felt her cheeks heat up. She bowed to Mr. E. "I'm sorry for embarrassing you. My emotional connection to this situation does not excuse my behavior."

"It's my fault, Mr. E," Olivia said. "I should have restrained myself."

"While you're Mr. E's guests, I expect all four of you to give him your full cooperation and respect. I expect nothing less. Do I make myself clear, ladies?"

After about an hour of driving through Osaka, the black Nissan van reached the offices of Shiawase Nomimono. Miyuki led Mr. E and the Gems back up to the fourth floor, where they found Miyuki's father standing outside his office, next to the large portrait of the old Japanese woman who owned the company.

"What are you doing here?" Miyuki's father asked. "This is not a good time for a visit."

"We know about the foreign minister coming for a visit," Miyuki said.

"How did you know about that?"

Miyuki didn't answer.

"Oh." Her father glanced at the Gems and the man in a black suit. "Through your secretive friends of course."

"Mr. Kaiko?" his secretary asked. "The front desk says there's a group of cars pulling up to the front of our building with government plates."

"Tell her it's the foreign minister."

"Why is the foreign minister here?" The room turned to see Mr. Nagumo standing in the outer office with five junior executives behind him. "Do you know why, Ichirou?"

Miyuki's father wanted to answer. But held his tongue.

Mr. Nagumo referenced the Gems. "Why are they here? And who is this man?"

"Mr. Isuku is a sales representative," Miyuki's father lied. "His company would like to bid on our new plant project in Kyoto. I planned to take him and my daughter's friends on a tour of our bottling facility down—"

"Well, your tour guide duties are canceled. Come with me."

Mr. Nagumo marched out of the office with Mr. Kaiko and his executives in tow. Other managers were gathering in the halls, wondering what was going on.

The foreign minister arrived with his entourage. They moved from the elevators as Mr. Nagumo and her father met them.

"A pleasant surprise. I was just informed of your arrival." Mr. Nagumo glanced around his office. "Everyone line up."

The officers of the company lined up as the foreign minister received each man and his business card. The process was formal and took a lot of time. One man with a shaved head assisted the minister.

"What are they doing?" Emma asked.

"Exchanging business cards. Very important in Japan. When someone gives you his card, it's an extension of that person and should be treated with respect."

After the minister exchanged cards with Miyuki's father, she noticed the man with a shaved head hesitating. Her father and this man shared a long, knowing glance. Miyuki studied the man with the shaved head. His eyes looked familiar and convinced Miyuki that this man was Ozawa, her father's longtime friend. When Miyuki last saw him, the man had a full head of hair.

Finally the process was done. The men all headed into a large boardroom. Mr. E motioned for the Gems to follow him inside.

However, one of Mr. Nagumo's young executives blocked his way. "My apologies. This is a private company meeting. Would you consider waiting in the lobby? I'll have Mr. Kaiko come downstairs after the meeting has concluded."

Mr. E nodded. "Of course. I understand." His eyes rested on Miyuki before they gestured towards the boardroom. He wanted her to get inside. Mr. E then headed for the elevators.

The young executive waited.

Nadia retreated a few steps before Olivia stopped her.

"My father said my friends and I could come to the meeting," Miyuki said.

"Your father mentioned he was taking you on a tour of our bottling facility. He said nothing about you attending this meeting." The executive began closing the boardroom's double doors. "Please proceed to the lobby. After the meeting is concluded, I'll tell Mr. Kaiko where you are."

Miyuki noticed the young man's powder pink tie. An impulse hit her and she went with it. She grabbed the man's tie and pulled him away from the doors. The man's face went into total shock.

"My father is a vice-president of this company and Mr. Nagumo holds him in the highest regard. I strongly suggest you find us seats inside that boardroom. Why? Because my brother…Mr. Kaiko's son…is finishing his management training program soon and will be looking for a new position inside the company. Do you want him to have yours?"

Miyuki let go of his tie, and the young executive swallowed.

The other three Gems exchanged glances; they were dying to know what Miyuki had just told him.

Now Miyuki felt invincible. She stepped around the executive and opened the double doors herself. The young executive regained his composure and stepped into the boardroom with Miyuki and the Gems. The executive escorted them to a faraway corner with four chairs before returning to Mr. Nagumo's side.

The room waited until the foreign minister sat down before everyone else did.

The boardroom became quiet.

"First, I want to thank Shiawase Nomimono International for welcoming my delegation to their offices," the foreign minister said.

"What's he saying?" Emma asked in a loud whisper.

A few heads turned.

Nadia placed her finger against her lips.

"I just want to know what's going on," Emma whispered in a lighter tone.

Miyuki moved closer to Emma, almost touching cheek to cheek. "I'll translate, but we must stay quiet."

The minister continued to speak to the room in Japanese. As Miyuki began translating his words at a whisper, Nadia snuggled in close so she could hear too.

"He says, 'We are concerned about the global reports about Thunderdog. Since our trade relations with the affected countries are critical to our nation's economy, I am here on behalf of the government to discuss the matter with you. With all due respect to the company, the government was wondering if Shiawase Nomimono would be open to the idea of reconsidering the distribution of their energy drink.'"

Mr. Nagumo rose from his seat and bowed before he spoke.

Miyuki paused a moment before translating. "Of course, we will reconsider this matter with priority."

Mr. Nagumo and the minister exchanged some pleasantries before the minister got up to leave. Everyone stood up and bowed as the foreign minister left the boardroom.

"Was that it?" Olivia asked.

"All he did was ask them to reconsider the drink," Emma said. "And even that sounded like only a suggestion."

"The minister made his point quite clear," Miyuki said.

"I think we're missing something," Nadia said.

"In Japan, a mere suggestion from the foreign affairs minister is interpreted by any company as an order," Miyuki said. "Their company is endangering the government's reputation with its trading partners. Therefore, the company should save face and pull the product themselves. Because a government order to do so would be seen as an embarrassment."

"The foreign minister didn't mention your father at all, right?" Emma said.

That was the one huge relief Miyuki had. Apparently Ozawa hadn't mentioned the source of the information he got about Thunderdog. Perhaps her father wouldn't be penalized for blowing the whistle on the company after all.

It took a couple of minutes for the foreign minister's entourage to crowd into the elevators and make their way down to the lobby. Once they did, Mr. Nagumo released his fury…

"I want to know who told them. Someone told the minister about Thunderdog. Who was it?" Mr. Nagumo walked in a complete circle. Eying each executive with disgust. "I will have their head on a spike."

Miyuki's father stood there stone-faced.

"If any of you have a shred of honor left within you, then you'll reveal yourself to me by the end of the day." Mr. Nagumo allowed that idea to float in the air a moment before facing Miyuki's father. "You will do as the minister requests. Withdraw Thunderdog from all our test markets."

A younger man in a suit ran up to Mr. Kaiko. "You can't do that!" he shouted in Japanese. But the man wasn't Japanese. Miyuki noted that his features suggested more of a Vietnamese or Southeastern Asian background; plus he was still struggling with his Japanese. "I won't sit here and let you destroy one of the most ingenious drinks of the twenty-first century. The government can go to hell."

"Control yourself, Mr. Cho," Miyuki's father said.

"I thought you were different, Mr. Kaiko, I thought you wanted to produce bold new products like Thunderdog. I thought you supported me. Yet when there's a bump in the road, you're ready to pull over and abandon your car. You're just like the rest of them." The young man referenced the older Japanese executives, "Scared old men clinging to the past."

"What's he saying?" Emma asked.

Mr. Nagumo suddenly grabbed Tyler Cho by the neck and forced him over to a wall. "You arrogant piece of Vietnamese trash. You do not make demands here. We tell you what to do. Your drink will be withdrawn and you'll go back to creating a drink we can sell."

Tyler Cho glared into the old man's eyes. "I made a mistake in trusting all of you. Well, that stops now. I quit!"

Miyuki's father went up to them. "Let's go into my office and discuss this. Please, we can manage this," he pleaded in a calm logical manner to both men.

"Go to hell," the young man said as he pushed Mr. Nagumo back and marched out of the boardroom. The other executives noticed and looked over at Miyuki's father for an explanation. Her father could only lower his head in shame.

Emma squeezed Miyuki's arm so tight it hurt. "What are they saying!?"

As everyone left the boardroom and emptied into the main office floor, Mr. Nagumo disappeared into his own office.

He came out with his samurai sword.

Tyler Cho ran to the elevators. His fingers frantically attacked the down button.

Miyuki's father swallowed and intercepted Mr. Nagumo. "You must control yourself."

"Stand aside, Ichirou." Mr. Nagumo's eyes fumed.

"You're embarrassing yourself, sir."

"Move aside," Mr. Nagumo repeated, quieter this time.

"With all due respect, Mr. Nagumo, go to your office and calm yourself." Miyuki's father didn't move. His face was like stone.

The coldness from her father's look affected Mr. Nagumo. The old man blinked and headed for his office, closing the door.

The elevator dinged and the doors opened. Tyler Cho jumped inside before the doors could close.

Emma was shaking Miyuki to death. "Oh my God! Please stop torturing me and tell me what's going on!?"

CHAPTER 21

The morning sunlight came in through the window, touching her sheets and reminding Miyuki that her restless night of sleep was over. All she could think about was how furious Mr. Nagumo had been yesterday. It sounded like he wouldn't rest until he found out who tipped off the government about Thunderdog. That meant he would eventually find out what her father did, and force him to resign. Her father had worked at Shiawase Nomimono for most of his life. It was all he knew. Being humiliated in front of his colleagues and workers would most likely break him, and Miyuki knew it.

After packing her bag, Miyuki took a shower, and dressed comfortably for the long flight home. As she put on a fresh new face for the day, Miyuki saw herself in the mirror and decided to purge those negative thoughts from her mind. Yes, Mr. Nagumo might become upset at her father, but surely the company wouldn't make him quit. She'd seen how her father had stepped in to calm the argument between Nagumo and Tyler Cho. Maintaining a team environment where everyone worked together was a valuable skill in Japan. If her father could convince Tyler Cho to stay and create a new drink that would make the company plenty of money... wouldn't the disaster of Thunderdog be forgotten? That thought put Miyuki in a better mood.

Her family gathered outside near the front garden to see her off. Kameko showed tears, but Miyuki encouraged her little sister to text her as often as she wanted since father had already promised her a phone for her birthday, and she agreed.

Her brother, Haru, released a smile and a hug. "Sorry for not spending more time with you. Being in the training program occupies all of my time."

"I understand." Miyuki knew it was more likely an excuse, but

Miyuki hoped her brother still had some love for his crazy sister hidden deep down in his heart like she did for him.

Her mother gave Miyuki a hug and a kiss that lasted for much longer than the first day she arrived. It lifted Miyuki's spirits more.

Miyuki then came to her father.

He didn't move.

She bowed slightly. And he returned the gesture.

"Take care of yourself," she said.

Her father nodded, but that was it.

Miyuki understood. Perhaps someday he would feel comfortable enough to hug his daughter.

* * *

Air Global flight 308 landed five minutes early at San Francisco International. During her ten-hour flight, Miyuki had found a movie on the aircraft's entertainment system that she fell in love with. *The Muppet Movie* had been made in 1979 and featured a bunch of Muppets such as Kermit and Miss Piggy, but the rest of the Muppets were new to Miyuki. But something about this movie lifted her out of the disturbance in her life force that had plagued her for days.

After finishing the movie by herself, Miyuki badgered Emma into watching it with her a second time. Emma had never heard of the movie either…but after another viewing, Emma loved it too.

"It's so simple…and funny…and heartwarming," Emma said. "Sometimes you just need a movie that makes you happy."

Miyuki agreed completely.

After managing to watch it a third time before landing, Miyuki and Emma were singing Kermit the Frog's solo rendition of *The Rainbow Connection* as they followed everyone off the jet bridge.

"You two are mental," Olivia said, wanting to roll her eyes but resisting the urge.

"What are you singing?" Nadia asked, more curious than annoyed.

As they waited for their luggage, Emma had downloaded *The Muppet Movie*'s soundtrack to her phone and had Nadia singing *The Rainbow Connection* to herself five minutes later.

"I don't want to listen to any stupid Muppets," Olivia said. "And if you play that on the way home, Emma, I'll choke you from behind and risk you driving us off the Bay bridge."

An announcement echoed through the busy terminal…

Paging Miss Ana Yamaguchi. Ana Yamaguchi. Please see the Air Global agent at the information desk. Miss Ana Yamaguchi, please see the Air Global agent at the information desk.

Olivia whipped her eyes to Miyuki who already knew why. Ana Yamaguchi was one of Miyuki's aliases during missions. Only someone from the Authority would know that.

"Isn't that your—?"

Olivia interrupted Nadia. "Let's all go to the information desk and see."

The four Gems rolled their luggage across the tiled floor of the check-in area and parked them near the Air Global information desk.

"May I see your passports, please?" Mrs. B was dressed in an Air Global uniform.

Olivia tried to hide her smile as she gave her their passports.

Mrs. B pretended to check them. "Our deepest apologies, but there's been a change to your travel itinerary. You'll be flying out later tonight on the last flight to Honolulu. Air Global apologizes for any inconvenience." Mrs. B gave them one of the passports back.

Olivia checked it. "What's in Honolulu?"

Mrs. B's eyes quickly scanned the area. Her voice lowered. "Tokyo station reports that Tyler Cho stole all the formulas and materials related to Thunderdog from the Shiawase Nomimono company servers. Including all the backup files."

"How do they know it was him?" Miyuki asked.

"Because Mr. Cho was kind enough to send all the company's executives an angry email. He plans to sell the drink to a rival beverage company."

Now Miyuki knew her father would be asked to resign. Her happiness evaporated.

"Today, Tyler Cho left Japan. We believe he flew to Hong Kong. However, we're still trying to find him and track his movements," Mrs. B said. "We've decided that all material related to Thunderdog must be recovered and destroyed. The beverage is far too dangerous to let anyone get a hold of it."

"Then why don't you send us to Hong Kong?" Miyuki asked.

"Tyler's family lives in Hawaii, and there's a chance he's been in contact with them. His family could also help to confirm what his real plans are for the stolen material. That's where you come in. Tomorrow, I want you to pose as representatives from Shiawase Nomimono. You'll be in Hawaii under the pretense of finalizing their son's employment contract and other company benefits. Your flight leaves in two hours."

CHAPTER 22

Miyuki watched all the people on the beach enjoying the Hawaiian sun. A large wave rose from the Pacific as a surfer captured it with a long ride. Watching him made Miyuki realize that she had done zero surfing since she'd moved to California, and that made her sad.

The traffic light changed. Their driver made a left, and their Ford passenger van moved away from the public beach.

"Doesn't Hawaii remind you of Tahiti?"

Miyuki followed the voice to Nadia, who sat right beside her in the middle seat.

"Yes, that was so fun." Miyuki remembered Tahiti's crystal blue ocean. The beautiful and friendly locals. And the end of a stressful mission. "Have you heard from Robert lately?"

Nadia paused and adjusted the glasses she was wearing. "No… it's been a while."

Reading her body language, Miyuki knew she shouldn't have asked her that. She had made her friend uncomfortable. Today Nadia wore a nice beige pantsuit with flats, her long black hair put into a lovely bun. But Nadia kept touching her new eyeglasses. Clearly she wasn't used to wearing such things. Overall, Nadia looked the part of her new alias, Jayanti Patel, a mature young Indian businesswoman who was Miyuki's assistant.

Miyuki didn't like her business clothes. Hilo station had done a good job researching Japanese business culture, and Miyuki's dark suit with tasteful skirt and low heels would do the job. However, it reminded Miyuki too much of the life she almost fell into back in Japan. The role her father was hoping that she would play. A part of the company. A part of the group. An honorable member of Japanese society. Miyuki wondered if her father still hoped she could change.

"Maybe I could be vice president of Hawaiian operations," Emma said.

Olivia and Emma sat in the third row of seats behind Miyuki and Nadia.

"You and I stay in the van, love. Sapphire and Ruby get to have all the fun," Olivia said. "Mrs. B was quite specific."

"But I have the most acting experience in the group." Emma scanned the other girls. "No offense."

"You're not even Hawaiian," Olivia said. "And you don't have a tan."

"When would a businesswoman have time to tan?"

Olivia laughed. "It's sunny and seventy-five degrees in Hawaii for three hundred and sixty-five days a year. A businesswoman would get a tan just by eating her lunch outside every day. Besides, you're as white as chalk, love."

Emma glared. "After school I have to do spy training, chorus practice, and student government meetings. On the weekends we do missions all around the freaking world—when do I have time to squeeze in a tanning session?"

The Ford passenger van parked near a shopping area.

"Remember, we'll be in the van listening to everything," Olivia said. "Good luck."

"Don't say that!" Emma said. "It's bad luck in the theater. You always say break a leg."

Miyuki and Nadia slipped out of the van before the two girls began arguing again. They moved towards a parked rental car provided by Hilo station to help sell their cover. Nadia got behind the wheel and waited for a panel truck with a local carpet business painted on its sides to show up in the parking lot. With the surveillance vehicle ready, Nadia then drove the rental out of the parking lot while the panel truck loosely tailed them.

Since Tyler Cho's family spent most of their time working at their business, Nadia drove to that address located in a touristy area of Honolulu. Nadia circled the area before finding a parking spot and shutting off the engine.

Miyuki noticed she was touching her glasses again. "Sapphire, may I make a suggestion?"

The girl turned her head.

"Perhaps you should keep your hands under the table."

Nadia stared at her hands like they'd grown a dozen warts. "Why? Do my nails look horrible?"

"Your nails look wonderful. However, I've noticed that since you put on your fake glasses…you keep touching them."

"Oh, am I being that obvious?"

Miyuki grinned.

"Thank you. I'll take your advice. Ready?"

Miyuki and Nadia climbed out of their rental car and blended in with the tourists. The Chos' business was in fact a restaurant. The Saigon Palace had a large window decorated with a mural of Vietnamese and Thai cultural images hand drawn using vibrant and beautiful colors. Something that would make a tourist stop to look at. Whoever the artist was, Miyuki thought they had real talent.

"Sapphire and Ruby in position," Nadia said under her breath, just enough for the hidden microphones they were wearing to pick up.

Through a small inconspicuous earphone, Miyuki heard the reply.

"Prize Patrol in position." It was Olivia's voice. "Proceed."

Miyuki took in a deep breath and squeezed her soft leather business pouch. Miyuki could feel the legal pad and pens inside. She could imagine the official (and fake) employment agreement from the company with their final severance offer for Tyler Cho. She imagined herself inside that world of working Japanese women who dedicated their lives in service to the company. This was a theater technique Emma had taught her. A way to ground herself back into character quickly.

When Miyuki was ready, she stepped inside the restaurant. The inside was smaller than a normal restaurant, but it was decorated as creatively as the window was. More colorful murals portrayed Thai and Vietnamese culture in a warm and thoughtful way.

"Two for lunch?" a Vietnamese girl asked. She was about the same age as them.

Miyuki went to work. "Would it be possible if we could have a moment with Mr. Cho?"

"What do you want with my father?" the girl asked, her pleasant tone fading.

"My apologies, but it's a private business matter."

"Does he owe you money?"

Nadia touched her glasses again. "It's about his son, Tyler."

The girl scrutinized both visitors. "Get out of here."

"Tyler doesn't—owe us money—as you put it," Miyuki said. "On the contrary, we owe him money."

"Who's we?"

Miyuki ignored her. "May we look around for your father?" She then noted a much older man bringing out a bowl of fresh spring rolls to a buffet. Miyuki glanced at Nadia. "We'll ask that nice-looking man over there."

The girl blocked them. "Leave my father alone or I'll call the police."

"Don't press too hard." Olivia was now talking in Miyuki's ear. "We don't want the police getting involved."

"Perhaps we should show her the agreement, Miss Yamaguchi," Nadia said.

Miyuki nodded and broke out her soft leather pouch and removed the employment contract along with the severance offer. Miyuki handed it to the girl. She took it and began reading. The girl examined the two visitors for a second time.

"We come bearing gifts," Miyuki added with a friendly smile.

The girl handed the material back to Miyuki. "Wait here."

The old man with the now empty bowl headed into the kitchen. The girl followed him inside. Soon, both of them emerged from the kitchen and came up front.

Miyuki handed him the company materials with a slight bow. "My name is Anna Yamaguchi, and this is Jayanti Patel. We work in the human resources department of Shiawase Nomimono."

The old man looked up from the employment contract. "You have come all the way from Japan?"

Miyuki nodded.

"You must be hungry. Please, have a seat."

"Dad, don't comp them a meal," the girl said. "How do we make money if you give away all our food?"

"Show them to a table." The old man wagged his finger at his daughter before handing Miyuki the contract back..

The girl scooped up two rolled napkins of silverware from a bin. She sighed. "Follow me." The girl led Miyuki and Nadia to an empty table near the buffet, where she tossed both sets of silverware on the table like rocks and left the girls alone. The aroma coming from the buffet was tantalizing, causing Miyuki's stomach to wake up with hunger.

The old man filled the yellow curry sauce bin with fresh ingredients before cleaning his hands and sitting down.

Miyuki brought out the contract and severance materials again.

But the old man's attention wasn't focused on that. "Where are your drinks?" The old man glared at his daughter. "Bring them drinks. What is wrong with you?"

The daughter stopped wiping down an empty table and threw the dish towel down. She grabbed a water pitcher with one hand and an ice tea pitcher with the other before coming over to the table. "Tea or water?"

"Do you have hot tea?" Miyuki asked.

"Hot tea would be lovely," Nadia added.

"We have a nice tea blend from Da Nang. My wife and I drink it often." The old man glared at his daughter before spouting a few tense orders in Vietnamese.

The daughter's attitude shifted. She nodded and headed into the kitchen.

Miyuki pushed the contract towards the father. "We are disappointed that your son decided to leave our company. As per his employment contract, this is a severance of almost eleven million yen that's owed to him."

"Around one hundred thousand American dollars," Nadia said. "The difficulty for us is that we don't know where he is."

"When he left Japan, your son didn't supply us with a forwarding address. So you see, we can't pay him his severance if we don't know where he is. Do you have any information that would be useful to us?"

"I understand," the old man said. "Tyler has informed us about the baseless accusations against him made by your company and why he was forced to quit."

"We're not here to judge your son," Miyuki said. "Our only task is to give him the money that's owed to him."

The daughter returned with a tea kettle, two cups, and an older woman, who sat down near the old man. He introduced the woman as his wife. The daughter poured two cups of tea for Miyuki and Nadia before sitting down at the table.

"I wish we could help you, but my wife and I do not know where Tyler is. We assumed he was still in Japan," the old man said. "If it's possible, you could give us the check, and when we hear from him, we will give it to him."

Olivia's voice came back into Miyuki's ear. "No way. We only hand over the check to Tyler in person."

"We can only hand the check over to your son in person," Miyuki repeated.

"Why?" their daughter asked. "The check is only made out to Tyler, right? So my parents and I can't cash it."

"Our company has strict procedural rules that we must follow," Nadia said.

Miyuki thought that was a good ad-lib. "My assistant is correct. I don't mind giving the check to you. I trust you. However, our company has rules."

"You're worried about him, aren't you?" the daughter said. "That's why you're trying to find him. Well, you should be. When Tyler finds a company to partner with, he's going to bury you."

"He's looking for a partner?" Miyuki asked.

"Tyler has so many brilliant ideas, some company will buy them for lots of money."

"Sounds like you've been in contact with him recently," Nadia said.

"Maybe. But I'm not telling you where."

"Why not? Does he not want eleven million yen?" Miyuki asked.

"I'm not stupid," the daughter said. "You want to find him so you can take him back to Japan and arrest him."

"Why would the Japanese wish to arrest Tyler?" the old man asked.

The daughter didn't reply.

But the old man and his wife waited.

Miyuki stared at her tea.

"Miss Yamaguchi is too polite to say it," Nadia said. "I must tell you that our company is charging Tyler with theft. Before he quit, your son took secret company formulas and other material from the company without permission."

Miyuki felt herself tense up. No one over the radio had told Nadia to do that. Revealing the truth could spook Tyler's family into not helping them at all.

"Those were his formulas. Not theirs. They have no right to them," the daughter said.

"Is that why you want to find my son?" the old man asked.

Since the secret was already out, Miyuki went along.

"Regrettably, yes, but our company only cares about retrieving the material. They do not wish to put your son in prison, Mr. Cho."

The old man sat there quietly for a moment. He then asked his daughter something in Vietnamese.

She didn't answer.

He then shouted something to her in Vietnamese. The resistance inside the girl weakened. Her gaze fell to the tabletop. She answered slowly in Vietnamese.

"My daughter says that Tyler is in Hong Kong. He's meeting with some investors who want to help him create his own beverage company."

"Thank you for your help. Can you tell us which hotel he's staying at?"

CHAPTER 23

Emma had never been to Hong Kong before. When her father was alive, he'd taken her to Singapore a few times when he had business there, but Singapore had an orderly way about it. Things were all in their proper place and tidy. So far, glancing outside their taxi, Hong Kong was not orderly.

The streets were swelling with people. Through her open rear-seat window, Emma could smell incense and fish drifting in from the outdoor markets and restaurants they were passing. The entire city was vibrant and bustling with noisy activity. She could also smell exhaust fumes. The traffic in Hong Kong was quite heavy.

Emma loved it. To her, Hong Kong was more like the New York City of the East. To her, it felt more like home.

"How did you know?" Miyuki asked.

The question drew Emma's attention away from the window. But Miyuki was addressing Nadia. All three of them shared the back seat of the taxi while Olivia sat in front.

"I felt it," Nadia answered. "The way the father talked to his daughter. The way he made her show respect to us. I felt that if we told him what his son did, he would feel ashamed and he could help us flip the daughter."

"I should have thought of that. It was a great idea," Miyuki said.

Emma remembered listening in on their conversation inside the cramped panel truck. She thought Miyuki and Nadia had done a great job at that restaurant. Emma was convinced it was her theater tips that made the difference.

Emma and the Gems soon arrived at Tyler Cho's hotel. It was a simple hotel, boasting a small lobby with free coffee and a check-in desk. Emma would rate it more of a three-star than a five-star. Given the choice, she would never stay at a hotel like this.

In the lobby, the Gems made contact with an operative from the Hong Kong station who was watching Tyler Cho. She told Olivia that Tyler was eating dinner inside the restaurant. He hadn't gone outside the hotel since she started watching him.

"We'll take it from here," Olivia said.

The operative agreed and left the hotel.

"Let's keep this simple," Olivia said. "We'll wait upstairs until he opens the door to his room, then we'll confront him. Emma, you stay in the lobby and give us a heads-up when he's on his way."

An hour later, Emma slipped a bookmark into her latest read in progress as she stretched against the uncomfortable leather couch. This Tyler sure treasured his mealtime. Emma placed her novel down on the glass coffee table and did another visual scan of the hotel lobby.

A Canadian family stepped out of the elevator. The mom's Air Canada travel bag and the son's Ottawa Senators NHL hat were big giveaways. The fourteen-year-old son noticed Emma and began checking her out. Emma turned away, making it clear she wasn't interested.

"Can you call us a taxi?" the father asked one of the English-speaking desk clerks.

"How will the driver know where to go?" the wife asked.

"The location's on my phone and it's in Chinese. Don't worry," the husband said.

The wife frowned and took a seat near Emma. Her son joined her.

Emma picked up her book and only pretended to read.

Soon the father sat down with his family and his wife began asking him a gauntlet of what-if questions. It was clear to Emma that the woman was more of a travel-group kind of tourist. Winging a vacation seemed to terrify her.

"Hey," a young male voice said.

At first, Emma wasn't sure that she actually heard it.

"Hey," the voice repeated.

Emma glanced at the boy.

He smiled. "That a good book?"

"It's okay," Emma said, returning her eyes back to it. She offered nothing more.

"I can read," the boy said.

"Oh, can you?" Emma asked without looking up.

The boy gave out a nervous laugh. "That sounded dumb, eh? Yeah, of course I can read. Duh. I meant—I like reading too. Books, I mean." He paused. "Do you read any fantasy?"

"Nope."

"Science fiction?"

"Only dystopian. I don't like spaceships or aliens."

"Then we have a lot in common."

"Yes…we both read books in English." Emma knew she was being harsh, but she was here on a mission. Picking up boys wasn't on the agenda. Besides, he was a child and didn't know what a mature young woman like herself required in a long-term relationship.

"You smell nice," he said.

Emma had shot him down. But the boy found a new plan and was trying again. She gave him a point for willpower.

"Thank you," she said.

"Are you staying here?"

"Maybe."

"You a hockey fan?" the boy asked.

"Nope. Do you love plays or musicals?"

The boy paused.

"I take that as a no."

The boy frowned.

Emma closed her book and folded her hands together. She needed to let him off the hook so he would stop wasting his time. But when Emma leveled her gaze upon the boy, she noted Tyler Cho leaving the restaurant and heading towards the elevator landing.

"It was nice meeting you, Ottawa." Emma grabbed her book and hopped off the couch.

"My name's Trevor."

Emma ignored him as she left the lobby and stepped inside the occupied elevator before the metal doors shut.

Tyler Cho only gave her a passing glance before pressing his floor number. Emma felt the elevator rise. The interior of the elevator was shiny, so Emma could study Tyler's face without looking directly at him. The man had nice dark hair cut to a more modern style. He wore some nice khakis along with a light-colored blazer and a beige T-shirt underneath. Emma guessed him to be in his late twenties. Maybe even early thirties, but not by much. His focus was not on Emma, but on the floor numbers as they lit up on the panel.

Emma was too close to Tyler to warn the Gems he was on his way. She would just have to wing it.

The elevator slowed and their momentum subsided. The doors opened and Tyler Cho got off on the fourteenth floor.

Emma hesitated. She waited until the doors were about to close before she put her foot in the way and made the doors retreat. Emma stepped into the hallway and noted Tyler was still walking towards his room, so she hid around a corner to observe. Tyler stopped at one door, inserted his card key, and entered one of the hotel rooms. Emma walked by, noted the number, and slipped into the nearby fire escape.

"What are you doing here?" Olivia asked. "Why aren't you in the flipping lobby?"

Her words echoed down the fire escape where the other three Gems were waiting.

"Slight change of plans," Emma said. "Some boy was hitting on me in the lobby, so I couldn't blow my cover and call you in front of him."

"Where's Tyler?"

"He's back in his room."

"Damn it, Emma."

"I couldn't blow my cover."

"Then why didn't you send a text?" Nadia said.

Emma thought about it. "Sorry…my bad."

Olivia glared.

"Right, like you don't make mistakes?"

"We should focus on what to do now," Miyuki said.

"Yes, we need to come up with a different plan," Nadia added.

Olivia shut her eyes and let the anger pass through her before speaking. "We need to rush in there quick and knock him out. That should give Nadia some time to look over his computer for the Thunderdog material while we search his room for anything else we need to destroy."

"How do we, 'rush in'?" Miyuki asked. "The door is too thick for us to kick in."

"We wait until he comes out again," Nadia said. "Then force him into his room."

"Awesome, more sitting around watching things," Emma said with sarcasm. "So exciting."

"Go watch his door," Olivia said.

"You go watch his door."

"You screwed up, so you get to watch the door…that's an order."

Emma hated when Olivia gave her an order. But she didn't have a good excuse this time. She did mess up. Emma sighed and walked up a few steps to crack open the fire door and glance down the hall towards Tyler's room.

"Maybe I could climb out the window and enter through the balcony?" Miyuki asked.

"The rooms in this hotel have no balconies, love. Only windows."

"How about posing as housekeeping or room service?" Nadia asked.

"Room service could make him suspicious if he didn't order it," Olivia said.

"And I doubt this hotel has acceptable room service anyway," Emma said.

Olivia fired a look.

"I'm watching the room. Oh my God, can I not comment and watch a stupid door at the same time?"

"What about maintenance?" Miyuki asked. "We could be searching for a leak that the room below complained about."

"I like that," Olivia said. "But we don't exactly look like typical maintenance blokes."

"Maybe he won't look through the security peephole," Miyuki said.

"I would."

"Me too," Nadia said.

"I can look like a boy," Miyuki said.

"But you'll need a uniform," Olivia said. "We'll have to break into the housekeeping closets and see what we can find."

Emma noticed someone stepping out in the hallway. It was Tyler Cho.

"Oh wow, he's out of his room."

"What?" Olivia asked.

An idea flashed into Emma's brain. "I'll fix this." She pushed on the metal bar and walked confidently out into the hallway.

CHAPTER 24

Emma headed down the hallway. Tyler was ahead of her, approaching the elevator landing. Emma sped up her walking pace, but did her best not to run. To her surprise, Tyler ignored the elevator and went inside the floor's vending machine room.

Emma grinned to herself, perfect.

Tyler scanned the drink choices on the machine as its cooler kicked on with a hum. All the offerings were in Chinese, but there were also visual representations of each drink as well.

Emma saw her chance. "Wow, I don't know any Chinese."

Tyler noted her presence.

"I'm, like, super thirsty and I don't want to take a chance on the water, you know?"

Tyler nodded.

Emma studied the machine. "What are you going to have?"

Tyler pointed at one drink. "This one is delicious and you can only buy it in China. It has a grape and lemon flavor that goes well after meals. This one is ginger beer, but has hints of cinnamon. Yellow Cream is a new flavor. It tastes like yellow cake with frosting, but not as sugary as you would think. A balanced and tasty dessert drink."

"Wow, you know a lot about soft drinks."

A wash of pride went over the man. "I'm the creator of Yellow Cream."

"You created it? What do you mean by that?"

"I'm a food engineer. I also created Double Choco soda, Lotta Lemon, and the energy drink Thunderdog."

"You created Thunderdog? Oh my God, I drink that all the time."

"It's the best beverage I've ever created."

Another thought hit Emma, and like a true actress, she went

with her gut.

"I wish they had Thunderdog in this machine."

Tyler smiled. "I have a case in my room."

"You do?"

"You'll need some ice, but you're welcome to a can."

"That's so nice of you. I'll grab some ice now."

"Please, allow me." Tyler grabbed an ice bucket from the stack next to the machine and filled it for Emma. Next he selected two cans of Yellow Cream from the machine. "You should at least try this one too."

Soon Emma walked next to Tyler as he balanced a plastic ice bucket and two cans of Yellow Cream soda pop as they moved down the hall.

Olivia, Nadia, and Miyuki approached them from the opposite direction. Emma knew what they were thinking, but jumping the guy in the hallway wouldn't be necessary. She had this all under control.

Emma distracted Tyler by resting her hand on his shoulder and thanking him again for being so nice. Tyler released a huge smile and was on the verge of blushing. Emma took that moment to flash the Gems a dismissive shake of the head and a wink.

Her friends took the hint as they passed them in the hall like strangers.

Tyler fumbled with his room key, ice bucket, and the drinks. Emma offered and he happily gave her his room key. She inserted the card and opened the door for him. Emma waited for him to step inside the room before she flicked the plastic room key into the hallway before moving inside and closing the door.

Tyler put the ice bucket and the two cans of soda on his dresser while Emma moved towards the window that overlooked Hong Kong.

Tyler hesitated.

Emma turned around and caught his stare. She smiled. "How's that drink coming?"

Tyler opened his closet and knelt to retrieve his case of Thunderdog on the floor. He ripped a hole in the plastic as he attempted to pull out a can from the case.

The lock on the front door clicked as someone inserted the card key. Tyler was too consumed with the case of Thunderdog to notice the three other Gems slipping into his hotel room.

Emma smiled at them and gestured down at the floor. The girls took positions around him.

Finally, Tyler Cho freed a can of Thunderdog and jumped up like the character of a pop-up book. His excitement quickly melted as he eyed three extra girls in his hotel room.

"Tyler, these are my friends," Emma said. "I hope you don't mind if they crash our party."

"How do you know my name?"

"We know all about you, Mr. Cho," Olivia said.

"You stole beverage formulas that belong to a Japanese company, and they would like them back, please," Miyuki said.

Tyler surveyed the room. "Is this a joke? Do you kids work for Shiawase Nomimono?" He then noted Emma and frowned. "How old are you?"

Emma didn't skip a beat. "Let's see, how old is your sister in Honolulu?"

Tyler knew the answer and it turned his face green. "What did you say about the formulas?"

"That you swiped them before you quit your job," Olivia said.

"I did no such thing," Tyler said. "First the company tries to destroy my drink, and now they want to destroy my reputation by saying lies about me?"

"You erased all the material from the company's servers," Miyuki said. "What else should the company do?"

"But I didn't do that."

"Then why are you here, love?" Olivia asked. "Decided to have a quick holiday, eh? You're not waiting to meet with anybody, are you?"

Tyler moved over to the table and scooped up his laptop. "You kids should leave." Tyler grabbed his backpack.

But Olivia snatched it from him. "We should take a look at your laptop. Just so we can establish your innocence, Mr. Cho."

"Give me back my property." Tyler couldn't believe this. "I don't know who put you up to this, but I'm not taking orders from a bunch of children. Give me back my property, or I will call the police."

"You're not calling the police or selling those drink formulas, especially Thunderdog," Olivia said. "That drink is dangerous."

"Dangerous? My creation is not dangerous," Tyler said. "Nagumo and those mindless robots in Japan only care about protecting their honor. They all lack vision. They don't see the future. But I do. They don't understand what's possible, and they're unwilling to push the boundaries of how we think of beverages. I need to find people who are willing to break those boundaries."

Since Olivia and Miyuki were playing bad cop, Emma decided to go the opposite way. She eased up to Tyler and showed him a helpful smile. "C'mon, don't be that way. We can help you work it out with the Japanese. We have important friends who can get you out of this problem. But that's only if you're nice and cooperate."

Tyler pushed her away. "I'm done being polite." He moved towards Olivia, who stiffened and prepared for his attack.

But it was Emma who swept her leg across the floor and caught Tyler's knees. The man fell forward into the carpet. When he rolled on his back, Emma raised the heel of her boot and let it float above Tyler's face. The move was flawless and it make Emma feel good about herself. Lioness would have been proud. Tyler's eyes were circles. His body twitched nervously.

"This boot is from Saks Fifth Avenue and I don't want to ruin it with your face. Now, can you be chill for, like, five minutes?"

Tyler slowly nodded.

"Awesome," Emma said. "Stay right there and don't move unless I give you permission, is that clear?"

He nodded again and swallowed.

Emma softened. "Thank you. Your cooperation in our investigation is much appreciated."

Nadia picked up the laptop from the floor near Tyler. She made herself comfortable at the desk and powered it on. Meanwhile Olivia searched the backpack and Miyuki went through the hotel room.

"What's your password?" Nadia asked.

Tyler pressed his lips together.

"Seriously? These boots cost five hundred dollars," Emma said.

Olivia went to her knees. "We'll toss you out of this bloody window if you don't tell us."

Tyler wasn't sure if these girls were serious, but he wasn't the superhero type either. He gave them the password.

Nadia logged into the laptop and scanned the contents. "The information is all here. He also has it stored on a DocLock online account. I'll delete those files first."

Olivia handed Nadia a portable drive. "I found that in his backpack. Probably another backup."

"Why are you deleting the files? I thought you were sent to retrieve them?" Tyler tried to rise.

Emma forced him back down with her boot. "Stay down."

Miyuki offered her a mascara pen. "We might have to knock him out."

"Sapphire, are you good with his passwords?" Olivia asked.

"Yes, I have access to all his accounts now."

"Then we don't need Mr. Cho anymore. Knock him out."

Emma took the mascara pen and double-clicked the end. She aimed the exposed dart towards Tyler. "Don't worry, it's painless and you feel kinda good afterward." She aimed the exposed dart towards Tyler and...

Someone knocked on the door.

"Who the hell is that?" Olivia asked.

"Help me!" Tyler screamed at the top of his lungs. "Help me!"

"Shut up, you, twit!" Olivia said.

"Help me!" Tyler repeated.

"Shoot him with the bloody dart before—"

The door burst open, and pieces of its wood frame dropped to the floor. The first man through the door had a goatee and was either Vietnamese or Korean, Emma wasn't sure. The man had a knife in his right hand and was ready to use it.

The second man was European with skin as white as death. What gave Emma pause was the man's strange, goofy eyes. One eye examined her while the other gazed off in another direction.

Whoever they were, Emma was convinced they were all in trouble.

CHAPTER 25

Miyuki backed away from the door when she saw the two men entering Tyler Cho's hotel room. The man with the goatee held the knife in his hand as if it were an extension of his body. His grip was so familiar with the weapon that Miyuki was convinced he was most likely an expert. She also knew he was Vietnamese by the symbols tattooed on the inside of his arm. The other man had strange eyes with pupils that reminded Miyuki of two hard-boiled eggs. He also walked into the room slightly lopsided. The only important thing about the man was the silver Glock gleaming in his hand.

"Where is Mr. Cho?" the man with egg eyes asked in a Dutch accent. His words were slow but filled with purpose.

Tyler scrambled to his feet. "I'm here. Thank God you've come. They were going to throw me out a window."

Egg Eyes studied each one of the Gems. "Whatever your purpose is...leave the room immediately."

Miyuki swallowed and checked with the other Gems. Nadia and Emma were ready to comply.

However, Olivia's jaw clenched. "We're not going anywhere, mate."

Miyuki swallowed again and prepared herself. She would have to attack Egg Eyes first since he posed the greatest threat. Hopefully, the man with the goatee didn't stab all of her friends before they could knock him out.

"Move aside, young lady. We have business with Mr. Cho," Egg Eyes said.

"Let me get my things," Tyler announced. He went over to the table and closed his laptop.

A drop of sweat glided down Olivia's forehead. "Mr. Cho is coming with us," she said. "Now, you two can go piss off."

Emma and Nadia threw a nervous look at one another. Miyuki quietly pivoted her body slightly, ready to spring into action. One hard kick might have enough force to throw Egg Eyes off balance and drop him to the floor.

"I know who you are." Egg Eyes tilted his head. "The Gems."

Miyuki's heart skipped. She put weight on her left foot. She was close enough to bring her right leg up and kick Egg Eyes in the face.

"The who?" the man with the goatee asked.

"Those obnoxious teens. The ones who blew up our satellite. The ones who exposed our secret terrorist training center to a Russian drone attack. The ones who destroyed our Norway project. Asset One will promote us if we kill them."

Olivia squinted. "And my boss will give us a lovely plate of biscuits and tea if we throw you two blokes out that window."

Emma turned. "That's British for cookies, right?"

"Not relevant now," Olivia said.

"We have a car waiting for you downstairs," Egg Eyes said to Tyler. "Let us clean up this mess so you can be on your way to becoming a rich man."

Tyler stood up and grabbed his backpack.

"Once they get what they want, they'll kill you, Tyler," Olivia said. "Don't trust them. Come with us and you'll still be alive."

Tyler slipped his laptop into his backpack as he warily eyed both parties.

"Speaking with people irritates me," Egg Eyes said. "Put a knife through the girl who talks too much."

The man with the goatee cocked his arm back.

And Miyuki jumped forward, planted her right foot, then swung her entire body around to bring her left leg up in the air. As the man's arm went forward, Miyuki's leg plowed into his stomach.

The knife still flew out of his hand...but it was low and off-center. Plunging into the wall, not Olivia.

As Miyuki planted herself back on to the floor, Egg Eyes aimed the Glock at her. Miyuki tensed up and wondered what being shot would feel like.

But a streak of blond hair came into view as Emma crashed into Egg Eyes, dropping both of them to the ground.

Goatee man was on one knee, but he was grabbing another knife from his belt bristling with cutlery.

Olivia lunged at him.

Nadia reached into her purse.

Miyuki quickly decided Goatee man was the immediate threat. She lunged at him also.

But the man was agile and fast. He brought up another knife that bit into Olivia's forearm. She cried out and grabbed her arm.

Miyuki rammed the heel of her palm into Goatee's face. The man shook it off and swung his knife at Miyuki's stomach.

He missed.

She tried a kick, but he brushed her leg to the side, knocking Miyuki off balance.

Before she could recover, Goatee man came in behind her with his knife, preparing to run his blade through her back.

That was when the man's body shook like a million volts were going through him.

Miyuki stumbled away from the man. She noticed two prongs stuck in Goatee man's back. Miyuki traced the wires to a hairbrush that Nadia was holding. Actually, it was a powerful Taser gun.

Miyuki checked to see if Emma needed help. Egg Eyes was flat on his stomach while Emma sat on top of him. The gun was on the floor but had been kicked away from the man's grasp. Apparently, he wasn't strong enough to knock her off.

Miyuki then remembered Olivia. She found her sitting on the bed, holding her forearm. Tears streamed down the girl's cheeks.

"How deep is the cut?" Miyuki asked.

"I don't know," Olivia said through clenched teeth. "Stings like flipping hell."

"Keep pressure on it," Miyuki said.

Olivia nodded as the tears poured out.

Nadia picked up the Glock and aimed it at Goatee man. With the man's nerve endings still tingling, he surrendered his belt of knives without protest.

"Sit against that wall, please," Nadia said, her voice calm and soft.

Goatee man crawled over to the wall and sat.

Emma got off Egg Eyes and pointed. "Join him."

"You little—"

"Manners, sir," Nadia said. "Do as the girl says."

Egg Eyes glared at her, then crawled on his knees to join his friend against the wall.

Miyuki searched the room. "Where is Tyler?"

Emma and Nadia looked around too. There was no sign of him.

Olivia grimaced as she stood up from the bed. "Head down the bloody stairs and catch him."

Miyuki was the first one down the stairs. She took two steps at a time, using her momentum to get down the concrete steps as quickly as humanly possible. She burst into the lobby and glanced over at the elevator landing for Tyler. Not seeing him, she checked the lobby. Again, no sign of him.

Miyuki passed through the glass doors of the hotel entrance. It was night outside, but the streets were well lit thanks to all the store signs and other numerous decorations. On her left, there were a few people on the sidewalk, but no Tyler.

On her right...

Tyler froze under a streetlamp as his eyes made contact with hers. He was halfway down the block.

Miyuki made a come-here gesture with her finger.

Tyler didn't. He stepped off the curb against the traffic light. Cars braked to a stop and horns blared as he ran across the street, dodging cars.

A grin curled up Miyuki's lips. If Tyler wanted a chase, she would give him one. Miyuki ran as fast as she could down the sidewalk. When she arrived at the same intersection Tyler had run across, Miyuki didn't stop. She scurried across the street like a rabbit, narrowly missing a bus that slammed on its brakes.

With his backpack in tow, Tyler raced down the sidewalk.

Miyuki switched on the afterburners. She was running faster and faster. The adrenaline raced up and down her veins. The excitement was back. The thrill of cheating death had returned.

Thanks to being in such good shape, Miyuki was closing in on Tyler.

The man took a hard left down the next street.

Miyuki took the same hard left and noticed a giant pagoda-shaped gate in the middle of the street. The gate had a sign composed of two large gold Chinese symbols. Below the symbols were the words *Temple Street* in English.

Tyler ran under the pagoda gate as Miyuki followed. This Temple Street area was some type of open-air market. The pavement was a wash of various lights from all the businesses on both sides of the street.

Tyler headed right for the heart of the crowd. Miyuki tried to catch up before he got there. But Tyler was short and snaked through the thickening crowd, making it difficult for Miyuki to follow him.

However, she still could see Tyler's red backpack as he navigated the crowd.

Then a clerk from one of the clothing shops held up a red blouse that blocked Miyuki's view.

"You would look wonderful in this," the salesclerk said in Mandarin. "It's on sale. I have a changing room in the back."

"No, thank you," Miyuki said as she darted around the woman. She scanned the crowd for the red backpack.

But it was nowhere to be found.

Miyuki jumped on top of a covered public trash can and balanced herself against a nearby light pole. She watched the crowd for any sign of Tyler Cho or his backpack. However, there were hundreds of people moving up and down this crowded street.

After scanning the crowd for a half hour, Miyuki jumped off the trash can and had to admit defeat.

CHAPTER 26

It was late afternoon by the time Miyuki and the Gems landed in San Francisco. Since they'd already missed school for that day, Mrs. B wanted them to do a mission debrief at headquarters before heading home. She met them behind the security checkpoint and escorted them to the "jungle," where another green pod waited. The Gems sat down and Mrs. B activated the cone of silence mode.

"Emerald, would you please go over the report you sent us?" Mrs. B asked.

Olivia went over how they went over to the hotel and took over the surveillance. How they confronted Tyler Cho inside his hotel room, and how everything went to crap after that.

With her finger, Mrs. B swiped and tapped on her tablet. Two familiar images hovered above the Gems. "Both of these men are known Venomous operatives. The Vietnamese gentleman with the goatee is simply known as Ho Chi. He's a master of all things with a blade. Rumor says he can throw a knife from seventy-five meters away with deadly accuracy. The other man is Oscar van Zanten, a Dutch national who moved his shipping operations to the Pacific after the European Union found out his company was laundering money for the Russian mob."

"Why are his eyes so weird?" Emma asked.

"What was that?" Mrs. B asked.

"I mean, they don't look in the same direction. It's kind of creepy."

Olivia sat back and crossed her legs, ready for Mrs. B to jump on Emma.

"I was curious too," Miyuki said, not wanting Emma to get in trouble. "If only for us to understand the man."

Mrs. B paused. "Van Zanten was born with a defect in his right eye. He's lived with it most of his life, I do believe." She scanned the Gems. "Does anyone have anything else to add to Emerald's report?"

No one did.

"Thank you. That's all for now. I'm sure you have plenty of neglected schoolwork to attend to." Mrs. B put up the tablet and opened the green pod.

"Excuse me, ma'am, but we're not going back to search for Tyler Cho?" Miyuki asked.

"The Hong Kong and Tokyo stations will handle it from here."

Miyuki didn't want to go back to school. She wanted to track down the formulas and bring them back to Japan so her father wouldn't lose his job.

"I'll give you updates the moment I receive them, Ruby," Mrs. B said, her eyes softening. "Rest assured that Mr. E is doing everything within his power to help your father."

Miyuki nodded, but she wasn't sure if that would be enough.

CHAPTER 27

This morning Emma felt like Leonardo DiCaprio standing on the bow of the *Titanic*. The air from the sea blowing through her long blond hair. The bow of the ship crashing against the waves as she shouted to the sky, "I'm king of the world!"

Today would be the best day ever. Why? Because today Emma would reveal her major project to the world. The major project she had been working on ever since the Gems got back from Hong Kong more than a month ago.

Project Kayla. Emma felt bad about giving the girl the runaround while they were in Japan, so she decided to help Kayla fit in at her new school in a big way. And what better way to do that than a total makeover.

A few weeks ago, Emma whipped out her gold credit card and took Kayla to the Westfield Centre Shopping Mall. She chose five different types of shirts, blouses, skirts, shoes, pants, sweaters—the basic building blocks to any decent wardrobe—and gave Kayla the option of using the clothes in different combinations to create numerous looks. But Emma had designed it so Kayla couldn't screw it up, even if she tried.

Over the weekend, Emma took Kayla to the salon for some major hair resuscitation along with a new bold color. Then came a skin detox and cleansing before applying new cosmetics that suited Kayla's complexion better. Emma was so proud of the result that she couldn't wait to introduce the new Kayla to everyone at school on Monday.

After locking up the Mercedes in the student parking lot, Emma used an excuse to ditch the Gems before heading for the girls' bathroom near the theater arts room. Kayla was waiting for her there, wearing one of the new skirts and a nice blouse. The classy ballet flats completed the look.

"Do I suck? Does this combination work? I hope it doesn't suck. I tried on every skirt and I think this works...but I don't know. Does it work? Did I do my face right? Do you see any zits? I so don't want to embarrass you," Kayla said with a frenzy. "You're not saying anything. Shouldn't you be saying something?"

Emma placed her hands on Kayla's shoulders. "Love the skirt, the blouse, and the flats. Your cosmetic work is exactly what I told you to do. Your hair is brushed out nicely. Eyeliner looks killer. No smudges. Nails painted and look great. I approve."

Kayla clapped like a little child. "Yay!"

"Alright, now is the fun part. I want you to do a dramatic entrance."

Kayla's eyes went wide. "I don't know how to act. You're the actress. I can't be dramatic. You know all about entering a room and that kind of stuff. I'm shy. Like super shy. Like I'll hide behind a table and totally embarrass myself—"

"Kayla..."

"Seriously, Emma. I'll do a nosedive under the table and everyone will laugh and I'll be known as the crazy girl who eats under tables at lunch."

Emma squeezed her shoulders. "Pull yourself together."

Kayla buttoned her lip.

"I'm not talking about acting on a stage. All you have to do is walk over to our table and sit down."

"Oh, really?"

"Really. The key to making an entrance is not acting like you're making an entrance."

Kayla paused. "I don't get it."

"Be normal. Just walk into the commons and sit down with us."

"That's it?"

"Yup."

"I can do that," Kayla said. "Okay, I'm ready."

"No, I want you to stay here and wait for my cue. I'll text you."

"Your cue? What cue? Why do I have to have a cue? Didn't you say—"

"Kayla, chill. I only want to be in the commons when you make your entrance so I can watch everyone's reaction." Emma referenced her phone. "And record it for history."

"Why are you putting all this pressure on me?"

"Pressure? Oh my God, Kayla, you're walking to a table. In

flats. That's it."

Kayla licked her lips. "I can do this," she said to herself.

"I know you can." Emma pushed the bathroom door open. "Remember, wait for my cue."

Emma made her way into the commons area, which was filled with students waiting for the morning bell. Emma maneuvered her way through the crowd and found their normal table near the south doors. Miyuki and Nadia were nibbling on some fruit while Olivia was showing Lewis her notebook.

"What's up?" Lewis asked Emma. The boy wore a plain red shirt and had smooth dark skin. His open bottle of chocolate milk sat on the table.

"Nothing much. What are you reading?"

"Olivia's book report. It's crazy," he said. "She's dissing him major time."

"Dissing Ernest Hemingway?" Emma asked.

"Crushing him. Wanna hear the title? 'Ernest Hemingway: Full of Bullocks.'" Lewis laughed. "If this Hemingway was still alive, he'd send a few of his boys over to mess this girl up."

"It's not a diss," Olivia said. "It's an honest opinion of his novel from the perception of a young female reader."

Lewis kept on reading and laughed so hard he slammed his sneaker against the ground. "Check this out. 'Judging by the way Mr. Hemingway tells his story, the only thing one can say is that he must see the world only through his—'"

Nadia snatched the paper away from Lewis. "You put that in your book report?"

"I'm being honest, love," Olivia said.

Lewis smiled. "You're taking literary criticism to a whole new level."

"Thanks," Olivia said, her eyes hanging on Lewis as the boy stood up and drank more of his milk.

"See you girls around," Lewis said before slipping away.

"He's sweet on you," Miyuki said to Olivia.

"When are you going to ask him out?" Emma asked.

"He's the bloke. He's supposed to ask me out. That's the proper way."

"Says the proper girl who accuses one of America's greatest authors of thinking through his love pump."

The other Gems giggled.

Emma's phone vibrated, so she checked it.

How much longer? I'm dying here!!!!

Emma cursed at herself. She totally forgot about Kayla. Emma hit her back.

Go!

She activated the record video function on her phone and pointed it at the large doors. Seconds later, the new Kayla emerged from the hallway and out into the commons area. Instead of holding her head up high and feeling the confidence that a fabulous wardrobe should bring to a girl, Kayla's eyes dragged along the shiny floor as she made her way towards their table. A few girls noticed and their faces showed approval. Even a couple of guys stopped talking to check Kayla out. But the rest of the Gems were occupied and weren't paying attention. They were missing it!

"Oh my God," Emma said. "Is that Kayla?"

Miyuki glanced over first. Olivia sighed and turned.

Nadia was still reading Olivia's book report. She shook her head. "You can't turn this paper in. You'll get expelled."

Miyuki and Olivia stared at Kayla as she approached.

"Hi, everyone! How's life?" Kayla asked in her chipper tone.

Olivia and Miyuki didn't answer. They were so overwhelmed by Kayla's new look that they couldn't speak.

Emma knew that she nailed it. It was a home run in personal makeovers.

"Hello, are you new to our school?" Nadia asked. She was dead serious.

Miyuki clapped her hands and giggled.

"That's Kayla." Olivia grinned. "She looks a bit different this morning."

"Oh, I'm so sorry," Nadia said.

Kayla laughed. "Emma was right. It's like I'm a different person."

The girl sat down next to Emma, who was so basking in her own radiance. The old Kayla had been obliterated and a much better version had emerged from the ashes. Emma's work here was done.

"Trying out a new look, love?" Olivia asked.

"Do you like it? Does it look good on me? Please be honest. Or you don't have to be honest. If you hate it, you can just say you like it and I won't know the difference."

"You look beautiful, Kayla," Miyuki said.

"Do I? Or are you just saying that?"

Olivia sat back in her chair. Her eyes moved back and forth between Kayla and Emma.

"She means it," Emma said. "Because you do look great."

"And you look so familiar," Olivia said with a smirk.

Emma wondered what that was supposed to mean.

"Really?" Kayla asked.

"I'm assuming that Emma helped you with your new look. Would I be correct?" Olivia asked.

"Oh my God, yes." Kayla told the Gems about all the clothes they ended up buying and the trip to the salon and to the spa. "Emma has been so nice to me. Some day I'll pay her back."

"Bringing joy to someone's life needs no reward, Kayla," Emma said.

Olivia tossed a snide glance over at Nadia. Of course, why would Olivia see this as a good deed? The girl couldn't go through one day without finding something negative to say about anything Emma did. And Emma saved her life too!

Kayla set her backpack on her chair. "All this fashion excitement is making me hungry. I'm gonna grab something before class. Want anything?"

The Gems shook their heads and Kayla strutted off to the vending machines. The girl swayed with much more confidence than before. If they weren't in public, Emma would be sobbing a few tears of joy.

"You're amazing," Olivia said.

Emma knew she was, but hearing it from Olivia was nice.

"And?" Emma waited for the burn.

"What did you do to that poor girl?"

Emma didn't understand.

"Do you understand the general concept of a makeover, love?"

"What the hell are you talking about?" Emma asked.

"Did you color Kayla's hair?" Nadia asked politely.

"Yes, I took her to my stylist and her hair looks fabulous now."

"Did you pick her clothes too?" Miyuki asked.

"Of course. She needed a lot of guidance, but with my help, we took it to the next level. Do you guys hate it?"

"Kayla looks beautiful and I can see the clothes give her new confidence."

"Exactly, that's the entire point. Thank you, Miyuki."

"We're not saying that we hate it," Nadia corrected.

"But?"

Olivia chuckled. "You don't realize it, do you?"

"Why don't you educate me," Emma said, her voice on edge. She was trying her best not to go off.

"Kayla looks exactly like you. You haven't improved her. All you did was make a copy of yourself and paste it into existence."

Emma froze. Her mind gathered evidence. The clothes she bought. The hair coloring. The type of cut she wanted the stylist to do on Kayla. No, the idea was absurd. She gave Kayla her taste in clothes. Her taste in hair. She would never create a clone of herself.

"Besides Kayla having shorter hair, the color and the cut does match yours exactly," Nadia said.

No way, these girls were wrong.

"You like it, don't you?" Emma asked Miyuki.

"Yes." Her eyes fell to the table.

"Do you agree with them?"

Miyuki shifted in her chair. "You were excited to help her. Perhaps you didn't realize it at the time."

Emma didn't believe it. Couldn't believe it. Wouldn't believe it.

And then Kayla walked back into the commons area with a bag of cookies. This time, the proud girl circled the area so everyone could notice her. Kayla's hair was blond and exactly like Emma's. And her outfit…

"Oh my God, I wore that outfit last week," Emma said out loud, cupping her hands over her face.

Miyuki gasped.

"You have to fix it. You owe her that," Olivia said.

"Make her the best Kayla she can be," Nadia said.

Finally, Kayla came back to the table and opened her bag of cookies. The girl was glowing like the sun. Emma examined Kayla from head to toe and wanted to kick herself. How could she not see it? It was embarrassing.

"Let's meet after school," Emma said. "There's more work I need to do on you."

"Some tweaks?" Kayla said.

"Yes, tweaks. Lots and lots of tweaks."

Kayla smiled and crunched on a cookie.

"Can you come along?" Emma asked Miyuki. "I might need you to…" Emma searched for the right words.

"To help keep you from yourself?"

"Exactly."

Miyuki gave her a thumbs-up. "No problem."

Emma's phone buzzed with a new message.

Hi Emma. How are you?

Ryan's name was displayed to the side. Emma had labeled the number the first time he contacted her. She glanced around the table. If Mrs. B or the other Gems knew that she was still talking to Ryan, Emma would be in big trouble.

She answered him.

Leave me alone.

Know a dude named Tyler Cho?

Emma swallowed. Why would Ryan ask her about him? She played dumb.

Don't know anyone by that name. Why?

How was Hong Kong?

Ryan knew about their trip. Was he trying to get more info out of her?

That's creepy. Stalking a girl's not the way to win her heart.

I was in Greece. My associates saw Gems in HK.
What's the about page on Thunderdog? Inquiring minds wanna know.

Why would Ryan be asking about Tyler Cho and Thunderdog?

Unless Ryan's "friends" in Hong Kong didn't find Tyler either.

Emma played it cool.

It's an energy drink. Go online & Moogle it.

I did. Lots of recalls. Why? What's so special about it?

Maybe Ryan wasn't that important to Venomous after all. He had no clue. Emma didn't feel like helping him either.

Turning off my phone now.

Parked @ Pacifica state beach right now. Love to see you again.

Emma hesitated, then typed.

You're in California?

Yes. Curious?

Emma kept her phone on her lap as she thought about it. Did Venomous send Ryan here to get info out of her? Maybe. But what if Venomous did have Tyler Cho and was planning to weaponize Thunderdog? Ryan could be the only way to find out and stop them.

She typed.

Do you expect me to trust you?

Expect no. Trust yes. You'll be safe. Promise. Please come w/o friends. Our visit not for them.

The bell for first period rang and students emptied out of the commons area. The Gems and Kayla stood up from their table.

Emma paused. She would have to skip most of the day in order to drive all the way down to Pacifica State Beach. She would also have to make up an excuse to the Gems about why she missed lunch period too. Emma said goodbye to everyone and slipped into the girls' restroom. She sent another message.

OK. On my way.

CHAPTER 28

Emma reached the front lobby, where the school offices were. A security officer posted near the main entrance watched her. Emma knew that if she didn't make it out by the third bell, she wouldn't be able to get out of school without a pass from the office. Her heels clicked against the tiles as she made her way towards the double doors as quickly as she could without drawing too much suspicion. The moment she shoved open the door and stepped outside, the third bell rang.

Emma rushed over to her Mercedes, pushed the start ignition button, and drove off-campus.

The drive down the coast to Pacifica State Beach took a while. Emma never liked to speed, so she went as fast as she felt comfortable going, and using the Mercedes's advanced cruise control helped a lot. When she arrived at the beach, Emma found a space in the crowded parking lot and waited.

Ten minutes passed.

No text from Ryan. No sign of him. If the boy was cruising the parking lot, he would have come up to her car by now.

She texted him.

I'm here. Where are you?

She waited for an answer.

Ten additional minutes passed. Nothing.

Was Ryan playing a joke on her? Did he use a Moogle map of California and pick some random place for her to drive to while he was somewhere else in the world? Next time Emma saw him, Ryan would die.

Emma slipped out of her car and locked it. While she was here, Emma figured she might as well have a walk on the beach, especially since the weather was nice and the sand between her toes would feel good.

She'd made it all the way to the beach's entrance when a car horn made her turn.

There was a convertible idling next to a tree. The top was down.

Curious, Emma moved closer to the vehicle. It wasn't an expensive car, more like something you would rent for the weekend. The driver was a boy with the deepest blue eyes. His hair was dark. His chin was strong with a cute dimple in the middle. His thick frame offered no fat, only muscle. He wore shorts and was playing a Beatles tune through the speakers. Paul McCartney singing about wanting someone and it was driving him mad.

It was Ryan. The boy turned down the music. "You came."

"I've been waiting, like, forever," Emma said with attitude, determined not to let this boy play her like a tuba. "Now, be honest with me. Did your friends kidnap Tyler Cho?"

"I've always wanted to drive down the coast. Beautiful day for it, don't you think?"

"You can do anything you want. I don't care. But only after you give me the information."

"Emma, you're out of school. I'm in town. Let's go for a drive and enjoy life."

"I'd rather see you drive off a cliff and enjoy death."

"Don't be like that. It's a drive down the coast. Two friends talking and enjoying the nice weather."

"I've told you that I'm not your friend."

Ryan playfully shook his head. "Meaningful acquaintances? Will that do?"

"Acquaintances will do. But I'm not getting into a car with you."

"Are you afraid of being kidnapped or something?"

"Pretty much, yeah."

"I haven't told them anything about you, Emma. There's no big trap out there. Just me, you, and a rented convertible that I need to return before five to keep my cheap day rate."

"Don't you have to be twenty-five to rent a car?"

"Our fake IDs are really good. I also have a set of diplomatic papers that say I'm related to a diplomat in the Canadian embassy," Ryan said. "Can we stop talking shop? I wanna go for a drive."

"Do you have a gun?"

"I have a knife."

"Give it to me."

"Can I have it back?"

"I'll think about it," Emma said, holding out her hand.

Ryan placed a large switchblade into it. Her finger found the button and the knife snapped open. With new confidence, Emma opened the passenger-side door and slid into the seat. But the girl angled her body so the sharp end of the knife pointed at Ryan.

"You sure know how to make a guy feel comfortable," he said.

Emma didn't want Ryan to feel comfortable. She wanted him to feel threatened. She wanted to show herself as dangerous and in control of the situation, because Ryan had a way of pulling down her guard.

"Let's get this over with," Emma said.

Ryan nodded and turned the Beatles back up on the car's audio system. He slipped his shades on and drove the convertible through the parking lot before making the turn south along the highway.

Emma's blond hair flapped against her left shoulder as their speed picked up. Ryan went maybe four over the speed limit. She watched him like a hawk.

"How's school?" Ryan asked, his tone relaxed.

"It's fine," Emma said. She wasn't in the mood to elaborate.

"What classes are you taking this semester?"

"Six."

Ryan waited for more details.

Emma peeled off a few strands of hair that had blown into her eyes as they kept watch over him.

"What subjects?" he asked.

"Where is Tyler Cho? I don't have time for games."

Ryan looked over Emma's shoulder. "Look at that view. All those waves crashing against the rocks. The ocean is so blue today."

Emma didn't move. She wasn't falling for that.

"You're not even looking," Ryan said, a bit frustrated. "This was supposed to be fun, you know? There's no need to be so hostile." Ryan eyed the knife still in Emma's hand.

Emma thought about it. The switchblade could be snapped open instantly if she needed it quick. Emma placed her finger on the dull end and snapped the knife shut. However, she still kept it inside her palm.

"Thanks," Ryan said.

Emma turned to face the front. She did a quick check of the view. The white cliffs dived sharply down into the blue ocean. Flocks of seagulls cawed as they floated on the wind. Ryan was right. It was a beautiful view.

The next Beatles song came on. Emma recognized it as "While My Guitar Gently Weeps," a song she liked. She reached over and turned the volume up loud. Ryan grinned his approval.

Emma allowed herself to relax. She listened to the music, watched the road and the view, and pretended she was alone. But her hand still gripped the knife tight.

When the song ended, Ryan used his steering wheel to turn the volume down. "Can we talk now?"

Emma paused. She began by telling Ryan about her six classes in detail. She didn't mention Kayla or any of the Gems.

Ryan guided the car to the left as the road curved. "Do your friends like living with your grandmother?"

"Who said we're living together?"

"I haven't told them, Emma."

She didn't like the fact that Ryan knew the Gems lived together. If anyone found out, her grandmother could be in danger.

"What if I stab you to make sure?"

"On a road like this, you'd be killing herself as well. Why do you want to stab me? I gave you flowers, remember?"

"That's the only reason you're still alive."

Ryan laughed.

Emma was only half-kidding. "So what have you been up to, Ryan? Stealing and hurting innocent people? Slapping a few babies in the face? Kicking a puppy or two?"

"Our group extorted money from a Russian mob boss. Stole a shipment of diamonds from a train in Africa. Banked around one hundred thousand dollars in my account already, and I still haven't taken a cent of my father's money."

"Does your mom know how you got all that money?"

The relaxed facade on Ryan's face disappeared. "My mom was awarded what's left of my father's estate...fifty thousand dollars. That's it. Do you believe that?"

"His estate?" Emma asked. "But your father is still in prison, right?"

Ryan didn't answer right away. He gripped the wheel tighter. "He killed himself."

"He what?"

Ryan smirked. "He used his bedsheet to hang himself in his cell."

"Oh my God," Emma said. "I'm so sorry, Ryan."

"He gave up. The coward gave up. He could have done his twenty years. Got out of jail and fixed his mistakes."

"Like the way he treated you?"

"Why wouldn't you want to give your son something that you worked so hard for?" Ryan asked. "Raymond Foods should have been mine. Even though the son of a bitch wasn't there as a father, my dad could have given me a future. A consolation prize for putting up with his shit all my life."

Emma moved closer to him. "You didn't deserve to be treated that way."

"Your father didn't do that, Emma. Your father gave you everything he had because he wanted you to succeed."

"It's just money, Ryan," Emma said. "Don't you want to be more than just a name next to a bunch of numbers on a bank account?"

Ryan found a scenic turnout and stopped the car. The boy took off his sunglasses and sat back against the door, facing Emma. "You're the only one who understands what I'm going through."

Emma's chest felt warm. He was right. She did understand him. Like the time they were both sitting on those rocks in Missouri, their feet soaking in the cool lake water. That peaceful setting brought out the honesty in Ryan, who spoke to Emma from deep within his soul. Now, they had both lost their fathers.

Emma slipped the knife into her pants pocket. She touched his arm. "Does your mom still live in Wichita?"

Ryan nodded.

"You still love her, don't you?"

"Yeah."

"Then why not go live with her? Help her with the estate and think about what you want to do with your life."

"She doesn't need me right now. When the money runs out, I'll take care of her."

"You need her, Ryan. You need to take a break from all this."

Ryan didn't answer.

"You don't need a criminal group like Venomous to give you a purpose in life. With one hundred thousand bucks, you could leave the group and use that money to do something awesome. If you keep working for Venomous, you'll eventually be forced to do something awful, and then you'll be condemned for the rest of your life."

"It's too late for me. Once you've joined Venomous, you never get to leave."

"There must be a way to take out those implants safely."

"Even if there was, Venomous wouldn't rest until I was dead," Ryan said. "I appreciate the concern, but there isn't anything you can do."

"I refuse to believe that."

Ryan watched the seagulls floating in the sky as he breathed in the sea air. "And you still wouldn't consider joining?"

"That's impossible," Emma said. "I won't betray my friends."

"I understand."

"If I gave you a million dollars, would you promise to leave Venomous and go live with your mother."

Ryan laughed.

"I'm serious."

Ryan cocked his head. "You don't have access to your father's trust. Your grandmother and Rothchild Industries control it."

"I can still get the money."

"You're crazy. Why give me a million dollars?"

Emma gave him a long look. "Maybe you're a guy worth investing in."

Ryan chuckled. "Am I on a secret episode of *Shark Tank* or something?"

"That's right. I'm investing one hundred percent in the Ryan Raymond I met at the lake. The boy who hadn't given up on his future."

That sentence registered on Ryan's face. Emma could feel his mind struggling with the idea.

"And how do you fit into this deal? Besides the money."

Emma traced her finger down Ryan's arm. "The investor would be heavily involved with the project. She would be determined to get her money back, plus a hefty profit of course."

"Is money her only reward?"

161

"She would want to keep her options open. But it would depend on what the project wanted to accomplish."

Ryan stared at Emma for what seemed like hours. His hand was soft when it landed on top of hers. "That's one hell of an offer."

Emma smiled and crossed her fingers.

Ryan let go of her hand and checked the clock on the dash. "We'd better wrap this up. Your friends should be missing you at lunch right now. Which means they've already texted you and not gotten an answer. So now they're contacting your Authority friends to track your phone."

Emma glanced at the clock. It read twelve forty-four in the afternoon. She had totally lost all track of time. Emma would have to make up an excuse. But first, she needed to push her agenda.

"Ryan, where is Tyler Cho now?"

CHAPTER 29

Miyuki saw the ocean waves crest below her as the helicopter she was in followed the California coastline. The sun made the surface of the water shimmer, and it tried to lure Miyuki into thinking happy thoughts, but she knew better. Emma had gone missing from school and the Gems were freaking out.

When they discovered her missing from lunch, they also noticed Emma's Mercedes was gone and tried to contact her. But Emma didn't answer her phone. Olivia contacted Mrs. B, who put a trace on Emma's phone and located it south of Pacifica State Beach.

Instead of calling the police, Mrs. B took personal charge. She and Aardvark boarded a helicopter and flew to a city park in Berkeley, where they landed to pick up the Gems, who slipped away from school at the end of lunch period.

Now their helicopter closed in on Emma's phone, which was now stationary near a scenic turnout just ahead.

Miyuki's heart pounded with the fear that some crazy man had managed to lure Emma from school, kidnap her, and was now doing awful things to her. She wanted to find her friend as soon as possible.

As the helicopter reached the scenic overlook, Miyuki could see a teen girl with blond hair sitting on a bench that faced the ocean. The girl stood up and faced the helicopter as it came in for a landing. Her long blond hair flapped from the artificial wind created by the helicopter blades.

The moment the helicopter touched the earth, Miyuki jumped out and was the first one to reach Emma.

"Are you alright?" Miyuki asked. "We were so worried."

"You didn't have to bring a helicopter," Emma said. "I'm fine, seriously."

"What happened?"

Emma paused. "It's not a big deal."

"What's going on?" Olivia asked as she and Nadia reached them.

"Oh my God. You called Mrs. B?" Emma asked.

The woman in question stepped off the helicopter, with Aardvark in tow.

"Your car was missing and you didn't answer any of our calls," Nadia said. "We needed her help."

"Everybody needs to chill," Emma said. "It's not a huge thing."

"I'll decide that," Mrs. B said. "Do you need any medical attention?"

Emma rolled her eyes. "Of course not."

"Where's your car?"

"It's back at the beach."

"How did you get here?"

Emma paused again. "Someone gave me a ride."

"Who gave you a ride?"

"That's not important," Emma said. "What's important is that I know where Tyler Cho is."

"Who is the source of this new information?" Mrs. B asked.

"Why do you need to know that? All you need to know is we can trust him."

"So it's a he," Olivia said.

Emma frowned.

"This source contacted you at school?" Mrs. B asked.

"Yes. He wanted to meet and take a drive down the coast."

"You drove down the coast with him? Sounds a bit casual for gathering information from a source. Is he a friend?"

"Do you want the information or not?" Emma asked.

"I want the truth, Black Opal. What friend is this?"

"My source tells me that Oscar van Zanten has Tyler Cho at his summer home outside Jakarta, Indonesia."

"Is your source a member of Venomous?" Mrs. B asked, her eyes firm and serious.

"I can't say anything else."

Olivia stood in front of Emma. "Have you been talking to him about us?"

"I haven't given him information that he doesn't already know."

"What does he know?"

Emma paused. "He knows we live together with my grandmother."

"That's brilliant, Emma. Brilliant," Olivia said. "Now Venomous can come murder us in our beds."

"Ryan would never let that happen." Emma realized her mistake and slapped her hand over her mouth.

Ryan Raymond...Miyuki remembered him from Norway. The boy who joined Venomous and betrayed his father in the process. Miyuki knew that Emma had a soft spot for him. She thought she could turn him. That his motivations for joining Venomous were not strong and, thus, highly vulnerable to her influence. But maybe Ryan was using Emma to get to them.

"You stupid cow," Olivia said. "He tried to blow you up once."

"He saved us," Emma said. "If Ryan hadn't untied me, we would've died."

"Nevertheless," Mrs. B began, "he's a member of a terrorist organization that would love to find out where the Gems live—"

"Ryan said he would not betray us and I believe him."

"On what basis?" Mrs. B asked. "He betrayed his own father. He lied to you and the Gems. Why would you trust him?"

"My gut says so," Emma said. "He's being honest with me."

"You're flipping in love with him," Olivia said.

"I'm not in love. We're friends."

"That's bull—"

"Stop it. Both of you." Mrs. B glared at Emma. "We'll discuss Ryan later. Right now, I want you on that helicopter, young lady. We need to confirm your information."

* * *

The next morning, the Boeing Dreamliner cruised above the clouds at thirty-four thousand feet. The flight was as smooth as glass, but Miyuki was sick of flying over the Pacific. It was such a long flight and being stuck inside a plane for fifteen plus hours was always an endurance test. Not like a physical one, Miyuki loved those kinds of challenges. The athlete within her enjoyed those. Climbing a rock wall, running a marathon, competing in a bike race...those challenges were exciting and made her feel alive.

Ever since they'd taken off from San Francisco, Emma's nose was stuck inside a book. This was normal on most of the flights they took together; however, this time Emma blew off all of Miyuki's attempts to talk to her. Emma was still upset after her private meeting with Mrs. B yesterday. Miyuki assumed it was about Ryan Raymond, but whatever they did talk about, Emma came out in tears.

Since then, Olivia and Nadia gave Emma some space and didn't push her to talk about it. They assumed Mrs. B gave the girl a verbal smackdown, one severe enough that they didn't need to voice their own frustration at Emma's actions.

Miyuki wasn't sure what she thought about it. She did see the danger of allowing someone from Venomous to know where they lived. When Van Zanten had confronted them in Hong Kong, he'd made it sound like the entire group was bent on revenge against the Gems. Miyuki was sure that Van Zanten would not hesitate to kill them in their beds like Olivia feared.

However, Emma saw something different in Ryan, and Miyuki wondered what that was.

Emma put down her book and stretched in her seat.

"Do you want to watch *The Muppet Movie* again?" Miyuki asked.

At first, Emma didn't react. But then, a grin curled up Emma's mouth.

"Okay."

Two hours later, Miyuki and Emma finished *The Muppet Movie* right as lunch service began. Miyuki selected the turkey sandwich and Emma had the chicken salad. It was during lunch when Emma finally began to open up.

"They're wrong about him, you know. Ryan wouldn't let Venomous hurt us."

Miyuki wiped her mouth with a napkin before answering. "Yet you see why everyone is so worried. If Ryan knows where we live, he could be a potential threat."

"We were all there the night of my stage performance, remember? Ryan was in the audience too, and he could have easily followed us home from the auditorium and murdered us in bed. Or had someone from Venomous do it. But Ryan left me flowers instead."

"He was trying to recruit you."

"I know that. But even after I said no, Ryan hasn't made any moves against us. And why did he give me the information about Tyler Cho yesterday? It's because he likes me. But so what? A spy can use a person's feelings against them, right? If I make him fall in love with me, then maybe we have a way to get inside Venomous, right? Or I can convince him to help us."

"Did you tell that to Mrs. B?"

"I tried. But she kept bringing up vulnerabilities and unacceptable risks. She doesn't trust me. Like, I'm not mature enough to handle manipulating a guy. I've manipulated plenty of boys." Emma paused. "Now don't give me the stink eye, Miyuki, I don't mean, like, in evil ways. I never humiliate a boy. But if a smile and a hug make them do things for me, I mean, what's the harm?"

"Ryan is a handsome boy. What if he's manipulating you?" Miyuki asked.

Emma's lips tightened. She didn't like that assumption. But she was thinking about it. "He's not. I can tell."

"How can you tell?"

Emma thought about it some more. "Alright, fine. He's cute enough that—I shouldn't let my guard down."

"That's what Mrs. B is worried about. She doesn't want that boy to get inside your head. However, if you want to use him, you need to stay inside his."

A light went on behind Emma's eyes. "You mean pretend like he's my leading man in a play? Act like I care about him?"

Miyuki knew she had her. "Isn't that how a professional actress would approach a role with an actor she doesn't personally care for?"

Emma straightened her back. "You're right. She would. I mean, you wouldn't believe the number of jerks in the entertainment industry. An actress has to use her acting skills just to get along with all the people she despises."

"And spies must do it too."

Emma nodded, then showed a frown. "But what if I...still kind of like him?" She sighed. "Maybe I do need to stay away from Ryan."

CHAPTER 30

Miyuki and the Gems landed at Soekarno-Hatta International Airport in Jakarta. The attendant at the IndoCar rental counter called out for the next person in line. Olivia went up to the Indonesian woman and gave her a special reservation number.

The woman asked in English, "Is your trip to Jakarta for business or pleasure?"

"Business. We're here to pick up a package," Olivia said.

"Does the package know that you are coming to collect it?"

"Not at all."

The woman slipped her a rental folder with a set of car keys inside. "Good hunting, Emerald."

"Thank you."

The Gems found the rental car parking lot and climbed into a new Subaru SUV. Following Mrs. B's directions, Nadia drove the vehicle east and then south from the airport, joining up with a major highway that took them out of the city.

Nadia parked the Subaru by the side of the road and shut off the engine.

Olivia checked their position on her phone. "I bet that's Van Zanten's place down there."

Miyuki peeked down the street and saw two men guarding the beginning of a driveway.

"Time for a nature walk," Olivia said.

The large single-level house had these giant A-frame type roofs made of dark teak wood. But unlike Europe or America, these roofs did not meet in the center. On this house, one side of the roof was longer than the other, causing it to rise meters above the smaller roof. It made the house appear to have several tall foreheads.

The jungle surrounding the house was cut back several meters away. The Gems hiked around the perimeter, keeping themselves hidden inside the jungle so they could do their reconnaissance without detection. There were two Indonesian men wearing T-shirts and shorts stationed around the driveway to the residence. Four more men patrolled the large open area around the main house. They appeared unarmed. However, Miyuki was certain the slight bulges in the back of their T-shirts were guns.

"This must be the right place," Olivia said.

The Gems took pictures of the perimeter and headed back to the Subaru.

"What do you think?" Olivia asked Nadia.

"I saw a few spotlights. And I detected some hidden surveillance cameras. I'm sure someone is watching them."

"How can you see hidden cameras?" Emma asked.

Nadia held up her phone. "CC television mode. It's a new upgrade to our phones."

"Don't you read the emails on equipment updates?" Olivia added. "They're sent out every Wednesday, love."

"They must go into my junk email folder," Emma said. "I'll fix that when we get back."

"Anyway…do you think you can hack into one of those cameras and disable it?" Olivia asked.

Nadia thought about it as she studied the pictures they'd taken of the house. She zoomed in on one picture and examined it. "I see the wires now…the cameras are wired together. I would have to hack into the computer controlling them. That's if the computer is online."

"But it's possible."

"Perhaps."

"Those men with guns," Miyuki said. "How do we avoid them?"

"And we need to know how many men are inside the house," Olivia said. "Van Zanten could have an army inside that house for all we know."

"Ho Chi and his knives could be there," Miyuki added.

Olivia didn't like that suggestion. "We need to stake this place out and confirm that Tyler Cho is actually inside. Plus we need to count how many different people we see going in and out. We need to see what we're up against before we try a rescue."

Olivia was being cautious, but for once Miyuki agreed.

A green Range Rover rolled into view as it left the house and stopped at the end of the driveway. The two guards acknowledged whoever was inside.

Olivia grabbed some binoculars and observed the Range Rover as it eased onto the public road and turned.

"Van Zanten's in that car," Olivia said. "Get down!"

The Gems dropped their heads as the Range Rover passed by their Subaru and disappeared behind the bend.

"Let's follow him, Nads," Olivia said. "I want to see what he's up to."

Nadia started up the Subaru, spun it around, and raced to catch up. Soon Nadia had the Range Rover back in sight, so she eased off. The Range Rover headed back into Jakarta, towards an industrial portion of town. After passing endless factories, offices, and other facilities, the Range Rover turned into the parking lot of a small warehouse. The lot's old pavement was cracked and crumbling apart. The yellow paint on the warehouse itself had faded years ago.

Van Zanten and three of his goons exited the Range Rover. Van Zanten paused as he unlocked a door and went through it. His men followed.

Nadia parked the Subaru in a secluded spot opposite the warehouse.

"Wonder what's in there," Olivia said. "Should we take a peek, girls?"

The Gems checked around the building first for any cameras or security equipment and found none. The docking area in the back had four bays, however, their doors were locked tight. The Gems saw no other entrances into the warehouse except for the one Van Zanten had used.

Olivia paused.

"What's wrong?" Miyuki asked.

"Those three goons could be on the other side of that door. We need another way in."

"There is no other way," Nadia said.

"Maybe there is." Miyuki pointed to a series of small iron bars climbing up one of the walls. It was a ladder to the roof. She jogged over to the lower steps and climbed up a few feet.

The other three Gems hesitated as they glanced up towards the roof.

Miyuki kept climbing higher and higher. "No one wants to join?"

Emma paused, but then placed her sneaker on the first step and hoisted herself up. Miyuki grinned to herself as she continued climbing higher and higher.

Soon she reached the top and used a railing to hop on to the roof. Miyuki then searched for a door, but there was none. Only a couple of air conditioners and some vents.

"Doesn't look too promising," Emma said, reaching Miyuki.

Soon Olivia and Nadia climbed over the railing and had a look around. They looked disappointed too.

Miyuki then tripped over something.

Emma rushed over. "You okay?"

"Yes," Miyuki replied. She retraced her steps and noticed a handle sticking up from a square panel lying flat on the roof. Was that a door?

Miyuki pulled up on the handle, but the panel was heavy. Emma noticed and helped her lift the panel up; it flopped open like a door. Looking down, both girls noticed a stairway heading down into the warehouse.

"Bingo!" Emma said.

"What's a bingo?" Miyuki asked.

"It's like...touchdown!" Emma shot both her arms up like an NFL referee.

Miyuki got that reference.

"What are you two yelling about?" Olivia asked before seeing the door. "Oh, that's brilliant. Let's go."

The narrow stairway was dark. Since the lights weren't working, Miyuki used the mini-flashlight hidden on the tip of her lipstick to see where she was going. The steps were small and steep. One bad step could drop Miyuki fifty feet or more to the hard cement floor she knew would be waiting for her down below. The air was also dank and smelled like mildew.

"Are there rats down here?" Emma asked. She was just behind Miyuki.

"Please don't ask questions like that," Nadia said, her voice echoing down the narrow stairway.

"You both need to be quiet," Olivia said. "They might be able to hear us."

The Gems continued down the stairwell.

When her feet reached the bottom floor, Miyuki heard some squeaking sounds.

She flashed the light along the ground. About ten sets of beady little eyes stared back at her.

Rats.

Miyuki almost swallowed her tongue. She clamped her hand over her mouth so she wouldn't shriek. Emma was behind her, ready to jump off the stairs. But Miyuki held her back.

"What's wrong?" Emma asked.

"If I could answer your earlier question? Would you freak out?"

"My earlier question—?" Emma realized and her mouth opened, ready to scream.

But Miyuki shoved her hand into the girl's mouth.

"They'll hear us," Miyuki whispered.

Olivia poked her head down between them. "Why would she need to scream?"

Miyuki highlighted the ten rats with her flashlight. They finally scattered.

"Gross," Olivia said.

Emma nodded with Miyuki's hand still stuck in her mouth.

"Is the floor moving?" Nadia asked, still behind Olivia on the stairs.

Miyuki gestured to Nadia. Olivia nodded and turned around carefully on the narrow stairs to tell Nadia.

Now Olivia's hand was stuffed in Nadia's mouth.

"Can I take my hand away now?" Miyuki asked.

Emma nodded.

"Would you move off the stairs, Emma?" Olivia asked.

Emma didn't want to, but she hopped off anyway. Her eyes were still focused on the rats scurrying up and down the hallway.

Olivia jumped off the stairway too.

"See down the hall? That looks like a mechanical room," Miyuki said. "The one with the lights shining out of it?"

"Yes, I see it. We need to take a look."

"But what about the rats?" Emma asked.

"They're disgusting, but they won't bother us," Olivia said. "C'mon, Miyuki."

Miyuki shined the flashlight down the hall as they went forward.

"Emma and I will guard the stairs," Nadia said, her feet still not touching the floor of the tunnel.

"Do you two want to stay here with the rats, or get out of the tunnel?" Olivia asked.

"I want out of this tunnel. It smells like a garbage dump," Emma said.

"C'mon then."

Miyuki led the way through the tunnel, brushing the rats out of the way with her sneakers. Emma glued her hand to her mouth the entire time, trying her best not to freak out. Nadia only closed her eyes and gritted her teeth as all four Gems went the full length of the tunnel and reached the mechanical room.

Inside the mechanical room was an old generator. It maintained a steady hum as it supplied power to the warehouse. No one was inside the room, but there was another door. One that Olivia was sure led into the warehouse itself.

"Place yourselves on either side of the door just in case there's a goon on the other side."

Miyuki took the right side of the door while Emma and Nadia waited on the left.

Gently, Olivia pulled open the door and peeked. She touched her finger to her lips before slipping out the door. Miyuki followed.

The warehouse was wide and open. Voices bounced off the walls as Olivia made a beeline straight to a stack of rotting wooden pallets. They were only five feet high but good enough to hide behind. Miyuki joined her and peeked over the top pallet.

On the other side of the warehouse was a temporary lab. A long white table had been brought in. On top of it was a microscope, a couple of Bunsen burners, beakers, ring stands, a few cylinders and test tubes in a rack along one wall. Next to the rack was a whiteboard with chemical equations scribbled across it.

Five goons stood around the lab. Three of them came with Van Zanten, so the other two must be guards, Miyuki reasoned. She then had a good look at Tyler Cho.

The man's right cheek was swollen with large purple bruises. He had one black eye, and judging by the way he listed over the table, Venomous had broken his spirit as well as his face.

Miyuki glanced back to the door. Nadia was crouching near the floor. She paused before launching herself behind the pallets. It was a tight squeeze.

Emma peeked around the door. Her eyes danced back and

forth between the pallets and the open space. Miyuki could tell she was losing her nerve. She flashed Emma a supportive smile and motioned her to come join them.

Emma hesitated.

"C'mon, Emma," Olivia whispered.

Van Zanten's voice bounced off the walls as his egg eyes tried to focus on Tyler. "Don't be so grumpy. We're almost finished with you."

The voice made Emma retreat behind the door.

"Damn it." Olivia whispered.

Miyuki watched Van Zanten's goons on the other side of the warehouse. Their attention was on their boss and Tyler, not the door. So Miyuki ran from the pallets to the half-open door, collected Emma, then ran back over to the pallets.

"Sorry, I panicked," Emma whispered. "Did you see what they did to him?"

The Gems listened as Van Zanten continued. "Soon your family in Hawaii will be out of danger and you'll be released."

Tyler stared at the hard concrete floor and said nothing.

"I hate talking to people as well. Much rather send an email. Or a letter. No one sends letters anymore. A shame, if you ask me." Van Zanten tossed a glance at one of his goons. "Do you write letters to your mother?"

"I send her a card," the goon replied in a German accent. "One for Christmas and one for her birthday."

"You send her cards, but no letters?"

The goon shook his head.

"Like I said, a damn shame." Van Zanten sighed and faced Tyler again. "Sorry for the conversation. Had to give you an update in person because I don't know the address to this stupid place. Otherwise, I'd send you a letter."

"You could have sent me a text and I would have related it to him," the German goon said.

"What?"

"If you didn't want to talk to him, you could have sent me a text and I would have read it to him."

Van Zanten stared the German down. "That was a joke."

"Oh."

"Do you think I'm funny?" Van Zanten asked. His face was so serious.

The German thought about it and began laughing. "Yes, that was funny I—"

Van Zanten punched the man in the nose with the butt of his gun. The German man keeled over and held his nose as blood leaked out between his fingers.

"Now that was funny," Van Zanten replied, not smiling as he put away his Glock. The Dutchman headed for the door with his three goons following. They all stepped through the door as Van Zanten closed and locked it. Miyuki could hear the Range Rover's engine come alive. Soon the vehicle's sound faded as it drove away.

The German goon with the broken nose went over to the sink and ran some water. He tore a bunch of paper towels to stem all the blood.

The second goon with curly blond hair smiled. "Told you he was a lunatic."

"Go get the first aid kit before I bleed to death," the German said.

"Can I have my lunch now?" Tyler asked, his voice tired and gravelly.

Curly Hair walked over to a plastic bag and took out a carryout food container that Van Zanten must have brought. He placed it on the table and turned away.

"What about plasticware?"

Curly Hair sighed and tossed the plastic bag over to Tyler. "Dig for it yourself." He then went over to a far table.

Both guards had their backs facing the pallets. Miyuki sensed the opportunity.

"Let's go get them!" Miyuki whispered.

"Wait, we need to plan this. Nadia and I will—Miyuki!"

Miyuki was already on her feet and running right at Curly Hair near the far table. Gaining momentum, Miyuki jumped in the air and rotated her body around...bringing her right leg around like a fist. Curly Hair turned just in time to receive Miyuki's full-powered kick in the face. He went down to the floor.

The German turned from the mirror, still holding his nose. "*Wo ist das?*"

Emma ran at him, sweeping her leg under his and flipping the man on his back. Nadia backed her up by kneeling down and readying herself for a palm strike to the man's face.

"No! Please, not the face," the German pleaded.

175

"Don't move," Nadia ordered, keeping her palm up and ready.

The German didn't move as Emma removed his pistol from its holster, then checked to see if the chamber was loaded before pointing it at the German. Nadia stood up.

"Miyuki, behind you!" Olivia shouted.

Miyuki turned. Curly Hair had shaken off her attack, and his fist was coming at her face. Miyuki ducked on instinct as the fist missed her. She then shoved him away with her foot.

Curly Hair stumbled but didn't fall down. He swiveled back around with a gun.

Miyuki was too far away to strike him. She braced herself for the shot that was coming her way.

The gunshot sounded like a cannon as it echoed throughout the empty warehouse.

Curly Hair gripped his forearm, as his gun was now pointed at the floor. Miyuki took the gun away and looked behind her. Emma was holding a gun using both hands. A trickle of smoke rose from the muzzle. The girl's eyes were wide open.

"Nice shot, Black Opal," Olivia said.

"He was going to shoot her," Emma said, more like she was reassuring herself not anyone else.

While Miyuki held Curly Hair at gunpoint, Olivia checked the man's bullet wound. "Going to need to put a tourniquet on before he bleeds to death."

The German complained, "What about my nose?"

"We'll think about it," Olivia said.

"Would you like me to take that?" Nadia asked Emma.

Emma handed her the pistol. The girl's white skin looked pale as she quivered a little.

Miyuki gave Emma a supportive hug with her free arm.

"Do you need the first aid kit, Mr. Cho?" Olivia asked.

Tyler Cho closed his eyes and a tear escaped, but the man didn't cry. "That man lied to me. He said he represented a Dutch beverage company wanting to hire me and produce their own version of Thunderdog."

Olivia leaned down. "Can you tell us what's going on? What's Van Zanten planning?"

CHAPTER 31

Miyuki watched as Olivia used the first aid kit to put a tourniquet on the shooting victim's arm. He was weak from the loss of blood, but he was still alive. Next, Olivia cleaned up Tyler Cho's face as best she could. He still looked like a boxer after ten rounds in the ring.

"They wanted you to make a stronger concentration of Thunderdog?" Olivia asked.

"Yes, they called it Thunderdog 2.0," he said. "At first, I resisted. I wanted no part of this scheme. I'm a food engineer. I want nothing to do with turning food into a weapon."

Olivia touched his swollen cheek with the antiseptic swab. "But they started beating you."

"And threatened to kill all my family in Hawaii. I had no other choice but to believe them, so I did the things Van Zanten wanted."

"How concentrated is the new drink?"

"Possibly fifty percent. As an energy drink, it would put most older adults into cardiac arrest."

"And teens?"

"Van Zanten wanted to be careful with that age group. Not strong enough to cause heart attacks, but any child with a weak heart would die if they drank it. No beverage company in the world would release such a dangerous drink to the public."

"You did," Olivia said.

Fire came back in Tyler's eyes. "The original drink was safe. It didn't cause anyone to have heart attacks."

"But it did mess up teens. Made their emotions go bonkers."

"There's no proof of that."

Olivia pointed to herself. "I'm the flipping proof." She went on to tell Tyler about the night she brought home a can of

177

Thunderdog from school, and after she drank it, how she almost killed her best friends. "Don't you dare tell me that drink is safe. Because I know it's not. And our group has evidence to prove it."

"Not all teens act out on Thunderdog," Tyler said quietly. "Perhaps it's only a percentage with the same common characteristics inside their brain chemistry that the drink is affecting in this way." Tyler looked up at Olivia. "I can fix it. I can alter the chemistry of the drink so it won't hurt people."

"It's too late for all that. You've helped a bunch of terrorists make a bad drink even worse. Now, what's Van Zanten planning to use this new version for? Poison a city's water system? Use it as part of some weapon system?"

"I don't know. He doesn't talk about that around me."

"Are you sure? Can't you think of anything?" Olivia asked.

Tyler shrugged.

"Fantastic. Fantastic that is. Guess we'll go take a lovely drive back to Van Zanten's house to go ask him." Olivia sighed. "I flipping hate the idea of trying to sneak into that place. He has cameras, spotlights, an open field surrounding his house. Guards patrolling outside. Not to mention a knife-wielding maniac inside along with more armed guards."

"Could we call in a strike team?" Nadia asked. "Let them do all the hard work."

Olivia thought about it. "A strike team takes about twenty-four hours to assemble. Here in Indonesia, it might take even longer. I'm worried that, if Van Zanten finds out we have Tyler Cho…"

"It could spook him enough to move his operation."

"And we'd have to look for him all over again." Olivia folded her arms together. "If Venomous is planning something, time is not on our side."

"That means we must sneak into his house," Nadia said, not excited about the idea.

"I don't see an alternative. Do you?"

"I do," Emma said. "Why don't we ask these dudes?" Emma went up to the German with the bloody nose. She grabbed a chair and sat next to him.

"These are hired goons, Emma. Van Zanten wouldn't tell them anything."

"How do you know that?"

Olivia turned over the German's wrist. "See? There's no small scar from an incision. No computer chip implant. All Venomous operatives have a chip implanted in their wrist."

Emma rolled her eyes. "I knew that."

"Oh, that's right. Has your boyfriend shown you his yet?"

Emma glared.

"Like I said, you're wasting your time."

Emma turned away from Olivia and focused on the guard with a new determination. "Is your nose still bleeding?"

"I won't tell you anything," the German said.

Emma blinked. "Please?"

The German laughed.

"Did Van Zanten create a new batch of this Thunderdog 2.0 drink?"

"I have no idea."

"So…you're just a guard?"

The German lowered the bloody rags from his face. His nose was red, but the bleeding had stopped. "I'm a mercenary."

Emma's eyebrow went up. "Wow, a mercenary? You do look pretty buff. Have you been to a lot of places?"

The German sat up. "Syria, Iraq, Thailand, Ghana, Yemen, Columbia…I've been almost everywhere."

Emma leaned in. "Do you get lonely?"

The German didn't respond.

Emma's face softened. Miyuki could tell the actress was in full control of her. "Do you miss…being with a woman?"

Nadia shot a glance at Olivia. Both girls appeared alarmed and wondered the same thing. What was Emma doing?

Miyuki was curious too.

"Are you married?" Emma asked.

The German paused, still unsure of what was going on. "I was…once."

"She left you, didn't she? Because you were gone so much."

He was surprised. "How did you know?"

"My mom left my dad because he was always on the road with his job. It was hard on her."

Miyuki was confused. Emma's mom died years ago and her parents were together. At least, that was what Emma had told them.

"Yeah…I guess it was hard on her. I didn't protest when she wanted the divorce," the German said.

"I could tell. You seem like a decent guy." Emma touched his cheek. "Are you feeling better?"

"Yes…thank you."

Emma went in closer; her lips hovered above the older man's lips.

Now this made Miyuki uncomfortable. The man was three times her age and didn't look at all like Matthew McConaughey.

"Black Opal…are you sure that—"

"Shut up, Sapphire. I'm busy." Emma said, still focused on the German.

She was quiet for a moment before asking, "Do you want to kiss me?"

Miyuki really hoped that Emma knew what she was doing.

The German's eyes danced around Emma's face, then turned away in disgust. "*Nein*—you're young enough to be my daughter."

Emma drew away from the man. "Oh…I understand."

"Sorry."

"It's okay," Emma said, tossing a wink at the Gems, who still had no idea what she was doing. Emma turned her focus back to the man. "Your daughter…what's her name?"

"Hanna."

"How old is Hanna?"

"Fifteen."

"That's how old I am."

Emma was lying. But Miyuki didn't say anything.

"Does Hanna know what you do?"

"Yes…she doesn't like it."

"She wouldn't approve of you beating a man up inside a warehouse or trying to kill four teen girls who are young enough to be her friends."

The German lowered his head. The subject bothered him.

"If Hanna were here, how would you justify all this to her? How would you explain to her why…you did all this?"

The German thought about it. "I can't."

"And if you knew that the man you worked for…was planning to hurt more kids her age with this new energy drink…and you did nothing about it…how would you justify that?"

Emma gently pulled his chin up so the man would look at her. "What would you tell Hanna right now…if she asked you to help her find out where they're producing that drink?"

CHAPTER 32

Miyuki followed the route on her phone as Nadia drove the Subaru back into Jakarta. Tyler Cho hadn't wanted to come with them. Fearing Van Zanten would capture him again, the man wanted to get out of Indonesia as quickly as possible. However, Olivia made Tyler feel guilty again about his involvement and his responsibility to help them make things right.

The German guard didn't know much about Thunderdog 2.0 or what Van Zanten planned to do with it, but he did remember one time having to deliver some of Tyler Cho's work to a place called Jakarta Chemical Limited. It sounded like a promising lead. One the Gems wouldn't have gotten without Emma's help.

"That was a clever interrogation, love," Olivia said from the back seat. "How did you know about his wife and daughter?"

Emma bathed in the adulation. It was rare coming from Olivia. "I pickpocketed the guy's wallet and there was a picture of his wife and daughter inside. Then I checked to see if he was still wearing his wedding ring and he wasn't."

"Wait, I didn't see you swipe his wallet."

Emma paused as a sly grin formed on her face. "I have a confession to make. When I was little, I wanted to be a magician."

"A magician, really?" Nadia glanced in the rearview mirror.

"I was into it. Magic kits. The wand. The black hat...everything. I was good at palming coins and making them appear in different places. And to do that well, you have to have nimble fingers."

"Oh...you took out his wallet, opened it, and searched through it using only one hand?" Miyuki asked. For them not to see it, Emma must have done it behind the German's back while still blocking their view of the interrogation.

Miyuki was impressed.

"But what possessed you to—" Nadia had trouble saying it. "—

come on to him?"

Emma leaned forward from the back seat. "I was thinking that if he loved his daughter and had any kind of conscience, then throwing myself at him should make him uncomfortable. If he rejected me, that confirmed that I could use the daughter angle to flip him to our way of thinking. And it worked."

"What if he had kissed you?" Nadia asked.

Emma frowned. "Then he was a pervert and I would have given him another bloody nose."

It was getting dark as Nadia parked the Subaru on a side street. The Gems observed the building across the street for a moment. It was a medium-sized corrugated metal building with big delivery bays in the back. Two smokestacks rose above the building, yet produced no smoke. A Jakarta Chemical Limited sign was on the exterior. There was an administration office or wing on one side of the building, opposite the delivery bays. There were no cars in the parking lot. The place looked deserted.

"I don't see anyone," Nadia said. "It could be closed for the night."

"I'm sure they'll have guards," Miyuki said.

"Right, so we'll be careful. Let's have a look around," Olivia said.

The Gems and Tyler went over to the administration wing. There was the main office entrance, but it was locked. They walked along the perimeter of the building and noted the outside doors used heavy bolt locks.

Olivia also noted a card reader near each door. "I wonder if they have any guest key cards at the front desk that we can swipe. Think you can open those front lobby doors, love?"

Nadia paused. "I might be able to if there's a latch on the back side."

"Why don't we walk into the building instead?" Emma asked, referencing one door that was cracked open. A small rock held it open enough for the automatic locks not to re-engage.

Olivia examined the door. "Either someone's been here and they're coming back...or they're still inside."

"I feel lucky," Emma said.

"I'd feel luckier with a gun," Olivia said.

Nadia gave her the one Emma took from the German.

"Are you sure?"

"I have my shockingly effective hairbrush. I'll be okay."

Miyuki checked the gun she had obtained from the curly-haired man. It was loaded and the safety was off. She gripped the weapon and pointed it towards the ground. "I'll go in first."

Olivia gripped hers too. "I'll back you up, love."

"I'll stay in the car," Tyler announced, already turning around.

"You must come with us," Nadia said. "We'll need your help identifying the material we find."

Tyler closed his eyes and sighed. He walked back over to the Gems. "Please don't let me die."

Miyuki ignored him as she carefully opened the door and stepped inside the building.

Each hallway was lit, as if it were any normal business day. The Gems passed by several administration offices, flipping on the light switches and searching the contents inside. So far they had found nothing of interest.

A sign pointed towards lab one.

Miyuki took the lead and headed inside the lab. There were several long countertops, but unlike Tyler's makeshift lab, this one had deep metal sinks and gas valves built into the counters. There were cabinets stocked with beakers, flasks, cylinders, Bunsen burners, and other lab equipment. Under the countertops were drawers. Miyuki assumed it was for more lab equipment storage. There were numerous posters about safe lab practices on the wall, written in both Indonesian and English. Along with a large periodic table of elements.

She also could smell the latex from the gloves.

Curious, Tyler Cho searched through the lab. He stopped at a white dry-erase board.

"I recognize this," Tyler said. "These are drink formulas. A beverage company gives this to the factory when a drink is ready to manufacture." He pointed to one formula on the board. "This is the new formula they made me create."

"We need to destroy this lab," Miyuki said.

"It's on the torch list," Olivia said. "But we still need to know what they're going to do with the formula."

"Maybe this will tell us." Nadia flipped up a notebook computer on a desk near one of the counters. She powered it on.

"But you don't have their password," Tyler said.

Nadia smiled and held up a yellow sticky note. "You mean this username and password stuck to the computer?"

"That's very sloppy," Tyler said. "I would never run my lab without basic security protocols in place."

"Luckily for us, criminals aren't exactly the most intelligent people in the world." Nadia's fingers zipped through a few menus. "Here's a folder labeled Thunderdog 2.0."

Everyone crowded behind Nadia.

"It was under the folder named Smells Like Teen Spirit."

"Oh…that's the title of a Nirvana song," Miyuki said, happy to add the detail.

Nadia clicked open the folder. Inside were numerous documents and videos. She clicked on one document. "Here are some chemistry and math calculations involving the ratio of Thunderdog 2.0 syrup to a cubic foot of drinking water."

Tyler squinted at the screen. "The base syrup is how a soft drink is delivered to bottling plants, and clients such as restaurants that have drink fountains. The syrup canisters are connected to the drinking water and balanced to the correct ratio. However, Thunderdog is an energy drink. It's designed to be put in cans not distributed like a fountain drink."

"Click on one of the videos." Olivia pointed at the screen. "How about this one, what's the title?"

Nadia leaned forward and read. "Papua New Guinea Village. Before Experiment 13."

She clicked on the video. It opened up and played.

The location was a small village composed of a handful of dwellings in poor shape. The camera moved through the village as kids ran around playing tag. Near them, a group of older teens played a competitive game of soccer while older villagers watched. It was a small, but active little community. The video stopped.

Nadia then clicked on the video labeled—After Experiment 13.

It was the same village. But now everyone was dead.

Adult bodies littered the ground while numerous dwellings were engulfed in flames as the camera showed it all. Someone screamed. The camera whipped over and settled on a teenage boy who was tied up, his face drowned in fury. Like a rabid animal, the teen boy fought against his shackles. He was so overwhelmed with emotions that he hadn't realized his arm was dislocated. The camera moved away from the teen and began showing the bodies of dead children.

That was Nadia stopped the video herself. She said something softly in Arabic. Miyuki assumed it was a prayer for the dead.

There was a collective silence. No one had been prepared to see that.

Nadia composed herself and clicked on another document related to Experiment 13. She cleared her throat and began reading. "Experiment thirteen was a complete success. Seventy-four men, one hundred and twelve women, and thirty-seven children under the age of twelve were killed by twenty-three teenagers ranging from ages fourteen to nineteen. After the teens finished with the village, they turned on each other. Out of the twenty-three teenagers, there was only one survivor."

Tyler Cho's hands quivered on the counter. "This is madness. Complete madness."

"How horrid. How bloody horrid," Olivia said.

Miyuki's chest burned with anger. She knew her father wasn't responsible for this new twisted use of the drink. Yet she also knew that she wouldn't rest until the people responsible for this were hunted down and captured. And if she kicked one or two of them in the face, it wouldn't be the worst thing she ever did in her life.

Nadia plugged in her portable drive. "I'll collect this information and send it to Mrs. B."

"I had no idea. Who could think of doing such things? And I helped them." Tyler fell to his knees, overwhelmed by the situation. The Gems swarmed around him. "I should have been a real man and killed myself before helping them. Yes, I should have killed myself."

"You didn't kill those people," Miyuki said. "The evil men who kidnapped you did, and we must stop them."

"I had a hand in their deaths…how am I not responsible?"

Miyuki didn't have an answer for him.

Nadia returned to the laptop and took out the thumb drive. "All done."

"Right, we should keep searching for more clues," Olivia said.

The Gems and Tyler Cho slipped out of lab one and searched through more of the offices. There were two other labs, but they didn't find anything new. They also noticed a controlled area where liquids were being produced, but that area was shut down and locked up tight. The Gems couldn't find a way into that section of the building.

Miyuki opened one of the double doors that led to the warehouse that was adjacent to the landing bays.

It was dark inside.

Miyuki found a light switch. Only a few lights above the large warehouse flickered on, but enough for her to make out the cement floors with painted lines to show walking paths that followed the industrial shelving along the walls. Most of the shelving was empty of product. However, there were many giant tanks on the opposite side of the warehouse. And that was where Miyuki saw five security guards on the floor.

"What is it?" Olivia asked.

Miyuki ran over to check on them. None of them had a pulse. They all had deep slash wounds that were fresh.

"This is why we didn't see any guards," Olivia said, joining Miyuki.

Soon Emma, Tyler, and Nadia walked over.

"Someone *was* here before us," Nadia added.

"But who?"

"I think you should tell us," Oscar van Zanten said. His voice made everyone turn around.

Near the double doors were eight Venomous goons. Their AR-15 rifles were now pointed at the Gems. Van Zanten was right in the middle of them.

Miyuki gripped the gun in her hand. Even if she did manage one shot, those AR-15s would kill them way before she got off a second.

"We don't know who did this," Olivia said. "Maybe they tried a can of that new energy drink you've been developing here." Olivia's eyes burned. "You're a bunch of evil bastards, you know that? Using a bunch of innocent villagers as your test subjects."

Van Zanten shrugged. "Can't sell a weapon that doesn't work. You need to show potential buyers a demonstration."

"Is that what Venomous plans to do with it?" Miyuki asked.

Van Zanten clapped. "Bravo, you've cracked the case. Gold stars for the Nancy Drew Mystery Club. Your only mistake was opening the side door and tripping the silent alarm." The man moved forward. "My boss would love to torture the Gems in the most horrible of ways. Delivering all four of you alive would be a major boost to my rank. Unfortunately, you've demonstrated time and time again to my predecessors that you're far too dangerous to be kept alive. So in that case, I pick option two."

Van Zanten motioned to one of the goons who took out his phone and began recording. "To satisfy my boss, I'll record your deaths for him. That way he can relish your demise just as much as I will enjoy executing it." Van Zanten looked up at the ceiling. "This lighting is not ideal. Can you still see them?"

"It's good enough, boss."

"Excellent. Are we recording?"

The goon nodded.

Van Zanten gave the Gems a smirk. "Remember to please scream for the cameras."

"Mr. Van Zanten!" A Malaysian man with a dress shirt burst into the warehouse.

The Dutchman sighed. "Stop recording. What is it? Can't you see we're making a movie?"

"Sorry, sir, but I checked the outside tanks. They're empty."

"What do you mean the tanks are empty?"

"The beverage is gone. Someone has emptied all the outdoor storage tanks."

"Check those over there." Van Zanten pointed at the indoor tanks near the Gems.

The Malaysian man went over to the tanks, being careful to keep his distance from the Gems. He checked the dials of each tank. "Yes. These are empty too, sir."

"What the hell is going on?" He eyed the Gems. "What did you do?"

"Is something wrong, Mr. Van Zanten?" a voice asked.

Mr. Nagumo emerged from the shadows alone, dressed in his familiar white business suit with a large lapel pin of the Japanese flag on his blazer. Had he been there this entire time?

"Mr. Nagumo, I wasn't aware that you were back in town," Van Zanten said, unshaken by the man's appearance.

"I came to protect my investment."

"Your trip was unnecessary." Van Zanten referenced the Gems with his gun. "As you see, we have the situation well under control. These girls will not be bothering us any longer."

"I'm afraid that will not solve all of our problems, Mr. Van Zanten. Take you, for instance."

Van Zanten lowered his gun. "Me? How am I a problem?"

Mr. Nagumo's expression hardened. "At its core, Venomous is only another criminal organization. A highly capable one, but still…you're basically one step above my country's *Yakuza* or the Russian Mafia."

Van Zanten angled himself towards Mr. Nagumo, the gun still at his side. "I should remind you…sir…that you might take better care in how you speak about your partners."

Without blinking, Mr. Nagumo's steady eyes scanned the eight men with guns. "My partners? My Euro-trash partners who represent the worst in Western decadence and greed. Inferior white men who are full of arrogance and cultural imperialism. You were only a means to an end. I would never trust *gaijin* such as you."

Van Zanten and Nagumo locked their attention on one another.

Each man assessing the strength of the other.

Van Zanten's grip tightened on his Glock. "Then this is goodbye."

"Yes." Nagumo was still. And unarmed.

"Good." Van Zanten aimed his gun at Nagumo…

But like a dark cloud, twenty men dressed in black dropped from the ceiling with their samurai swords.

CHAPTER 33

Before Van Zanten could fire his Glock, the tip of a samurai sword went through his chest. He died instantly as he fell to the ground. The men in black swarmed over the Venomous goons, their swords slashing and hacking with expert precision. One shot was fired randomly but had no effect. Within twenty seconds, Van Zanten and his Venomous goons were all dead.

Miyuki began to breathe again. These men in black were terrifying. Was Mr. Nagumo here to save them? Why was he here anyway?

Emma stood close to Miyuki and touched her arm. This entire situation was scary and Miyuki agreed. Even Olivia and Nadia closed ranks near them as Tyler Cho hid behind the Gems.

As the men in black watched, Mr. Nagumo eased up to Van Zanten's body and spat on it.

"White trash," the man said in English.

Mr. Nagumo's "samurai" formed a half-circle around Tyler and the Gems. Thanks to all the blood, their swords had a rose-colored sheen to them.

Miyuki went into a shooting stance.

Olivia noticed and did the same.

"Can you shoot all of them before they hack us up?" Nadia asked in a hushed tone.

"Looks like we'll have to find out," Olivia said, her voice serious.

"We will do what we must do," Miyuki added.

"I love you, guys," Emma said, her voice wavering. "I just want you all to know that."

"Shouldn't we try to negotiate?" Nadia asked.

"If you've got an idea, love, now's not the time to be shy."

Miyuki aimed with care. Her finger rested on the trigger.

I will do what I must, she told herself.

"*Yameru!*" Mr. Nagumo yelled.

The men in black put away their samurai swords in one fluid motion.

Mr. Nagumo's steady eyes found Miyuki. "It appears that Ichirou's oldest daughter is much more than I first anticipated. Often I have heard Mr. Van Zanten talk about the Gems with the most scathing hatred. I must say, I'm impressed that you're a part of this, Miyuki." Mr. Nagumo paused. "It is Miyuki, yes?"

"*Hei*," she says.

"Your father is a good man. Ichirou has his weaknesses, but he's a good manager. Someone you can rely on. And he has a moral compass. Believes in right and wrong. I needed a man like that to report us to the government."

Miyuki cocked her head to the side.

"Yes," Nagumo continued, "I knew that your father had a good friend at the Japanese foreign minister's office. It was logical that he would eventually contact him as the problems with Thunderdog mounted."

"You wanted the government to stop you from distributing Thunderdog?" Miyuki asked.

"When it was apparent that Thunderdog was dangerous, I wanted to study it. See if it could be adapted into a silent weapon. Volunteering to recall the drink ourselves would avert any government attention as to what I was planning to do. Any changes to Thunderdog would be seen by the outside world as the company making the product safer for the consumer."

"Thunderdog was never intended to be used to harm people," Tyler said.

"Your new drink was a happy accident, Mr. Cho. An accident that fell right into my lap." Mr. Nagumo shook his finger at Tyler. "And the process would have gone smoother if you weren't such an ass. My plan was to work with you at the company to improve Thunderdog after the recall. That way my secret plans would be hidden under the Shiawase Nomimono company bureaucracy."

Mr. Nagumo sighed. "But you did a naughty thing, Mr. Cho. Your ego couldn't take the voluntary recall, so you stole the formula and wiped it from the company's computers. Do you see? I had to come up with a different strategy. Therefore, I made a deal with Venomous. They would lure you back with a fake job offer.

Then kidnap you and the formula so we could both develop a weaponized version of Thunderdog." Mr. Nagumo referenced Van Zanten's body. "But as you see, I've altered our original deal."

"You created a new batch of the energy drink. That's what was in those tanks, right?" Olivia asked. "Where did it all go?"

"That shipment left a few days ago. I was slowly siphoning off each tank right under Mr. Van Zanten's nose."

"Why? What's the hurry?"

"That information is irrelevant to our discussion. Do you mind lowering your weapons? I see no swords being presented in your direction."

Olivia lowered her gun.

As Miyuki lowered hers, Mr. Nagumo approached her. The man's hardness softened. His face reflected a loving grandfather. Not a man who just ordered the death of nine men.

"There is no need to fear me," he said in Japanese. "You are among patriots. I will not kill a pure-blooded Japanese girl. Our country needs strong young women to help with the cause." Nagumo referenced the Gems with his eyes. "Why do you make friends with such people? The blacks are hopeless and the Arabs are just as bad. And the white girl? She is the very ideal of Western arrogance. A blond symbol of its decadence. All of them are far below us. Japan has always been the jewel of the world. She has evolved into a world power by the force of her will. The will of the samurai. Japan went from making swords to making aircraft carriers in less than one hundred years. After American bombs flattened our land, we rose to become one of the most dominant economic powers on earth. Miyuki...can you not see that we are the highest developed race on the planet? America. China. South Korea. They all once *feared* us. We were *their* masters."

A fire burned inside the old man's eyes. "Never forget that you are Japanese."

Miyuki thought it was a moving speech. An emotional outpouring of sincere passion from the old man. But he was wrong. Mr. Nagumo referred to her friends as if they were only colors on a wheel. Like most racists, he ignored the unique human trapped under the label they snap on top of each person they see. And Mr. Nagumo's views about Japan were from another century. That wasn't the Japan she wanted her brother and sister to live in.

"I've always loved my country," she said, which was true.

"Then you should fight for her future," Nagumo said. "You should join us."

The suggestion shocked her.

"Is it such a foreign concept?"

Mr. Nagumo's words sparked an idea. A crazy idea. A reckless idea. An idea that could get her killed. But like most ideas Miyuki came up with, she brushed aside the danger because the thrill of doing it was far too enticing for her to resist.

However, Miyuki would have to give the performance of her life to pull it off. Something that would make a professional actor like Emma swoon with praises.

Miyuki sighed and relaxed her stance. "I don't know. I—I'm loyal to my friends. What you ask…it's difficult."

"I understand. Loyalty is important. I respect that. We must be able to trust one another." Mr. Nagumo's eyes scanned the Gems. "If I release your friends unharmed, would you stay with us as you consider my offer?"

"As your prisoner?"

"As my guest."

"The Gems will still try to stop whatever you're planning," Miyuki said.

"Perhaps. Unfortunately for them, my plans are already in motion. They're too late."

"What if I stay with you, and then I say no to your offer?"

"Then I will fly you back to Osaka and you can see your family again. As I said, we do not kill full-bloods."

Miyuki pretended to think about it. "I'll stay if you let everyone go. Including Tyler Cho."

Mr. Nagumo frowned. "I was looking forward to using my sword on Mr. Cho's neck."

"Everyone is allowed to leave. Or I must refuse your offer immediately."

It was a bold ultimatum. One that could easily blow up in Miyuki's face. But like a good poker player, Miyuki could feel the cards turning in her favor…it was time for her to act upon it.

"You test my sincerity like a shrewd businessman, young lady," Mr. Nagumo said. "Very well. As a token of my sincerity, we have an agreement."

Mr. Nagumo gave the order and his men backed up against the walls. "You are free to go. However, if you come back, my men will hang you on the walls with their swords. Are we clear?"

Olivia shot a puzzled look at Miyuki. "What's going on?"

"Mr. Nagumo has graciously allowed you to leave the building without dying. I highly suggest you do so…quickly." Miyuki laid out the command with some arrogance. As if she were frustrated with Olivia. As if Miyuki were having second thoughts about the group too.

Olivia straightened her back. She didn't like what Miyuki said. "Right, let's go, then." She headed for the exit with Emma, Nadia and Tyler following her back to the double doors. When they reached them, Emma hesitated.

"Come on, Miyuki."

"I'm staying."

Olivia turned around. "No, you're coming with us, love."

"I choose to stay with Mr. Nagumo. It's okay. I'll be fine."

"We're not leaving without you," Emma said.

"Please," Miyuki said. "It's okay. I won't be harmed."

"My sincerity has limits," Mr. Nagumo said. "I wouldn't test them."

"You must go," Miyuki said.

"Why are you staying?" Emma asked.

Nagumo stood next to Miyuki. The man's hand rested on the square of her back and Miyuki did her best not to be repulsed by his touch. "Your friend is seeing the light. She feels the spirit of her Japanese ancestors living within her. She requires the freedom to find out who she really is."

"You're a Gem and you're coming with us, love," Olivia said, the gun still by her side.

Miyuki appreciated her friends willingness to stand up to Mr. Nagumo in order to save her. But they were messing up her plan, even though they didn't realize it yet.

"A lot has happened with my family in the last few days," Miyuki said. "You all know this. I've been separated from them for years, and now I've realized that I've forgotten what it means to be Japanese. I need more time to explore these feelings. I need time to consider my options."

"Consider your options? What the hell does that even mean?" Olivia asked, her voice on edge.

"It means…perhaps, I don't want to be a Gem anymore."

"What rubbish is that?" Olivia asked. "You took an oath."

Olivia was already on her high horse. That made Miyuki happy. Perhaps her plan would work after all.

"Please leave. It's okay," Miyuki repeated. "I want you all to be safe."

"Not if it means you're a prisoner," Emma said.

Miyuki had to make them leave or they would upset the entire apple cart.

"It's my choice, Black Opal. Please respect my decision and get out!" Miyuki yelled, sprinkling her words with anger and contempt.

Emma's eyes softened. She exchanged glances with Olivia and Nadia. Her friends all looked equally mad and confused. Tyler Cho didn't care. He walked through the double doors without hesitation.

"We should go," Nadia said. "There are higher priorities at stake here. We need to consider that." Nadia backed up towards the doors. Olivia reluctantly followed.

As Emma turned to leave—

"Black Opal?" Miyuki walked over to Emma and lowered her voice. "Always remember that anyone can be a Ryan Raymond."

Miyuki then retreated towards Mr. Nagumo.

"C'mon, Black Opal," Olivia said over at the exit.

Emma hesitated, as if unsure about what her friend had said. The girl then jogged back to the double doors. The Gems left the building and Miyuki behind.

CHAPTER 34

Miyuki felt uneasy on Mr. Nagumo's company jet. Even though the flight attendant was friendly to her, Miyuki knew that Mr. Nagumo didn't automatically trust her like some long-lost sister. The man wasn't an idiot. He had confiscated her phone and anything else that appeared suspicious enough to be a secret device. Her "cosmetics" were tossed in the trash and she herself was searched meticulously.

No, it was crystal clear that Mr. Nagumo was giving her a chance to prove her loyalty. To prove she was a "pure-blooded" Japanese girl, as Mr. Nagumo would say. Miyuki also had a sinking feeling that if she failed this test, he would kill her. However, if this gave Miyuki an opportunity to find out his plans and stop them, it would be worth the risk. If she had to die in order to save thousands of innocent people, Miyuki was ready to make that choice.

During most of the flight, Mr. Nagumo talked about his family. His father had worked in a Toyota factory. His mother was kind, yet very strict. They were people Mr. Nagumo grew up to respect. And his family was proud of the company he led.

Miyuki acted interested…but secretly she was bored.

"Are we flying to Japan?" Miyuki asked.

"Eventually," Mr. Nagumo answered. "We must make a stop in Hong Kong first."

"Oh?"

"I have business at the company's China offices. Even though my outside activities are important, a Shiawase Nomimono president's job never stops. However, before we land. I have a test for you."

"What test is that?"

Mr. Nagumo handed Miyuki a satellite phone. There was a number already selected.

"You see, we've planted a bomb inside the Chos' family restaurant in Hawaii. At this moment, it should be lunchtime there. Rest assured that I will kill Tyler Cho in my own good time. However, I wish to send him a message first." Mr. Nagumo pointed at the phone. "When that number is called, and the person on the other end hears the word *Hei!* Then he will detonate that bomb."

Miyuki froze. Her mind went through images of Tyler Cho's father, mother, and sister working at the restaurant. Not to mention all the customers enjoying lunch, unaware they would become casualties in a senseless vendetta from a man who couldn't stand anyone who talked back to him.

Mr. Nagumo brightened. "It's time to show your loyalty to the cause, my dear Miyuki."

"I don't understand," she lied, trying to delay him as long as she could.

"You will give the order to kill them. You met his family, did you not? Tyler told Mr. Van Zanten that his family was contacted by two young women representing the company. He assumed it was the same ones who came after him in Hong Kong. That was you and the Gems, correct?"

Miyuki nodded.

"I know this may sound cruel. However, we all must do unpleasant things for the cause. A true Japanese patriot must put aside her personal feelings. She must be dedicated to eradicating anyone who is not of pure Japanese blood. We must make our nation strong, Miyuki. We must show the world that Japan is reawaking. That the giant is rising from the ashes once again. That her people are willing to do whatever must be done in order to forge a new future. Now, give the order and show your loyalty to Japan."

CHAPTER 35

Emma weaved her way through all the tourists as she followed Tyler Cho, Olivia, and Nadia along the sidewalk of the outdoor shopping center. A couple of hours ago, their flight from Jakarta had landed in Honolulu as the Gems escorted Tyler back home to his family's restaurant. Visiting any shopping center would normally brighten Emma's mood and stop her from worrying about anything. Add to that an outdoor Hawaiian shopping center —where the weather was perfect and the sales were numerous— the girl should be in heaven right now.

But Emma worried about Miyuki. Worried about what was going through her mind. Worried that she might never see her friend again.

The Saigon Palace had a large window decorated with a hand-drawn mural of Chinese characters that Emma didn't understand. As she followed everyone inside the restaurant, Tyler's sister was the first one to greet her brother. The commotion drew Tyler's father and mother out of the kitchen. They were also happy to see him. His father guided everyone to sit down at some empty tables.

"My job prospect didn't pan out as I hoped," Tyler explained to his family. He then introduced the Gems by their code names while Olivia explained to Tyler's family about the organization they worked for. It was very general information. Something Mrs. B had always coached them to say if anyone was ever curious. It was enough to let the world know that the Authority was out there, but without giving any specifics.

"Please stay for lunch," Tyler's father said. "I insist."

"That's not necessary, sir," Olivia replied.

"You don't have a choice now," Tyler said with a grin. "My father will not allow you to leave without a belly full of food."

The delicious smells rising from the buffet were making Emma a little hungry. Soon, the Gems were given samples of all the main dishes. Tyler's father even prevented them from getting the food from the buffet, preferring to deliver it to their table instead.

While Tyler and the Gems enjoyed lunch, three familiar faces stepped inside the restaurant.

"Table for three?" Tyler's sister asked the unusual-looking group.

"Actually, I think that table over there is expecting us," the older woman said in an English accent.

Emma couldn't believe it. Mrs. B, Mr. E, and Aardvark walked over and sat down at their table. Olivia introduced them to Tyler Cho and his family.

"Our large friend here is very hungry." Mrs. B referenced Aardvark. "Can you please show him your lovely buffet? If you don't mind, I would like a private moment with your son."

After Tyler's mom and dad left with Aardvark, Olivia briefed Mrs. B and Mr. E on what had happened in Jakarta.

"We reviewed the information Sapphire sent us. It was unnerving. Thunderdog 2.0 is a threat that must be dealt with immediately. We have issued a worldwide alert for Nagumo and any information regarding him or his Emperor's sword associates."

"Every station has been notified including other national intelligence agencies," Mr. E added. "Nagumo mentioned that his plans were already in motion, yes?"

"That's correct, sir," Olivia said.

"Can we please talk about Miyuki?" Emma asked.

Mrs. B sat back. "You do mean Ruby isn't that correct…Black Opal?"

"Sorry, ma'am. Yes, can we discuss Ruby's situation?"

"Are you sure she switched sides? Ruby offered to stay so you all could leave. In light of the situation, the decision was a logical sacrifice in order for the information you found to be sent to us,"

"Do you have evidence that she's given Nagumo any useful information?" Mr. E asked.

Olivia glanced at Emma and Nadia. "We don't have any evidence of that."

"Ruby could be acting as a conduit to leak us information on his plans," Mrs. B said. "However, based on what Ruby has been through with her father the last few months…I'm concerned that Ruby could be vulnerable to Nagumo's influence."

Emma thought about what Miyuki had said to her.

Anyone can be a Ryan Raymond.

What did she mean by that? Did that mean she was going to be a traitor like Ryan was?

But wait…Ryan was still helping her with information. And he still never told Venomous about the Gems true identities. Ryan was playing the middle and doing whatever he could to survive. So… was Miyuki doing whatever she could to survive? Or did that phrase mean she was going to feed them information like Ryan did?

That must be it! Miyuki gave her a message only Emma would understand.

"Ruby is only pretending to consider his offer so she can leak us information."

"How do you know that?" Nadia asked.

"Before we left, she mentioned Ryan to me. *Anyone can be a Ryan Raymond*…that's what she said. She only told me because I understood Ryan."

"Ryan's a traitor," Olivia said. "She means anyone can be a traitor."

"Not in that context. Ruby meant it in a different context. She meant someone who can play down the middle. I mean, seriously, do you think Ruby would turn on us?"

"Well, you were talking to Ryan without us knowing about it," Olivia said. "We could have easily suggested you were a traitor."

"Stop that right now," Mrs. B said. "Black Opal brings up a valid point. It's more likely Ruby is playing along with Mr. Nagumo's game in order to get closer to him."

"The Emperor's Sword are a militant group, yet they're desperate for acceptance into mainstream Japanese society," Mr. E said. "If Nagumo is as passionate to the cause as I feel he is, then the man might believe that he can actually turn Ruby into a follower."

"And Ruby could have felt that from him and acted upon it," Mrs. B said. "Sapphire, you have excellent observation skills. Do you think Ruby is a traitor?"

Nadia thought about it. "No, ma'am. I think you're right. Ruby could have felt the opportunity and went with her intuition. She tends to do that a lot."

"She always has been a jump-first-and ask-questions-later kinda girl," Emma said.

Olivia was quiet for a moment. "Perhaps you're right. I shouldn't throw her under the bus so quickly."

"Intelligence work can be like chess," Mrs. B said. "You must examine every possible move...before you make it. Perhaps Ruby didn't examine her move, but she saw an opportunity to take out the queen...so she took it."

"May I say something?" Tyler asked.

"Yes, of course," Mrs. B said.

"I owe a lot to you all. The Gems saved me from captivity, and my family and I are grateful. I don't think I've deserved it, but I want to help you stop whatever Mr. Nagumo is planning. And I want to help get Mr. Kaiko's daughter back to him. I've done him a great disservice and I must make amends for what I've done."

Mrs. B nodded. "Your cooperation will be of value to us, Mr. Cho, if you can assist our scientists in finding a way to counteract the effects of the drink...if the worst-case scenario happens."

"If Mr. Nagumo is as ready as he says, we can expect an attack at any moment," Mr. E said.

CHAPTER 36

Miyuki stared at the phone number. Such a simple thing to do, but with such deadly consequences. The engines of the corporate jet droned on continuously. The luxurious cabin didn't seem so comfortable now. It held a dirty secret. The president of a respected Japanese company was a madman wanting to blow up a restaurant full of people to prove someone's loyalty.

Or was this to be only the start? The opening notes to a violent opera that would bring grief to millions of people. It was the violent opera that Miyuki feared. If she didn't do what Mr. Nagumo wanted, she would never find out what he was planning. There would be no chance to stop the audience from gathering. To stop the curtain from rising as the performers entered the stage. To stop the orchestra from playing the first act.

What was the right thing to do? Should she sacrifice a handful of innocent people in order to save thousands or perhaps millions later?

If Miyuki chose the restaurant, could she ever forgive herself? How could she ever look into the mirror and see herself as a person working for the benefit of mankind?

Yet…what else could she do?

Mr. Nagumo sat back down and put on his seat belt. This allowed his white suit to partially open, revealing a gun and a holster hidden on his belt.

The gun gave Miyuki another crazy idea. However, if one took the idea of killing innocent people off the table…this crazy idea became the only logical choice she had. If she captured Mr. Nagumo, there was a chance she could somehow make him talk or give up enough information to help the Gems stop his plans. It was a slim chance. However, it was enough to risk her life on.

Miyuki's thumb hovered over the call button of the satellite phone. She breathed deeply and readied herself.

Her thumb pretended to hit the button as she brought the phone up to her face.

Miyuki waited. "*Hei.*" She put down the phone and closed her eyes.

When she opened them back up, Mr. Nagumo greeted her with a smile. "I'm proud of you, Miyuki. You have taken the first step towards a larger purpose. Congratulations."

Miyuki slipped off her seat belt and brought the phone back over to Mr. Nagumo. He took it and checked the screen. His expression changed.

"You lied!"

Miyuki struck him in the nose as hard as she could. Mr. Nagumo grabbed his nose and tried to lean forward, but the seat belt kept him in place. Miyuki pulled open his suit and took the gun. Mr. Nagumo tried to grab her hand, but Miyuki hit him in the face with the handle of the gun, causing him even more pain.

She pointed the gun at Mr. Nagumo. He tried to stand, but the seat belt pulled him back down once again. "You will answer all of my questions or I will blow a hole in this plane. Perhaps even take out an engine or two."

"And you will die as well." Mr. Nagumo checked his bruised nose for blood.

"I'm willing to die. Are you?" Miyuki asked. Her voice sounded crazy and on edge.

A man dressed in black entered the cabin from the cockpit side. The man unsheathed his samurai sword.

"Stand down," Miyuki said. "Will your sword stop my bullets? Put it down. Now."

The man in black checked with Mr. Nagumo, who nodded. His associate put down the sword. Miyuki motioned him to switch places with her.

Now, Miyuki had both Mr. Nagumo and the man in black at gunpoint. But her back now faced the front of the plane.

Miyuki failed to notice the flight attendant sneaking in from her service nook near the cockpit.

"Who are you going to see in Hong Kong?" Miyuki asked, confident she had the upper hand.

The flight attendant slipped off one of her pumps and turned the heel side up. She pressed a hidden trigger and a blade snapped out, making the heel a knife.

The sound made Miyuki look behind her just as the woman made her attack.

Miyuki spun out of the way, but the move caused her to lose her grip on the gun, which dropped to the cabin floor.

As Miyuki shoved the woman down, the man in black plowed into Miyuki. His momentum shoved both of them into the front portion of the cabin.

The flight attendant raced over to help. She stepped over Miyuki and raised her deadly-sharp pump.

Miyuki kicked her in the thigh, disrupting her attack.

The man in black tackled Miyuki to the carpet. She rolled on top of him in an effort to break free...but that was when his hands found her neck. He rolled on top of her and squeezed tight. Miyuki squirmed and shook and did everything she could to push him off. But the man's arms were strong and they couldn't be dislodged. The flight attendant recovered as well. She slipped her pumps back on and kicked Miyuki hard in the side, over and over again.

Miyuki tried to ignore the pain and focus on getting the man to stop choking her.

But she was failing.

Miyuki could feel the energy leaving her body, evaporating like dew when the morning sun came up.

She was losing the battle.

Her eyes searched for something...

Anything that would help.

All she saw was the cabin door and the yellow handle.

The pain of the kicks radiated through her side. Her mind wanted to drift away, to forget reality. Miyuki wanted to fight the feeling, but she didn't have the strength. Crazy thoughts circled her mind like caged rats knowing they were about to die. Miyuki let the animal inside her take control. To do whatever it would take to stay alive. The animal bit down hard on the man's hand.

The man in black grunted and his grip loosened just enough for her to push him away.

Miyuki heard herself scream as she stumbled over to the cabin door. Gripped the big yellow handle. And with whatever strength she had left, Miyuki pulled the handle all the way up.

The world exploded.

CHAPTER 37

After the loud bang, the first thing Miyuki felt was a massive pull as the cabin door, the flight attendant, and the man in black were sucked out of the plane like pieces of fuzz near a vacuum cleaner. A torrent of trash followed, hitting Miyuki in the face and making her squint. The rush of air screamed into her ears. Then came an awful metallic grinding noise as the jet's engines surged. Half of her own body was hanging outside the door as this mysterious force clawed at her, wanting Miyuki to get out of the plane too. Her shoes were already gone and her jeans were barely hanging on to her body. The only thing keeping Miyuki inside the aircraft was the death grip she had on a handle just inside the cabin. Her fingers throbbed, unable to cope with the force trying to rip them away.

Miyuki shut her eyes and focused on holding on as best she could.

The aircraft dropped like a rock. So rapidly that Miyuki felt like she was floating above the floor. But she knew if she let go, she'd be floating over the clouds without a parachute.

Eventually, the aircraft went below ten thousand feet and the pressure equalized. The force pulling at her, wanting to kill her, had slackened, allowing Miyuki to pull herself back into the cabin. She took a moment to celebrate the fact that she was still alive.

After her ears popped due to the altitude change, Miyuki picked up more unsettling noises from the end of the airplane. The engines didn't sound normal. They were still surging up and down.

Miyuki stumbled towards the main cabin. Her mind was dizzy and she felt like she would pass out at any moment. Her eyes caught a few oxygen masks swinging from the ceiling. Maybe that was why she was feeling dizzy.

Miyuki shook off the feeling and headed towards one of the oxygen masks. She put the cup over her mouth and breathed in.

The cool air filled her lungs and her body relaxed. She had to take a few more deep breaths before she looked around the once luxurious cabin. There was nothing on the floor or the tables. All the dishes, cups, bags of chips, everything that wasn't nailed down was gone, sucked out through the door.

Mr. Nagumo was still in his seat, his seat belt preventing him from being sucked out. There was a large gash on his forehead. Something must have struck him on its way out the door. Mr. Nagumo wasn't moving.

When Miyuki felt like she had enough oxygen, she moved over to him and checked his pulse. He was still alive. In response to her touch, Mr. Nagumo's eyes drifted open. He mumbled something Miyuki couldn't make out. She placed an oxygen mask over his mouth and the man breathed on his own. Miyuki hoped he would be well enough to answer her questions.

That was if they survived the landing.

Miyuki went to the cockpit. The two pilots still had their oxygen masks on. "What has happened back there?" one pilot asked in Japanese. "We had to make an emergency descent."

A warning horn blared.

"Engine one is on fire," the other pilot said.

"Let's shut it down." The first pilot repeated his question to Miyuki. "What happened?"

"The door was opened by accident. Two people were thrown out of the aircraft."

"I see," the first pilot said. "They must have been sucked into engine one. Strap yourself in. We'll have to make an emergency landing in Hong Kong."

Miyuki left the cockpit and sat near Mr. Nagumo. His eyes fluttered as he drifted in and out of consciousness. The man's head wound appeared deep and it was bleeding. Miyuki searched some of the cabinets in the galley for a first aid kit.

The jet made wide turns, a sign it was maneuvering into an approach for a landing.

Miyuki found a kit inside one cabinet. She also saw Mr. Nagumo's personal luggage. Since the cabinets closed with latches, the contents inside had escaped the typhoon. She took out the first aid kit and the luggage. First, Miyuki treated his wound, then bandaged it up as best she could. Miyuki then dug around in Mr. Nagumo's luggage and found his laptop.

She powered it up.

The pilot came over the cabin speakers. "Ten minutes to an emergency landing. Get into crash positions, please."

Miyuki didn't have time to prepare for a crash. She didn't want to let this chance to find out Mr. Nagumo's plans elude her. First, Miyuki went through his emails, scanning them for anything out of the ordinary. She did find one email from a festival event company. They thanked Mr. Nagumo for his generous sponsorship of something called TeenPeace. She glanced over the emails and found another one regarding TeenPeace. Mr. Nagumo had told the organizers that Shiawase Nomimono was planning to unveil a new drink called Teen Spirit. And Mr. Nagumo thought TeenPeace would be the perfect venue for it.

Miyuki's heart skipped. Was Teen Spirit actually Thunderdog 2.0?

"Five minutes to landing."

She did a local search of his laptop for anything referring to Teen Spirit. Miyuki found a folder with a PDF map and a few highlighted Shiawase Nomimono bottling plants. According to the map, not all the company's bottling plants were being used. Only certain ones near a few select cities.

Miyuki looked over the emails from TeenPeace again. There was a brochure attached to one email. She clicked and it opened. *TeenPeace, the biggest music festival since Live Aid. Ten cities. Four continents. Over one hundred artists. And one great cause.* Miyuki continued reading. And as she did, it became more and more obvious what Mr. Nagumo was planning. She had to call someone and warn them.

Miyuki searched the cabin for the satellite phone. But it was gone, most likely sucked out of the aircraft.

The jet's landing gear rumbled under her. They would be on the ground soon.

Miyuki found a chair, put on her seatbelt and assumed a crash position. It was okay, she told herself. Emma's grandmother had made all the Gems memorize her home phone number so they would always have someone to call if they lost their phone and needed help. Once they landed, Miyuki would borrow someone's phone and call California.

A few minutes later, the wounded jet touched down on the

runway. Even with the damaged engine, the pilots were able to stop the aircraft on the runway. The engines were shut down. Miyuki could hear the sirens of the fire engines approaching. Hopefully, there would be an ambulance for Mr. Nagumo. Despite what he was planning, she didn't want him to die. Maybe if the man still respected her, Mr. Nagumo could be convinced to do the right thing and call the entire scheme off.

A Hong Kong firefighter climbed through the open cabin door. Since Mr. Nagumo had a head injury, the firefighter took him out of the parked jet first as Miyuki followed him down to the airport tarmac. Additional fire crews arrived and doused the engines with fire retardant while Mr. Nagumo was placed into a waiting ambulance.

Miyuki needed to stay with him. She ran up to the medics. "Excuse me, that man is my uncle," she said in Mandarin. "May I ride in the back?"

The medic opened the back door for her.

"Wait, just a moment please," An airport policeman jogged up to her. "You must stay here. We have some questions for you."

"That is my uncle." Miyuki pointed. "He has a bad head injury." She summoned a few tears just in case.

The policeman checked with the medic, who told him Mr. Nagumo's condition wasn't critical.

"I'm sorry, you must stay," the officer insisted.

"Which hospital are you taking him to?" Miyuki asked.

The medic told her before jumping into the ambulance. The lights flashed and the siren wailed as the emergency vehicle sped off down the airport service road.

Miyuki noted that she wasn't the only one the police were talking to. Another officer was speaking to the two pilots. They were referencing Miyuki a lot with their hands. When that police officer spoke to the other police officer, Miyuki found herself in handcuffs.

"What's going on?"

"You are being detained." That was the only thing the policeman said before they placed her inside a windowless police van and shut the door.

When those doors opened again, Miyuki found herself being pulled out and escorted inside the Hong Kong terminal. Curious passengers watched this teen girl in handcuffs as the officers took her to the airport police substation. Miyuki was put into an interrogation room, where they chained her handcuffs to a metal table and made her sit there for at least an hour.

"What am I doing here? I have done nothing wrong," Miyuki said in Mandarin.

An airport police sergeant took a seat opposite her. The sergeant examined her wallet and passport that she had in her pockets. He did not answer her question.

Miyuki repeated it. "What am I doing here?"

The sergeant tossed her passport to the side and cleared his throat. "Did you pull the release lever to the cabin door while the aircraft was in flight?"

Something told Miyuki she'd better not admit to that. "No, the door must have failed somehow."

The sergeant watched her for a long moment before speaking again. "Two people fell from the sky. From about seventeen thousand feet. A very awful death. Some might say being burned alive would have been better."

Miyuki felt that some might say the way those two "innocent" people were trying to kill her...and the fact they were most likely part of Mr. Nagumo's racist hate group...well, some might say tossing them out of a jet would be most appropriate under the circumstances. Still, Miyuki took no pride in what she had done. If there were another way, she would have chosen that option.

"I see you feel remorse after what you've done." The sergeant was good at reading her face.

"May I have access to a phone?" she asked. "If you allow me this...I will confess all that I know."

"A full confession from a member of the Gems?" a male's voice said in English. "I'm all ears."

Miyuki's eyes wandered over to the interrogation room door. There, standing in a business suit, was Volleen Woo.

"Nice to see you again, Ruby."

CHAPTER 38

The lunch they had at the Chos' family restaurant was some of the best Thai food Emma had ever eaten in her life. The yellow sauce in particular was extra yummy. Aardvark ate seven plates of food (yes, seven!) before the man acted like he was full. Tyler's father joked that if Aardvark was a regular customer, they would have to open another buffet just for him.

That was when Mrs. B received a call and went outside the restaurant to take it.

"I've eaten enough noodles to float back to Japan." Mr. E smiled.

"The food was delicious," Nadia said. She asked Tyler's father about Vietnam and about how he and his wife settled in Hawaii.

But soon Mrs. B came back inside with some news. "A Shiawase Nomimono company jet made an emergency landing in Hong Kong. Reports say a door blew out, causing an emergency decompression. There was also an engine fire. We checked the flight plan and the jet took off from Jakarta."

Emma sat up. "Do you think Miyuki was on board?"

"I would say it's likely."

"Yes, that's not a coincidence," Mr. E added.

"Reports also indicate that two people died," Mrs. B said. "There's no information as to who they were."

A cold and awful realization pressed against Emma's heart. "You mean Miyuki is…?"

"We don't know that," Mrs. B said.

Darkness fell around Emma as if someone had switched off the light. She covered her face as her body began to shut down. It was like her father's plane crash all over again. Emma couldn't face another death of someone she adored.

Someone held her. "We can't assume anything yet," Nadia's

soft voice reassured Emma. "Don't lose hope. She's so smart. I'm sure she found a way to survive."

But the grief rolled out of Emma like a tidal wave, and there was no way she could hold it back. The sobbing began in earnest as Nadia held her tighter. Someone else touched her shoulder.

"Give her a chance, love," Olivia said, her voice positive. "Sapphire is right, She's a resourceful girl. If there was a way to get herself out of a jam, Ruby would find it."

"I agree," Mrs. B said. "Go to Hong Kong and find her."

As their flight from Hawaii landed in Hong Kong, Emma was still upset about Miyuki. What had happened on that plane? Was Miyuki injured? Was she still alive at all? It drove Emma crazy with worry.

She still had nightmares about her father's death. Her mind always tried to reconstruct the last minutes of her father's life, even though she was not there to witness it. Sometimes her father told Emma he loved her. Sometimes he was so disappointed not to be in her life. Sometimes Emma died with him. Her father's regrets changed a lot in her nightmares, but the ending was always the same. Now Miyuki would be a part of that same nightmare.

Emma shook away those thoughts. Nadia was right, they just didn't know what had happened, and killing Miyuki off before knowing the facts would be unfair to her friend. Emma had a right to be hopeful.

Getting on board this commercial jet in her current frame of mind was torture. She almost refused. Even thought about taking a boat from Hawaii to San Francisco so she would never have to fly again. However, Emma was willing to go through the emotional torture of flying to Hong Kong if it meant there was a chance to find Miyuki alive.

A hand touched her arm. "How are you feeling?" Nadia asked, concerned.

"Better. Now that we're on the ground," Emma said.

"Some detective work should keep your mind occupied, love. We'll go to the airport's administration office to gather some information about that emergency landing, then work from there." Olivia turned to Nadia. "Think you can do your assistant for the company act again when we meet them?"

"Yes, I packed my business suit in my carry-on."

"I only hope Miyuki's okay," Emma repeated.

"We'll find her. One way or the other, we'll find her," Olivia said.

"Let's hope it's the alive way," Nadia added.

Emma agreed.

The Gems followed the passengers across the Jetway and into the main Hong Kong international terminal. They circled around the massive blocks of seats filled with passengers near the gate area and followed signs that directed them to the women's bathroom. Nadia headed inside to change clothes. To kill time, Emma's nose tracked down a nearby coffee place, and she bought herself and Olivia two lattes. She also picked up a tea for Nadia before waiting near the bathroom.

Soon, Nadia emerged looking like the sharp businesswoman she'd projected while visiting the Chos' restaurant.

"Well?" she asked.

Olivia handed her a steaming cup of tea. "You look perfect."

Nadia blew off the steam and sipped. "Do I have enough time to enjoy my tea?"

Olivia glanced at her phone. "Sure, why not? There's a table over there."

The three Gems sat down and relaxed. As Nadia and Olivia went over how Nadia would approach the people in the airport administrative office, Emma watched all the passengers making their way across the concourse. A tall Australian man with a backpack. A family from Iran trying to find their gate. An Indian mother and her daughter laughing. A businessman walking briskly across the floor while speaking Russian into a phone. So many different kinds of people. So many different languages. It was a people-watcher's dream.

Emma sipped her latte and wondered if there were any shops near them. Not that this was the best time to go shopping, but it would help her relax and get her mind off less pleasant things. The faraway jewelry store caught Emma's attention. Its glass displays of expensive jewels sparkled even from this distance. It wouldn't hurt to look, would it? She didn't have to buy anything.

That was when Emma caught sight of two airport police officers watching her. At first, she blew it off. Emma was used to guys staring at her because...well, she was good looking. But soon it became clear to her that these Hong Kong airport policemen were interested in all three of them. And that could be bad.

Emma leaned casually to the other Gems. "Hey, those policemen are watching us. Over by the jewelry store." Emma leaned back, trying to project calmness.

Olivia took a moment before glancing. "Don't panic. There's no reason for the police to pay us any attention. We've done nothing wrong."

Emma turned slightly and noticed another group of policemen approaching. One of the officers spoke into his radio.

"Sorry, but I think they have a reason."

Olivia saw both groups of officers. "Let's walk that way, but don't make it too obvious."

The three Gems gathered their things and moved away from the officers.

"Excuse me," a policeman called out to them in English. "Excuse me, please."

"Walk faster," Olivia said under her breath and the Gems did. They wove around a few stores inside the concourse before heading straight for the exit to the baggage claim. And that was when a massive Polynesian man blocked their path.

Emma recognized him. Kawiki was a henchman they had encountered on a train in Utah when the Gems were helping Robert escape. Kawiki was one of the three Chinese intelligence agents who wanted to force Robert to work for their government. Emma remembered how strong Kawiki was, and there was no way the Gems were getting through him. Or the ten armed policemen who now surrounded them.

When Volleen Woo emerged from behind Kawiki, Emma knew they were doomed.

The Chinese spy with dangerous eyes wore a nice suit, and his smile made Emma's skin crawl. "It's so nice to have such loyal and dependable friends. Welcome to Hong Kong. We have much to talk about."

CHAPTER 39

Miyuki didn't know how long she had been held inside this interrogation room. They gave her water but didn't allow her to use the restroom or get up from the chair and stand. Volleen Woo asked her about the thumb drive she'd stolen from them in Tokyo. Miyuki told him it had been destroyed and no duplicates had been made. The Authority was ruthless when it came to eliminating new chemical weapons that could be used against civilian populations.

Miyuki didn't know what else to tell him. She feared the next subject would be the Authority itself. Mr. Woo could demand information about who ran it. About who she reported to. And about the identities of the Gems.

The door opened and instead of seeing Volleen Woo, she saw Emma. Her best friend gushed with happiness as she ran over to Miyuki, almost knocking her over.

Emma's hands were restrained, so she rubbed faces with Miyuki like a cat as tears melted her eyeliner. "We thought you were dead."

"It's so good to see you alive," Nadia said, entering the room with Olivia.

"I don't understand," Miyuki said.

"You obviously didn't get sucked out of a plane," Olivia said.

"Oh…" Miyuki realized they were talking about her in-flight mishap.

The airport policemen chained them to the same table Miyuki was at, then brought in four chairs before leaving the Gems alone.

"What happened?" Olivia asked.

Miyuki told them about the bomb Mr. Nagumo wanted her to detonate in order to prove her loyalty to the cause.

"There's a bomb at the Chos' restaurant?" Nadia asked.

"We were inside that restaurant, love."

Miyuki froze and closed her eyes. Her friends didn't know it, but she'd almost killed them.

"What happened then?" Emma asked.

Miyuki told her about trying to take Mr. Nagumo's gun. The struggle with the man in black and the flight attendant. And what happened when she opened the cabin door.

"You opened it during the flight?" Olivia asked, astonished. "You silly cow, you could have killed everyone, including yourself."

"I'm well aware of that now," Miyuki said.

Emma propped her chin on Miyuki's shoulder. The closeness helped Miyuki feel better about her situation. At least she wouldn't face whatever Mr. Woo would throw at her alone.

"So Mr. Nagumo's at a hospital right now?" Olivia asked.

"Far as I know, yes." Miyuki told them about a drink called Teen Spirit that was being distributed to select bottling plants throughout the world, plus the company's sponsorship of an event called Teen Peace.

Emma leaned back. "I've heard about that festival. Kayla wanted me to go with her to the one in San Francisco, but we've been so busy that I turned her down."

"What do you know about it?" Miyuki asked.

"It's like a huge music festival with concerts all over the world. But they plan to start the concerts at the same time so they can claim to be the biggest music festival in the world. TeenPeace is raising money for a bunch of charities, but their main mission is to bring all teens together for world peace or something like that."

"Where are the other TeenPeace concerts?"

"Let's see. Um…I remember Singapore, Melbourne, Seoul, Tokyo, Beijing, London, Paris, Amsterdam, New York, and San Francisco."

"Mr. Nagumo wants revenge against the people who have hurt or humiliated Japan," Miyuki said.

"Besides Tokyo, all the other cities are located within countries that fought against the Japanese in World War Two," Nadia said.

"South Korea and China are direct competitors on the economic front as well," Miyuki added. "I did see one email where Mr. Nagumo planned to distribute the new drink for free in order to promote it. And the festival was going to help him."

"Oh my God," Olivia said "If they hand out that new drink to all those thousands of kids—"

"They'll go crazy and kill each other," Emma said.

"They'll do more than that. Remember that video from the village?" Nadia asked. "They'll riot in the streets and destroy everything in sight."

"It's like the zombie apocalypse…but for real." Emma realized something. "You know what? I think TeenPeace begins tonight."

"Are you sure?"

"Positive."

"And we're stuck in here," Olivia said. "We have to get out." She raised her voice. "Oy, you lot behind the door, I know you coppers are listening to us. Get in here. We want to talk."

Miyuki repeated Olivia's plea in Mandarin and added her own. It was imperative that they didn't waste more time.

Finally, the door opened and Volleen Woo entered along with the always angry lady Miyuki had encountered on Takeshita Street. The other Gems remembered her too.

"Hello, Gems," Mr. Woo said with a grin. "The pleasure is all mine."

The always angry woman dragged in a chair and handed it to Mr. Woo as she fixed a permanent glare at the Gems.

"What's he doing here?" Olivia asked Miyuki.

Mr. Woo sat down. "Your question sounds…a bit silly under the circumstances. Don't you think, Emerald? Or did you forget that Your Majesty's government surrendered Hong Kong back to China? Surely you didn't make such a comical error in choosing to come here."

"We've already been in and out of Hong Kong without you even knowing about it."

"Yes, the Authority uses excellent travel documents and itineraries that fool our immigration officers a little too well for my liking. However, after our encounter in Tokyo, I put Ruby on a special security list. To be honest, I didn't think it would work. However, Ruby was kind enough to cause an air emergency. Her actions provided the airport police with enough cause to hold her for questioning."

"They put my image in their computer," Miyuki added.

Mr. Woo smiled. "And their screen lit up like an American Christmas tree. So they called me."

"Wonderful, you caught us," Olivia said. "But that's not important right now. We need you to send a message."

The man laughed. "The pizza in Hong Kong may not be to your liking, but I will see what I can do."

"We're not joking,"

"People are in danger," Nadia said. "We must send a message to our handler."

"It's of the highest priority," Miyuki added.

"And why would I do that?"

"Because we have information of a pending terrorist attack."

Volleen Woo's eyebrow lifted. "A tainted soft drink that causes teenagers to fight each other? Sounds like an awful Disney channel movie"

So Mr. Woo had been eavesdropping on their conversation. Miyuki thought that was a good thing. Surely he could be made to understand how serious this situation was.

"It's true," Olivia said. "All of it is true. And if you don't let us warn our people—"

"Your request is denied. However, I would like to spend our time together discussing another topic. One I'm more invested in." Mr. Woo eased forward with purpose. "Where did the Authority take Robert and his android friends? You do remember them, do you not?"

Miyuki saw Nadia tense up upon hearing Robert's name again. The other Gems exchanged glances. Miyuki agreed, now wasn't the best time to bring up old adventures.

"We don't have time for that spy rubbish right now," Olivia said. "Thousands of people are about to die and you'll be held responsible because you didn't let us contact our people."

"Haven't you been following the news about those Thunderdog-related attacks?" Emma asked.

Mr. Woo chuckled. "The Western media certainly enjoys their titillating headlines, don't they? I prefer reading literature instead of the news. Much better food for the mind. Don't you think?"

The always angry woman whispered into Mr. Woo's ear, causing him to nod in agreement. "She asks...why should anyone in China care if Japan poisons her allies? I must say, my colleague has a point."

"Wait, she understands English?" Emma asked.

"Yes, it's a requirement for service in the People's Ministry of State Security. But my colleague chooses not to speak to you because you four girls fill her with disgust. I believe she used the term...*biaozi*."

The Gems checked for the translation.

Miyuki's cheeks felt warm. "It basically means...whores."

The females in the room stared each other down.

Even Mr. Woo felt the tension. "We're getting off point here. All I want is the location of Robert and his friends. Tell us that and I'll release you. Then you can run off to stop the big energy-drink disaster."

"You know, if the world finds out that Chinese intelligence knew all about this attack and did nothing to prevent it, you'll lose credibility with every single country in your sphere of influence," Olivia said.

"And it could affect your trade with the West as well," Nadia said.

Mr. Woo stood up and slid his chair to the side. "I see your minds are too preoccupied at the moment. Perhaps spending time at a labor camp will help you focus. Tonight, you'll stay here. In the morning, you'll be transferred to a military prison. But don't worry, I'll make sure each of you has a private cell adorned with soft comfortable sheets for your beds. Then we will continue our discussion over breakfast." He turned to leave.

Miyuki made one last attempt. "The Beijing concert is at Tiananmen Square, isn't it? How many teens can fit inside that square? Thousands? Hundreds of thousands? I will tell you one thing, Mr. Woo. If they all consume that energy drink and something sets them off, those teens will kill every person around that square. Imagine the Great Hall of the People or the National Museum of China engulfed in flames as a mob of thousands rips Beijing apart. Your army will have no choice but to kill that angry mob. All the blood on the streets. Thousands of young Chinese kids dead in the square. This will make the 1989 uprising look like a tea party by comparison."

Miyuki addressed Nadia in English. "Sapphire, do you still have access to those videos? The ones involving the Thunderdog experiments in New Guinea? We need to show Mr. Woo what this drink can do."

CHAPTER 40

Volleen Woo watched the video files of the New Guinea village experiments that Nadia retrieved from her cloud drive. The burning huts. The dead children. The crazed teen survivor. Next, she showed him all the information they had gathered about the logistics of manufacturing five thousand liters of Thunderdog 2.0.

Miyuki watched the man's eyes. He was studying it, taking it in like a computer. Did the man have any compassion? Did he even care about his own people? How could he maintain such a neutral face while he witnessed such horrors? Was the man a human being?

Miyuki reiterated what she'd learned from Mr. Nagumo and his Emperor's Sword group. "Mr. Nagumo allowed the organizers to distribute the drink for free at every concert venue. If we can stop them from doing that, we could put an end to this before it begins."

"They're calling the drink Teen Spirit now," Olivia said.

Again, Mr. Woo was silent, as if his mind were still processing the information. He then left the room with the always angry woman who wanted to kill them.

"Damn it," Olivia said. "I thought we had him for a moment there."

"He's a monster," Emma said. "He didn't shed one tear over that video."

The Gems complained among themselves for about five minutes before Mr. Woo came back inside with four policemen. The men took off their handcuffs.

"I've confirmed some of the information you've given to me," he said, putting a phone on the table. "I will allow you to contact your people and tell them what you've told me. But nothing more."

Olivia hesitated, then picked up the phone. She dialed a public number that the Gems knew the Authority monitored. "Emerald says hello. My internet is down. But I love a good soap opera. Here's one I think you'll enjoy…" Olivia left the appropriate series of code words that identified her as the caller before she gave out every detail that they'd learned about TeenPeace and Mr. Nagumo's plans.

When Olivia hung up, the Gems relaxed. Their warning had gone out. Soon the Authority would use its worldwide network of resources to shut down the distribution of the free drinks or at the very least stop every concert before anything triggered the audience to riot. Meanwhile, Mr. Woo was also on the phone with his superiors, no doubt trying to shut down the Tiananmen Square concert.

When he was off the phone, Olivia thanked him. "I know we've been literally at each other's throats before, but thank you for helping us save thousands of innocent lives."

Mr. Woo only stood there. "I'm afraid our efforts have been in vain. TeenPeace started over twenty minutes ago."

"What about the drink? Did they give it out to the crowd?" Miyuki asked.

Mr. Woo answered with a simple nod. "Perhaps you've overestimated the drink's effectiveness. Perhaps nothing will happen."

The Gems looked at each other. They knew something would happen.

"Is there a way you can fly us to Tiananmen Square?" Olivia asked.

CHAPTER 41

Miyuki and the Gems waited on the airport tarmac with Volleen Woo. Two airport police vans were parked behind them with their yellow flashing lights.

The always angry woman complained to Mr. Woo in Mandarin. "How can you trust them? They will toss you out of the helicopter and kill everyone on board."

Miyuki couldn't believe the woman even asked that. None of her friends were monsters. Now, the Gems had tossed her out of a moving train once, but the woman landed on soft ground and received maybe a few bruises. Miyuki felt that they were kind under the circumstances. The woman did want to kill them.

"I want to go with you, boss," Kawiki said in English.

"Your concerns for my well-being are appreciated, but unnecessary in this instance. Besides, you would not fit into the crowded helicopter, my friend." Mr. Woo glanced at Kawiki's girth.

"I hope you know what you're doing," the woman continued in Mandarin. "I don't want your job if you get killed." She glared at Kawiki. "Come on." The woman marched to one of the police vans as Kawiki lingered.

"I'll be fine," Mr. Woo said.

"Get over here," the woman yelled in Mandarin.

Kawiki reluctantly did as she commanded and left Mr. Woo.

A loud sound diverted Miyuki's attention to the northern sky as a large military transport helicopter floated into view and landed on the tarmac in front of them. A squad of soldiers dressed in full battlefield gear jumped out of the helicopter and formed a ring around the Gems.

"This squad is from the Special Operations forces," Woo said loudly over the helicopter's engine. "If you do not follow any of my commands or make any attempt at hijacking this aircraft, these men have orders to kill you without hesitation. Even if it means sacrificing their own lives in the process. Do we have an understanding?"

"We both have the same goal," Olivia said. "There's no need for threats."

"I'd prefer to think of this as a mutual understanding of the ground rules to our temporary alliance. Shall we get on board?"

Five minutes later, Miyuki felt the transport helicopter rise from the ground as the Gems sat along one wall of the cabin. The inside of the helicopter was sparse and all-purpose, configured for holding paratroopers and supplies not comforting civilian passengers. Miyuki could smell the musky odor from the uniforms of the Chinese soldiers who were stationed all around them. She thought they could use some deodorant.

Mr. Woo had the Gems put on headsets and briefed them on the way. "The police found ten empty Shiawase Nomimono beverage trucks near the square. It would seem the organizers have already distributed the new drink to the crowd. They estimate the number is well into the thousands."

Miyuki closed her eyes. It was bad news. Now all it would take was one small thing to set the crowd off and they would burn the city to the ground.

"How long until we get there?" Olivia asked.

Mr. Woo checked his watch. "Ten minutes. We will land in the square itself."

"Is there a way we can get our phones back?"

"Why?"

"Because Tyler Cho is working with us to find a way to neutralize the effects of the drink. He might be able to help us with this situation if we maintain contact with him."

Mr. Woo took a moment to analyze Olivia's request in his mind before reaching into a bag and handing her one of their satellite phones. "This is only temporary. To contact your people in case they can assist us here. If you use it to escape—"

"You'll kill us. We got that part." Emma smiled at the Chinese soldier next to her. The man didn't react at all.

Olivia turned on her phone. "I'll see if they have any updates." She called another public number, one she had to use more code words for. It took a couple of handoffs until she reached Mrs. B.

After a few minutes, Olivia put up the phone. She looked concerned.

"What's wrong?" Miyuki asked.

"London, Amsterdam, Singapore, Melbourne—everyone is rioting. As soon as the music began, kids began attacking the stages and the venue itself. It's chaos, according to Mrs. B."

"But we warned them."

"Apparently it wasn't enough time."

"What about San Francisco?" Emma asked.

"Mrs. B tells me that the crowd is breaking out of Pacific Bell Park and starting to wreak havoc on the city."

"Do you think Kayla is there?" Miyuki asked.

"I don't think so. Not without me there," Emma said, but then a worried look came over her face. "But Lewis is probably there with his friends."

Now Olivia shared a worried look.

"There must be a way to counteract the effects of the drink," Nadia said. "Some drug or compound that can block it from affecting the brain. I wish I had a better knowledge of the chemistry involved."

"Mrs. B says Tyler Cho's in the lab working on it," Olivia said.

"I'm afraid that won't help us right now," Mr. Woo said. He then gave an order to the pilot in Mandarin as he motioned toward the windows.

Their helicopter circled above the immense plaza known as Tiananmen square. Two giant buildings anchored the square on opposite sides. To the west was the Great Hall of the People, which had hundreds of red Chinese flags along the perimeter of the roof. The entrance boasted twelve giant pillars in front with a large row of steps leading to the ground. To the east was the National Museum of China, one of the largest museums in the world. The structure was four stories tall and sat proudly like a national institution.

In between the buildings, a giant mob of teens was spread out across the plaza. Numerous fires burned around them. Chinese security forces were already on the ground, hitting the angry kids with tear gas. But the enraged crowd only surged forward, pushing the security forces back as more rocks and projectiles were being thrown at them. The Great Hall of the People was protected by a thin line of Chinese soldiers guarding the perimeter. Their guns pointed at the mob. Their eyes nervous. Their fingers lingered on the triggers of their weapons. The teenage mob had spread out like an amoeba, flowing into the neighboring streets in all directions. Smashing cars, breaking windows, beating up anyone in their path.

It was like the end of the world was just beginning.

"We're too late," Olivia said. "Even if Tyler creates an antidote, how in the world do we make all those kids down there take it?"

"Yes, they're raving lunatics now." Nadia stopped herself. The wheels of her mind began to whirl. "Mindless kids highly susceptible to their most primitive instincts."

Miyuki watched her with fascination. Nadia was working out the problem in her head, without a computer, without writing notes to herself. It was like a rush of information was pouring into her mind from who knows where.

"Wait a moment," Nadia said. "I've been thinking about this as a chemical problem needing a chemical solution. Perhaps it's not. Perhaps I should examine this as a psychological problem needing a psychological solution."

Miyuki still didn't understand what she was talking about, but that was okay.

"May I borrow that satellite phone?" Nadia asked.

Olivia gave it to her and Nadia became frustrated.

"What are those blasted code words again?" she asked Olivia.

Olivia called the number and gave out the correct code words for her before handing the phone back to her.

"Thank you." Nadia smiled and waited. "Mrs. B, this is Sapphire. Can you put Tyler Cho on the phone, please? Thank you."

"Got something ticking up there in that brain of yours, love?"

"Maybe. I'm not sure. I have to check on something." Nadia said. "Tyler? Yes, have you come up with anything that will counter the effects of the drink?" She listened. "I understand. Well, I have an idea and I want to run it by you."

CHAPTER 42

The Chinese transport helicopter hovered above Tiananmen Square as thousands of enraged teenagers rioted, tearing apart everything they could get their hands on and setting a lot of fires. The strong smell of tear gas mixed with smoke polluted the air.

Inside the helicopter, Miyuki watched Volleen Woo do a double take.

"You want us to do what?" he asked.

Nadia flashed him a polite smile. "Could you please land us on the stage? I need to use its soundboard."

"Those kids will rip the helicopter apart. Then they will rip us apart. Besides, the stage has a light canopy over it, we can't land there."

"I don't need the stage, really. I need to use the sound system."

"For what?"

"We don't have time, Mr. Woo," Olivia said. "Believe me, if this girl has an idea, we'd better pay attention."

"She's a genius," Miyuki added.

"Let her at least try," Emma said.

For a moment, Mr. Woo watched the mayhem below. Some smaller government buildings on the outskirts of the square were on fire as emergency crews struggled to put them out. Thousands of teens now surrounded the Great Hall of the People. They could easily breach the gates and destroy the inside of the building at any moment. Miyuki could tell the situation was pushing Volleen Woo's limits as well.

"Fine, we'll try to land near the stage," Mr. Woo said as he went forward to tell the pilots.

Soon, the helicopter flew over to the broken stage and began to circle. Miyuki listened to Woo and the captain argue. The pilot was trying to find a place to land near the stage, but it didn't look good.

The ground was still thick with kids and now the downdraft created by the helicopter blades was irritating them.

"They're throwing projectiles at us!" the captain yelled in Mandarin as a rock thumped against his window, leaving a crack. Miyuki could hear rocks and other things pelting the fuselage.

"This is too dangerous!" the captain said as he pulled his stick and the helicopter climbed from harm's way.

"What's going on?" Olivia said.

Mr. Woo came back into the cabin. "The pilot refuses to land. Too dangerous."

Olivia looked out the window. "Can he hover over that part of the stage? There's a portion of it still standing, see that? He could back up the helicopter and lower the back ramp on to that part." She pointed. "Do you see that?"

Mr. Woo nodded, then repeated the instructions to the captain, who shook his head no.

Miyuki listened to the captain's reasons and relayed them to Olivia in English.

"Too difficult? I could do that," Olivia said, "Mr. Woo? Let me switch places with his copilot and let me have a crack at it."

"You know how to fly a Chinese helicopter?" Emma asked.

Olivia blew her off and focused on Mr. Woo. "This is a variation of the Russian MK-912, right?"

Mr. Woo stared at her, trying to figure her out.

"I don't think he believes you," Miyuki said.

"Oy, you have lots of info about the Gems, don't you, Mr. Woo? In your official files?"

"Of course we do."

"Then you know all about my piloting skills, don't you, love?"

Mr. Woo's mouth tightened as if he were forced into making decisions that he didn't want to make. But the man ordered the copilot out of the cockpit and put Olivia in his place.

"I'm in command of this aircraft and I refuse to carry out the maneuver," the captain said, still defiant.

Mr. Woo showed no emotion as he pulled out his pistol and pressed it against the back of the captain's head.

Everyone on the helicopter froze.

"As a commander in the People's Ministry of State Security, I order you to hand over control of this aircraft to this teenage girl or I will make it a sad day for your family."

The captain's defiance melted as he nodded to Olivia.

"I have control of the aircraft," Olivia said.

Miyuki repeated the command in Mandarin and the captain nodded in defeat.

Olivia brought the helicopter around to near the back part of what was left of the stage. The captain leaned forward, his eyes nervous as he said something to Olivia.

Miyuki translated, "He says…there could be wires still attached to parts of the stage. If the blades get caught up in them—"

"Tell him I'll back us in nice and slow," Olivia said. "Just enough so the ramp can reach the stage."

Olivia focused as she rotated the helicopter around, making its back end point towards the portion of the stage still standing. Gentle on the controls, Olivia inched the helicopter backward. Carefully she brought the helicopter's rear within about twenty meters of the partial stage. The captain was shouting out suggestions as he worried like a mom teaching her daughter how to drive. But Miyuki didn't relay his concerns to Olivia. The girl knew what she was doing.

Olivia lowered the back door and extended the ramp as far as it would go. The ramp kissed the stage with two meters to spare. "You'd better hurry up and get out. A gust of wind could throw me into a wire."

Nadia ran across the ramp now acting as a makeshift bridge between the helicopter and the stage. She reached the partial stage along with Miyuki and Emma. The three Gems looked around and it was a mess. Microphone cables were strung out all over. Guitars, a drum set, keyboards, and other instruments had been left behind as the musicians and stagehands ran for their lives. Rocks, shoes, and all kinds of junk littered the stage after the crowd had thrown them at the musicians.

"Look out!" Emma pulled Miyuki down as a rock narrowly missed her face.

"This place is crazy," Miyuki said.

The helicopter moved away from the stage and gained altitude. They were now on their own.

"Over here!" Nadia shouted as she ran towards a large soundboard sitting at the edge of the stage. When she reached it, an old man with excessively long white hair popped out from under the soundboard and pushed Nadia away.

"Stay away from me," the man yelled in an Australian accent.

Miyuki and Emma ran over. The old man saw them and backed up against a wall, putting up his hands like a child about to be beaten. "Please don't kill me!" His voice cracked.

Miyuki could tell the man was terrified. "We won't hurt you."

"We haven't been affected by the drink," Nadia said.

The man didn't understand, but he did lower his hands.

"Sir, do you know if this sound system is still working?" Nadia asked.

"Or do you know someone who can help us with it?" Miyuki asked.

The man was still not sure about them.

Emma gave the frightened man a hug. "It's okay. We're here to help." After that, the man finally closed his eyes and relaxed. "Are you a member of the stage crew?"

The man with long white hair nodded.

"Do you know how to operate this?" Nadia pointed to the soundboard.

"Yes." The man swallowed. "I'm the sound engineer. They went bonkers. The band began to play and the kids went bonkers. They began slamming themselves against the stage like zombies. Strangest thing I ever saw in my life."

"Is the sound system still working?" Nadia asked with a note of desperation in her voice.

"I think so," the man said.

"Do you have an adapter that I could use to plug my phone into your soundboard?"

"Yeah, but why? Music is what made the kids riot in the first place."

"Can you please set that adapter up for me?" Nadia asked. "And I'll need a live microphone too."

Nadia gave the sound engineer her phone while he gave her a microphone. The man then dug through his equipment for an adapter. Nadia walked forward on the stage while tapping her fingernail on the microphone to see if it was working. She shrugged at Miyuki and Emma.

Miyuki turned to the sound engineer. "Is the microphone working?"

The sound engineer was busy working in the back of the soundboard. "Yup. Mic is on and the fader is up. She's good to go."

Miyuki gave her friend a thumbs-up.

Nadia then touched her lips to the mic and shouted, "Hello?"

Her voice thundered across Tiananmen Square, causing Nadia's eyes to inflate with shock. She froze as thousands of angry eyes now turned to her on the stage.

"Say something!" Miyuki shouted.

This was no time for stage fright.

Emma ran over and grabbed the microphone away from Nadia. She addressed the crowd. "Hi, everyone! How are we today? I mean, minus the rioting part of course."

The yelling and angry words were now directed at Emma as the mob slowly closed in on the stage.

"Hey, there's no need for that kind of anti-women language, people," Emma said on the microphone. "We need everyone to calm down. I know we're all super excited about destroying buildings right now...but you guys don't understand. You're all under control of this drink, this very bad drink that was given to you—"

Emma ducked as a shoe flew over her head. "Now that wasn't very nice."

Nadia ran back to the soundboard and Miyuki joined her. The engineer put the finishing touches on an adapter and plugged Nadia's phone into it.

Nadia brought up a menu of her media files. "Play this!"

The sound engineer brought up his fader, and the sound of falling rain on a tin roof echoed over Tiananmen Square.

Emma turned away from the crowd. "What's this shit?"

"Make it loud," Nadia said, "—as loud as you can!"

The sound engineer pumped up the output so loud the ground almost vibrated.

Nadia then ran up to Emma and reached out for the microphone.

Emma frowned; she didn't want to give it up.

Nadia tilted her head and Emma relented.

"Hello?" Nadia asked into the microphone. A loud, scary feedback loop began, but the sound engineer reduced the gain.

"Try it again," he yelled.

Nadia swallowed and spoke into the microphone. "Feel the rain. Feel it touching your face." Her voice was smooth, gentle, and calming. "Feel the rain cascade down your arm. Your neck. Your nose. Feel the chill in the air."

"What the hell are you doing?" Emma asked.

Nadia ignored her and continued speaking about the rain to the mob. How it wet their clothes. How it chilled their skin. How the drops rolled down their arms.

Miyuki looked around the square. Thousands of teens were listening to Nadia. They were standing in space, closing their eyes, and touching their arms and skin. It was an amazing thing to watch.

"Can someone please clue me in on what's going on?" Emma asked.

Miyuki ran over to them. "Let me translate your words so they all understand," Miyuki said. Nadia gave her the microphone. Miyuki repeated the same phrases in Mandarin over and over again, using the same calming voice Nadia did.

Now all the teens were standing in place with their eyes closed. They were touching their skin and listening to her suggestions. The noise of chaos faded as the rain sounds dominated the air for at least a kilometer around the square.

"Relax. Breathe. Feel the water cascading down your body. As if you were taking a shower," Miyuki said.

The crowd acted out everything she was saying as if it were real.

Emma's mouth hung open. She finally understood. "Wow, they're all listening to you."

"Now tell them to sit on the ground and keep calm," Nadia said.

Miyuki repeated the soothing idea in Mandarin. Soon thousands of Chinese teens sat down on the square in unison.

"Oh my God, that's amazing," Emma said.

Nadia touched Miyuki's shoulder. "That should do for now." Nadia gave the microphone back to the engineer and he killed the fader. "Please keep playing the rain sounds until they snap out of it."

Olivia, Volleen Woo, and his soldiers arrived on the partial stage.

"Look at that. It's brilliant," Olivia said.

"I still don't quite understand," Emma asked. "Why are they listening to you?"

Nadia explained, "Thunderdog makes us very sensitive to any kind of emotional trigger. In this case, the music triggered them to act out and become aggressive. Well, I tried to think of something that had the opposite effect. Something calming and soothing."

"So as easily as they could be triggered to become angry and violent—"

"They could also be triggered to become calm and quiet," Miyuki added. "So simple."

"Yes," Nadia said. "I remembered this media file on my phone. I use the rain sounds to help me study. It always calms me down and clears my head."

"And it's very soothing," Miyuki adds.

"Then after we calm them down, we offer a few words of suggestion that help them be more docile."

"What if the music runs out?" Olivia asked.

"It's a looping audio file. It should last long enough for the effects to pass. Tyler Cho believes the drink should wear off like alcohol does."

Miyuki noticed Emma walking back over to the soundboard. She picked up the microphone and pointed to the fader. The sound engineer brought it up and Emma tossed him a smile before walking back on to the stage.

"What is Emma doing?" Olivia asked.

Emma relaxed her face. "Feel the soothing rain as it rolls down your skin. Doesn't it feel so nice, everyone?"

Many teens nodded; they were all in their chill zone.

"How many boys do we have in the crowd tonight? Raise your hands, please."

The ones who understood English did.

A mischievous grin curled up Emma's lip. "Doesn't your shirt feel soaking wet? Doesn't it feel so uncomfortable? If you're a boy, maybe you should take off that shirt."

Nadia ripped the microphone from her hand. "Stop acting silly."

Miyuki noted that many of the boys were removing not just their shirts…but all of their clothes. This made her laugh and clap her hands with delight.

"Oh my God," Emma yelped though the microphone. "They're actually doing it."

"Order them to stop," Volleen Woo yelled. "Such disgusting behavior in front of the Great Hall of the People will not be tolerated."

CHAPTER 43

Three days later, Miyuki found herself alone inside a jail cell, wondering if she would live to see her seventeenth birthday.

After the riots stopped and the kids were peacefully dispersed by the police, Volleen Woo and his soldiers took the Gems back into custody. True to his word, Mr. Woo did furnish them with nice single beds and cushy pillows, but the rest of Miyuki's cell was not so pleasant. The stainless-steel sink and toilet were filthy. The cell block smelled like a mix of mildew and cleaning products. The pitted concrete walls of her cell were gouged out in places. Past inmates had carved out their last words in Mandarin for whoever found them. Other carvings were rambling sentences that didn't make any sense. But Miyuki reasoned that those authors were suffering from an obvious mental breakdown of their sanity.

Miyuki's new reality was perfectly captured by her cell's only source of illumination…one light bulb surrounded by a cage.

Even though the Gems had saved thousands of his people from dying at the hands of the angriest mob in recorded history, Mr. Woo and the People's Ministry of State Security still saw Miyuki and the Gems as enemies of the state.

This morning six guards appeared. One of them opened her cell and motioned for Miyuki to come out. Even if she were capable of taking out six large men, Miyuki would still have to break out of the prison itself. Then somehow escape the Chinese army base that surrounded their prison. Then move undetected across China while the People's Ministry of State Security hunted her down.

Miyuki gave up on the idea as the guards escorted her through two security checkpoints, each protected by new steel doors that the guards themselves didn't have keys to.

Finally, they opened a big door that revealed a large concrete-walled interrogation room. Bolted to the ground was a stainless-steel table with a full breakfast waiting, along with Emma, Nadia, and Olivia.

Mr. Woo was at the head of the table. "Please join us, Ruby."

Miyuki was happy to see her friends, but their sad eyes all told the same story. They were all prisoners too and no one had any hope they would ever get out.

There was a Western-style breakfast on the table. Steaming scrambled eggs. A choice of buttered toast or croissants. Slices of cheese. Bacon. Sausage. Fruit. It was a five-course gourmet meal compared to the plain bowl of mushy white rice they'd gaven Miyuki the past three days.

"Please help yourself," Mr. Woo said.

Emma was the first one to fill up her plate. Her blond hair was dirty and matted together. If Emma's sink was as disgusting as Miyuki's was, she didn't blame Emma for not using it to wash her hair.

Olivia's hair was limp and lifeless too. She crossed her arms. "I'm not hungry."

Nadia hesitated. She wore no headscarf. Her dark hair ran straight down her back and she had managed to braid it at the end. Nadia pushed her empty plate away. She refused to eat too.

Miyuki could smell the cinnamon baked into the rolls and the aroma of fresh bacon. After days of mushy rice, her stomach craved real food. A buttery croissant with some gouda and strawberries would taste so good right now. Miyuki glanced at her empty plate, then over at Olivia and Nadia. Reluctantly, she pushed her plate away as well.

"Not hungry?" Mr. Woo asked.

Emma was slow but picked up on all her friends not eating. She stared at her plate of piping hot eggs and sausage with sadness.

Mr. Woo grabbed his own plate and filled it with two fried eggs, bacon, toast and some fruit. "This is from a five-star restaurant in Beijing. Hate for this to go to waste." He finished putting food on his plate and took a few bites. His mouth savored the food. "The eggs are delicious. Are you sure you don't want any?"

Olivia lifted her chin and shook her head.

Nadia and Miyuki glanced over.

Emma stared at her plate. Miyuki could tell she wanted to eat it so bad. But she put it down and pushed it away. Only choosing some water instead.

"Your choice," Mr. Woo said as he took a bite of his bacon. "Mmm. Crunchy and delicious. So, what should we talk about?"

"Our freedom?" Olivia joked.

"You want to know where Robert is," Nadia said.

"Precisely. You're the smart girl in the group, Sapphire. What you did at the square was clever. I was impressed. Surely you will understand my logic. I want to find Robert in order to study him."

"We've been down this rabbit hole," Olivia said. "We don't trust you and Robert doesn't either."

"He's happy where he is," Nadia said. "And he's not working for anyone, so you don't have to worry about him. He's not a threat."

"What about the androids that made the choice to work with the United States Army? They are a threat to my people."

"That's between you and America," Nadia said. "Robert and his friends are neutral. All they want is to be left alone."

Mr. Woo paused as he buttered a piece of toast. "Well, I did invite you here for a nice breakfast and stimulating conversation. We are getting both."

"We'll never tell you where Robert is," Olivia said.

Mr. Woo chewed on his toast and swallowed. "Perhaps not at the moment. However, we've just begun our little game, and I should remind you that I have many ways of extracting information from people." Mr. Woo smiled and it was the most terrifying smile Miyuki had ever seen from a human being. "If I were you, I would take this opportunity to eat as much as I could. Who knows when I will decide to feed you again."

The steel door groaned as two guards and a man with a miniature pin of the Chinese flag on his black suit entered.

Mr. Woo immediately stood up.

The man with the pin glanced at the Gems. "Are these the girls?" he asked in Mandarin.

Mr. Woo nodded.

"You must release these prisoners immediately."

"Who is making this request?"

"The president. He wants state security to release them."

"Why?" Mr. Woo asked the man. "These girls are spies for a foreign agency. They are enemies of the people."

"The president doesn't have to give you a reason," the man

said, his body becoming rigid.

Mr. Woo weighed his options, then straightened his back. "These prisoners have valuable intelligence that is critical to the security of our country. I refuse to let them go."

"You would refuse a presidential order?"

"I took an oath to the people of China, not to the president. If you have a beef—as the Americans like to say—you can take it up with my boss. The head of state security."

The man with the Chinese flag pinned to his suit acted flustered. Miyuki could tell he wasn't used to people speaking back to him like this.

The man's face then relaxed. A smile cracked through his lips. "I salute your dedication to our country's security. No doubt, her security is safe in your dedicated hands. I will be honest with you. You see, both of the president's teenage daughters were inside Tiananmen Square for the festival. They had snuck out without their security details—this is most embarrassing—the two girls were trapped inside that angry mob. They feared for their lives. The girls mentioned to the president about these foreign girls on stage who calmed down the crowd and saved their lives. Do you see? The president is convinced that your prisoners' actions saved their lives and the lives of thousands of young Chinese citizens. He wants them released as a show of goodwill."

Mr. Woo placed one hand on the steel table and leaned against it. "With all due respect, I can't do that."

"The president is only asking for a favor." The man grinned. "A favor your boss has already graciously accepted."

Mr. Woo looked at him.

"Next time the president asks you for a favor, I suggest that you curb your stubbornness, my friend. Such stubbornness can affect one's career in state security." The man with the flag pinned to his suit headed for the door. "Clean them up and give them back their clothes. We will exchange them tonight in Hong Kong." The man left the room, and the door shut behind him.

The Gems all flinched as a plate shattered against the concrete wall. Two fried eggs slid down the tiles.

Mr. Woo's face burned with anger.

After Miyuki translated the conversation to the others, Olivia grabbed a plate and spooned out a generous helping of eggs and sausages. "Think I'm getting a bit peckish now. What about you, girls?"

"Absolutely!" Emma said.

"The cheese looks quite tasty," Nadia said.

Miyuki smiled and joined in as the Gems enjoyed a delicious and satisfying breakfast.

CHAPTER 44

A few days later, Miyuki and the Gems were back in California. All the girls felt exhausted but were happy that the mission was over. Aardvark picked them up at the airport and drove them out to Napa Valley for one final debrief. The Gems followed Mrs. B into the "jungle," where a green pod sat open. Waiting inside was Tyler Cho. Once Mrs. B and the Gems stepped inside, the pod closed and the cone of silence mode activated.

Mrs. B took out one of the pads from its charging cable and tapped her finger against it. A 3-D display of various rioting images hovered above them.

"Thanks to your warning, Emerald, we did manage to prevent the circulation of the drink in New York City since their portion of the event ran late. However, the situation at the other venues deteriorated rapidly. I must admit, it seemed rather dire there for a few hours. However, your simple solution to the situation, Sapphire, made all the difference. We were able to give that information out to the other cities, and they were able to disperse the rioters peacefully."

Mrs. B switched to images of ambulances and other emergency first responders doing their work.

"Was anyone killed?" Tyler asked. His eyes were tired as if he had gone through many nights of not sleeping.

"There were thousands of injuries. Kids being trampled or beaten up. Attacks on civilians, first responders, police, and military units. It's a miracle, but no one was killed."

Tyler's eyes glistened, but the man didn't cry.

Miyuki felt for him. She knew he didn't wish for any of this to happen. Still, she wished the Gems had been able to stop it from happening at all.

"If the Gems had not been there, many parts of Beijing would have burned to the ground, and there would have been a lot of dead people. The same goes for the other cities." Mrs. B sighed. "I know it doesn't feel like a victory, but it is. Your actions still saved lives. I think you've conducted yourselves admirably and I'm proud of you."

"Did they arrest Mr. Nagumo?" Miyuki asked.

"I haven't heard yet," Mrs. B said. "Mr. E is supposed to—"

An alert message flashed on the 3-D display.

"Ah…speak and ye shall find." Mrs. B tapped her finger on the tablet. "We were just speaking about you, Mr. E."

His image appeared above them. "My sincere apologies for the delay. I just received some new information."

"We had a question about Mr. Nagumo. Have the Chinese authorities arrested him?"

"After he was treated for his injuries in Hong Kong, Mr. Nagumo apparently found a medical technician's uniform and disappeared from the hospital. He hasn't been seen since."

Mrs. B closed her eyes. "That is most annoying. I must tell Chinese intelligence what I think about their lackluster security measures."

"I do have news about Ruby's father. I've learned through my sources that he's about to be fired by Shiawase Nomimono's board of directors. I'm sorry."

The news zapped Miyuki's heart, making it beat faster and faster. Her father would be devastated. His entire life revolved around the company. It gave him a purpose. It gave him an identity. Now the company would kill him. Miyuki was convinced that her father would commit suicide if he had to leave.

Miyuki felt someone move over to her. It was Tyler.

"The board of directors wants to dump this fiasco on your father so they can wash their dirty hands," he said. "They went along with every decision Nagumo made. Even when your father brought up the negative news reports about Thunderdog, they accepted Nagumo's interpretation of the situation instead. They should have questioned his decisions from day one and they didn't." Tyler hesitated. "They should blame me. I lied to your father about Thunderdog. I should be the one who is punished."

"The board has asked Ruby's father to meet with them tomorrow," Mr. E said. "I'm afraid they'll ask for his resignation then."

"He should fight them," Emma said. "Tell the board they're full of—"

"My father would never do such a thing."

"I agree. There is not much her father can do," Mr. E said.

"I'm not Japanese," Tyler said. "But I'm a Vietnamese-American and I'm pissed off. I'll fly there myself and confront those bastards. I'll tell them what I think about them and their cowardly actions."

Miyuki lifted her head. "And I'll go with you. To stand with my father."

"Time-wise that may be difficult," Nadia said. "You'll have to wait until morning to get a flight back to Japan."

Mrs. B turned to Aardvark. "Have my jet ready to go immediately." She addressed Tyler and Miyuki. "It's one of the fastest business jets in the world, plus we've made some special modifications. The jet should get you there in time."

* * *

Eleven hours later, Miyuki and Tyler Cho landed in Japan. Mr. E sent a car to pick them up and take them to the bright yellow office building with multicolored Japanese letters printed at the top.

Miyuki took the elevator to the fourth floor and headed for office 411 with Tyler by her side. She stepped around the office partition and noted the large portrait of that Japanese woman again. She remembered it from her last visit. Miss Tenchi, wasn't it? It was hard not to see her picture around the building.

The secretary was surprised to see Miyuki. The woman dabbed her eye with a Kleenex and bowed. Had she been crying?

Miyuki bowed. "Is my father in?"

"*Hei,*" the secretary said. "He is gathering his things."

Miyuki's heart skipped. Were they too late?

"Did he have his meeting with the board of directors?" Tyler asked.

The secretary acted surprised to see Tyler. "No, he has not." However, the secretary's watery eyes betrayed that she did know what was in store for her boss.

Miyuki slipped into the office and noticed it was almost bare. Some personal items were packed neatly into boxes sitting on the desk.

"What are you doing here?" her father asked.

"I heard about the meeting with the board of directors. Is there anything that can be done?"

Miyuki's father wilted. "There is nothing else. It's merely a formality."

"Tyler Cho came with me. He wants to take full responsibility. This wasn't your fault, Father."

"I don't agree."

"Mr. Nagumo manipulated the situation. Used the company's resources to carry out his evil plans. You're not responsible for that."

"The board does not see it that way, Miyuki."

"Then make them see the truth. Fight for your job."

"The truth is…I supervised Tyler Cho. I gave the approval for Thunderdog. The responsibility lies with me."

"But Tyler lied to you and the company. He's willing to admit that."

Miyuki's father softened as he gripped his daughter's hands. "I appreciate your concern. But I must do this the correct way."

There was a knock on the door as the secretary and Tyler stepped inside.

"The board is ready to see you in the conference room," the secretary said, her voice straining. She was trying not to lose it.

Miyuki's father turned to Tyler. "It's good you are here. We both need to speak the truth."

"Ichirou, you don't have to take responsibility for this," Tyler said. "This disaster rests on my shoulders. I'm the arrogant fool who led us to this calamity."

"It's over," Miyuki's father said. "Let us face the consequences together and be an example to our families on how an honorable man behaves."

The boardroom was large. On the gray walls were large pictures of happy kids and families enjoying delicious and colorful soft drinks. It was the images the company wanted the public to see. Yet, inside the boardroom, there was no happiness. No color. Only six aging Japanese businessmen sitting on one side of a large rectangular desk.

Miyuki was allowed to observe as her father stood before these men and took responsibility for not only Tyler Cho and Thunderdog, but also for not stopping Mr. Nagumo as well.

The board members then spoke in low voices to each other. Their chairs creaked as they leaned towards one side and back.

The air-conditioning came on and released a steady drone through the vents as everyone waited.

Then it was Tyler Cho's turn to speak. He also took responsibility for Thunderdog. For lying about the previous research on the drink. For stealing the Thunderdog materials and trying to sell them. Tyler admitted that even though he'd helped develop a weaponized version of the drink under the threat of death…it was still no excuse for helping a monster like Nagumo.

In the end, Tyler didn't attack the board of directors like he'd threatened to. After he was done, grief pulled on Tyler's face, as if confessing everything he had done had even convinced his own soul that it should be damned.

"The board of directors will now vote," the oldest man on the board said. "Those in favor of keeping Mr. Kaiko in his present position, please raise your hand."

No one did.

"Those opposed."

All six men raised their hands.

"The vote is unanimous. Mr. Kaiko, I regret to inform you…" The older man stopped and stood up immediately.

Everyone turned to notice a very old Japanese woman. She moved across the floor slowly, but with purpose.

All six men stood up and bowed to her.

"Miss Tenchi…we were not aware that you were in the building," the most senior board member said.

Despite her weakened appearance, the woman's voice was strong and vibrant. "I've been listening to what these men have to say. I've also been reading all the reports about what happened in regard to Mr. Nagumo." Miss Tenchi took her time, but she made her way to the middle of the room.

One of the old men carried a chair over for her.

"I prefer to stand for this."

The old man retreated to the table and shoved the chair back into place.

Miss Tenchi examined the room with sharp eyes as if making sure everyone was listening to her before she continued. "In my opinion, Mr. Nagumo's dishonor towards our company and our country was not the result of Mr. Kaiko's or Mr. Cho's actions. The ultimate responsibility for Mr. Nagumo's position and the oversight of that position rested with my board of directors."

The old men exchanged glances.

"You chose not to intervene when the drink was shown to be dangerous to children. You were complacent and did not take action until the government made you take action. Nor did you properly monitor Mr. Nagumo or his decisions. You have failed in your duty to protect the company. My company."

"May we speak to you in private, Miss Tenchi?" one old man asked.

"You may speak to me on the street."

The old men exchanged uncomfortable glances.

"Because I have come to the conclusion that I can no longer trust you to run my affairs. Your services to this company will no longer be required. As the majority shareholder, I hereby dissolve this board of directors."

The six old men looked stunned.

Miyuki wanted to give this old woman a hug.

Miss Tenchi moved over to Miyuki's father. "I accept your apology. Would you honor my company by accepting the position as its next president? I have no need for a chairman of the board anymore."

Miyuki stopped herself from clapping.

Her poor father couldn't answer. He was in shock.

"I have watched you over the years, Ichirou. You have shown yourself to be honest and an effective leader. You have never lied...unlike Mr. Nagumo." Miss Tenchi held eye contact with Miyuki's father. "I am impressed that you were willing to sacrifice your career on behalf of my company's welfare. Your sense of honor is strong and I respect you for that."

Miyuki's father presented her with a deep bow and held it for a moment. "Thank you, Miss Tenchi."

Miss Tenchi wrapped her arm around his. "We have wandered too far from what Shiawase Nomimono was always meant to be. A place that makes happy drinks. Drinks that put smiles on people's faces. It is in our name. It is in our soul. It is what my father and I have always strived for. Mr. Kaiko, I want to get back to that way of thinking again. Do you agree?"

Miyuki's father released the biggest smile Miyuki had ever seen her father make. "*Hei*."

* * *

The cupcake looked too cute to eat. The mountains of pink icing sitting on top of the lemon cake. The white chocolate kitty poking his head out of the icing and winking at her. It was all too cute for Miyuki to eat, like most of the food you can buy on Takeshita Street. But Miyuki's sweet tooth had a will of its own, forcing her mouth to bite into the sugar-coated yumminess. The lemon cupcake tasted as good as it looked.

"Do you not like it?" she asked.

Miyuki's father hesitated. His cupcake was chocolate on the bottom, but on top was a mound of white icing with a chocolate kitty cat sitting on top and waving hello. "I haven't tried it yet. How do you eat it without..." He rotated the cupcake.

Miyuki wiped her mouth with a napkin. "You don't. You let the icing go everywhere and just enjoy it."

Her father examined the cupcake, then went in and attacked. His mouth took out a chunk of icing and cake but left a smudge of chocolate on the tip of his nose.

Miyuki wiped it off for him.

Her father thanked her, then adjusted his chair and watched all the cute pedestrians wearing pinks, polka dots, and hearts on their clothes as they passed by their outdoor table. "This street reminds me of a circus, especially with all the colors. It's like a city of clowns."

Takeshita Street was a city of clowns. Cute and happy ones.

The image made Miyuki smile. "When Kameko is out of school, you should take her here."

"She would like that. She would like it more if you went with her."

"I'll miss her."

Her father looked up.

"I'll miss you all," Miyuki corrected.

Did she just insult her father? Miyuki wanted to say something else, but she bit into her cupcake instead.

Her father drank some water and ate a smaller bite of his cupcake.

They watched all the cute people walking down Takeshita Street.

"When does your plane leave?" he asked.

"About three hours."

"In that case, we should be walking to the station. The trains into Narita are always crowded."

Miyuki nodded, then caught her father staring down at her arm. Miyuki's fingers were rubbing the scar under her wrist. She pulled her hands down to her sides and pretended to watch the street again.

"Miyuki…" Her father stopped and cleared his throat.

She waited for him to continue.

But her father cleared his throat again and said nothing.

Miyuki blew him off. It was the same type of conversation they always had. He would struggle to say something nice without criticizing her while she bit her tongue in order to not embarrass him in front of the family.

"I—I've dishonored you," her father said.

That sentence made her look up. Did she hear him correctly?

"What?"

"I've dishonored you. I did some things…that I'm not proud of."

Miyuki could still feel the cigarette burn. How it stung against her flesh. It had happened four years ago and the sensation was still vivid in her mind. She had spoken out that day. Argued. Pushed her father to the limit of his tolerance. And he snapped.

"I was difficult. I spoke out. I fought back. I did not respect you or Mom."

Her father cleared his throat again. His eyes watered as if the man was holding it all in. Determined that he would not cry no matter what.

But tears fell from Miyuki's eyes instead as she watched her father struggle with the words.

"I realized long ago…that my oldest daughter was a unique flower. She was special. She was a purple blossom living among thousands of pink ones. Yet…I wanted to paint you pink. My daughter had to be a pink flower. No matter what. She would not be different from the other flowers. I wanted that reality so badly that I…I…" Her father stopped.

Even the confession was too painful for his lips.

Miyuki cupped her wrist in his hand. "It's okay. It doesn't hurt."

"That isn't true. It has injured you," her father said. "It has injured both of us. It has injured the way our family has become."

Miyuki couldn't argue with that. "Still, it happened long ago."

"Time does not excuse my actions. I was a coward lashing out at a child. A child who only wanted her father to pay attention to what she was saying."

Miyuki wiped away a tear.

"Despite my cowardly actions, you are still here to support me. You have helped saved my company from Mr. Nagumo. And you have saved me from myself, by reminding me about the duty of an honorable man." He cleared his throat again. "I will be forever in your debt."

Miyuki turned her wrist over and exposed the scarred burn. "This scar is a reminder of our past. It shouldn't be a reminder of our future."

"*Hei*," Her father said as he leaned down and kissed her wrist. Then the man broke down at the table.

Miyuki slipped out of her seat and swallowed him up in her arms.

She held him like that for a long time.

She missed her train.

She missed her flight.

But she would never miss this moment for all the sweet cupcakes on Takeshita Street.

THANK YOU FOR READING!

Dear Awesome Reader,

I hope you enjoyed *Thunderdog*. When I finished the first draft of this book, I realized I had no real villain. Venomous was involved in trying to make the energy drink into a weapon they could sell, but in that draft Oscar van Zanten was only a henchman, not a master villain. The real bad guy didn't show up until late in the second half of the book. This made the third act feel disconnected from the rest of the story, so I had to delete half the book and start over. That's when Mr. Nagumo came into being. Mr. Nagumo would be the puppet master who created problems for everyone in the story. Even Venomous. That's when the present version of the book took shape. Even the appearance of Volleen Woo and his comrades was an added bonus to the rewrite and helped me find a satisfying act three.

What did you think about the novel? What kind of stories would you like to see in future Gems novels? I'd love to hear from you! Please feel free to write me at dougthewriter@gmail.com or visit www.dougsolter.com for more options to stay connected.

Thank you again for reading ***Thunderdog!***

Doug Solter

ACKNOWLEDGMENTS

Another large shout-out to Laura Benedict for doing a beta read through my awful draft. Her honest feedback always makes these books so much better.

Travis Miles, for yet another wonderful book cover. He's amazing and I'm so lucky to have found him way back in 2012.

Pauline Nolet, for her eagle-eye editing skills. I'm lucky to have found her as well. She's always been amazing.

Max Adams, for her support and her amazing screenwriting classes.

For their constant support: Jeff Benedict, Jerry Bennett, Lela Fox, Joe Kinkade, Trevor and Talon Lane, Valarie Lawson, Erin and Tatum McHenry, Brenda Maier, Ginny Myers, Anna Myers, Ann Whitmire, Helen Newton, Sherry Spurrier, Courtney Summers, Amy Tipton, and Angela Townsend. The Oklahoma chapter of SCBWI. My filmmaker comrades through Max Adams' AFW program I love you all!

A big thank you to all my friends and family.

Finally, a giant thank you to my dad.

ABOUT THE AUTHOR

Doug Solter began writing screenplays in 1998, then made the switch to writing young adult fiction in 2008. His first novel *Skid* was a screenplay before it was adapted into a book. Doug has worked in television for over twenty years. He has also directed rap music videos and short films. Doug lives in Oklahoma.

So far in his life, Doug has enjoyed wine on the streets of Barcelona. Hiked the mountains. Loved a cat. Rang up vanilla lattes at Starbucks. Enjoyed a Primanti's sandwich in Pittsburgh. And one summer he baked pizzas and crazy bread for money when Michael Keaton was Batman.

Doug is also a member of the Society of Children's Book Writers and Illustrators.

Connect with Doug through his website...

www.dougsolter.com

ALSO BY DOUG SOLTER

ISBN-13: 978-09981466-1-4

Keep reading for a sample of the first chapter!

SEASON OF SPEED
SAMPLE

Samantha
Creek County, Oklahoma

The stadium lights expose clouds of dirt hovering above the track as I line up my Mustang inside the pack of mini-stock cars rolling in formation. I glance at the oil level. The red needle still hasn't moved the last fifty times I've checked it. I found a small oil puddle under the race car before the call to start all engines and I still have no idea where it's leaking from.

I should stop worrying. My '98 Ford Mustang always comes through no matter how badly I abuse her. She's my best friend on the racetrack, and when two best friends like us are surrounded by a bunch of guys like this, we girls have to stick together. I even painted my toenails the same shade of yellow as her hood. You know, like a best friend would.

Do I sound crazy?

It's time for me to focus as we round turn number four of the oval. The green flag waves and I stomp on the throttle. My best friend surges forward as the noise from twenty engines rumbles the ground. My best friend grips the dirt like her tires were made of spikes. She's fast tonight. It only takes us ten laps to reach second place.

Gil Webb's red and gold Dodge is the last car in front. Gil hates me.

No, seriously. I'm seventeen and a girl. For an old guy like him who thinks women should stay in the kitchen, those are two excellent reasons to let me have it.

Do I want to mess with him tonight?

I hold down the throttle and steer my car to the outside as I go on the attack.

Gil clings to the low part of the track because he doesn't like to give up the inside. He wants the other car to go high on the outside because Gil loves to—

His car swings hard into my left side, and I feel the Mustang's frame quiver like a freezing kitty.

We head into turn four, and Gil crowds me near the outside wall. I lift off and his car slides right in front of us.

Crap, I can hear my dad screaming inside my head. "Stop driving like a little girl."

As he enters turn one, Gil leaves the outside open again. He's daring me to try again.

Tonight I dare.

His Dodge closes in like a steel door and I brace. Gil slams hard into my car, pressing my best friend against the outer wall as it shaves off her bodywork like a saw. Gil slows us down enough to swing his car back in front to keep the lead.

I can't see the sides of my car, but I know she's taking a beating and I feel bad. I should quit and fall back before my best friend falls apart.

But I have an idea.

Entering turn two, I move my car to the outside and wait for Gil to make his move.

It doesn't take long. He throws his race car at me like a fist.

So I stand on the brakes. My car ducks away from his "punch" as it misses me and rams the outside wall instead. I'm back on the throttle and swing around him for a quick pass. The yellow flag then comes out as Gil's race car crawls along the inside with two deflated tires flapping the dirt like pancakes.

I flash Gil the finger as I lap him.

We get the green flag with only three laps to go. I feel another trophy is headed to my bedroom. But where can I put it? My desk is so full that I don't even have enough room to do my homework. Yeah, I need to build a wall shelf to show off my prizes.

Wait. What's that smell? It kinda smells like microwave popcorn that's been overcooked.

I check my oil pressure. The red needle hovers close to zero. Crap, I've lost tons of oil. That fight with Gil must have reopened my mysterious oil leak. Should I call it a night and save her poor engine for another race? It's not like I have a spare one.

But you're winning, Samantha!

Yeah, I didn't come here for second.

I apologize to my best friend as I hold her throttle down. I would add a prayer too, but I'm too busy right now.

Another lap down and I don't like how my girl's engine sounds. She's too rough. Much rougher than normal. I also don't like the blue smoke that's curling up inside the driver's compartment.

My heart knocks against my chest. I resist looking at the dash because the gauges will only tell me what I don't want to know. I plead with my best friend not to explode. She's brought me home safe and sound in every race so far, and now is not the time for a betrayal.

They show the white flag. One more lap to go.

The blue smoke thickens and makes me cough. The soles of my sneakers feel hot against the firewall. This would be the one night I forgot to put my flame-retardant racing shoes back into my duffel bag.

Stop panicking, Samantha! You do not have a fire under the hood.

The sound of grinding metal rattles my spine as the engine rips itself to pieces.

We enter turn three, and orange flames shoot out from under the hood.

Yes, you do! You DO have a fire under the hood, you stupid—

My engine dies, so I shift into neutral. Hopefully, I can coast her over the finish line.

I feel the heat of the fire through my racing suit. I bet it's hot enough to start melting the engine block. The blue smoke is now black and thick as it seeps into the car. I can't see through the windshield, so I use the right-side window to watch for the finish line.

There it is!

I cross over it and my heart swells with pride. Then, I check the windshield, and my hood is glowing orange with flames. I should have said that damn prayer.

I cough and gag as the smoke chokes my throat. Somehow I manage to bring my best friend to a stop as I struggle with my safety harnesses. A blanket of soot forms around me as blackness swallows the interior. I'm sleepy. I want to drift off, close my eyes, and sleep.

The feeling is so strong.

So overpowering.

I can't help myself.

I give in to it and black out.

I crawl out of the darkness as cold oxygen fills my lungs, a gift from the plastic tube stuck up my nose. I look around and see tiny compartments packed with medical equipment. A smooth white ceiling is above me as well as a young Creek Indian paramedic with a friendly smile. I must be in an ambulance.

"How are you feeling, miss?" the young paramedic asks.

I feel great, like I took the best nap ever. But if I say that, I might lose the attention of those hazel eyes.

"Still a little woozy," I lie.

The paramedic gives me a few minutes for being "woozy" before taking off the oxygen. He helps me sit up.

"Samantha, what were you thinking?" Megan leans against one of the open back doors of the ambulance. "You could have burned to death."

"But I didn't."

"Why did you keep going? Don't you remember that old saying? Where there's smoke, there's fire?"

"I was winning."

"So?"

"What do you think I'm trying to do out here?" I ask.

"From what I saw? Trying to kill yourself."

Megan enjoys worrying about things. My older sister thinks she's so mature because she has a kid and can legally drink a beer. But on nights like this, when Megan pulls all her black hair into a ponytail, I think it cuts off some blood to her brain. Especially the part of her brain that enjoys life.

"You've done some crazy stuff," she says. "But tonight was a new chapter. Even for you."

Oh God. She's channeling Mom again. I hate it when Megan does that.

"It's racing. Stuff breaks on cars all the time," I say.

"And normal drivers pull off the track when that happens," Megan says.

"I didn't know the car was in that bad a shape."

"What, you mean the large flames didn't clue you in?"

"Okay, I shouldn't have done it."

"Who are you trying to impress? Is it me? Because I'd rather see my sister alive."

"Like I give a crap about impressing you."

Megan grits her teeth. I don't think she liked my comment. I don't think I liked it either.

Her face darkens. "It's Dad, isn't it."

My silence only confirms it.

"I should have guessed."

The guilt catches in my throat.

"Why are you trying so hard to impress—"

"Shut up," I snap.

"We all miss him, but you shouldn't be—"

"Seriously. Drop it, Megan."

The guilt squeezes my throat tight. I can't breathe.

Megan keeps going. "We've lost somebody already, and I don't —"

"Fine, I'll give up racing."

"Samantha…"

"No. Screw anything I want. Keeping everyone happy is so much more important."

Tears form in Megan's eyes and smudge her heavy eye makeup. "That's not fair."

"Why are you crying?" Toby asks, holding Megan's hand, his stubby little fingers only covering a few of hers. My little nephew's blond hair dangles in front of his eyes like a small terrier's. Crap. I forgot she couldn't get a babysitter tonight.

Megan wipes her eyes, and the makeup stains her face as she fakes a smile. "I'm just happy Aunt Samantha is okay."

The burning popcorn smell still lingers in the air as what's left of my poor Mustang smolders on the back of a flatbed truck, her metal carcass ready for the nearest junkyard. The black mass that used to be my best friend now has these new added features: melted racing tires, a crispy black hood, curled-up black fenders, and a metal-wire frame that was my seat.

She's a total loss.

I wanna cry. Dad's pride and sweat went into building her for me, and now I've killed her. Out of respect, I should paint my toenails black tonight.

"Ready to go whenever you are." Megan heads for our Ford pickup.

I should stop her and apologize for losing it inside the

ambulance. Megan's so calm and puts up with a lot of my drama. And despite my outburst, I'm glad Megan still cares. I should say something, but I allow my sister to climb into the truck without one word.

There's always tomorrow, right?

I double-check the hitch on the empty trailer before sliding behind the wheel of the pickup. I start the engine, release the parking brake, and move the shifter into drive as a drop of water splashes across the windshield.

I freeze.

Water droplets pepper the glass as a shower moves over the track.

Every muscle inside me tenses up. Except my hand…

It's trembling on the wheel and I can't make it stop.

The shower changes to a downpour, creating a steady roar inside the cab of the pickup. I press the brake as far down as it will let me. The Ford hasn't moved an inch, but I keep forcing the pedal down like the truck is moving. And I can't make myself stop.

I close my eyes. I can't release the stupid brake.

"Want me to drive?" Megan asks, reading me so well.

We switch places in the driver's seat. I relax as Megan guides the pickup outside the gates of the raceway and heads into the wet and stormy Oklahoma night.

ISBN-13: 978-09981466-1-4

Order your copy today at your favorite bookseller.

Printed in Great Britain
by Amazon